Murder In The Blood

A DOYLE AND ACTON MYSTERY

ANNE CLEELAND

ARTEMIS
—PRESS—

The series in order:

Murder in Thrall
Murder in Retribution
Murder in Hindsight
Murder in Containment
Murder in All Honour
Murder in Shadow
Murder in Misdirection
Murder in Spite
Murder in Just Cause
Murder in the Blood

For Sir Winston Churchill, who twice turned down a dukedom; and for all others like him.

CHAPTER 1

———————o———————

Detective Sergeant Kathleen Doyle stood outside the garden gate, awaiting the arrival of the Senior Investigating Officer, who also happened to be Doyle's wedded husband.

This particular homicide case had taken an interesting turn, because the victim lying dead in the garden—the one who the property owners claimed to have never seen before—was listed as a witness in a homicide case that Detective Inspector Thomas Williams was already investigating. In such a situation, the senior on-site detective would call-in the detective who was handling the pending case, and the ranking SIO would decide if there appeared to be enough of a connection to combine the new case with the original one—oftentimes, this type of secondary murder was a key to solving the first.

Inspector Geary—the on-site detective originally assigned to the case—had therefore called-in DI Williams to have a look, and because Doyle was currently assigned to be Williams' temporary assist, she'd come along with him.

After they'd all greeted one another, Williams leaned in to take a quick survey of the enclosed garden through the gate's wrought-iron bars. "What do we know?"

Geary, a big, bluff Irishman who was currently on loan to Scotland Yard from Dublin, replied in his usual brusque manner. "Single shot to the head. Carried no ID, but he didn't look to be a vagrant, so I ran a quick facial ID and—lo, and behold—the fella's on the list of witnesses from your

Cavanaugh case. The owner of the property is a Carlos Navarro, who's a visitin' professor at Winchester University. He lives here with his wife, and they say they've no idea why the victim was shot in their garden."

"Now, there's a wrinkle," Doyle offered. The garden was enclosed by a high wall, and the gate had a formidable-looking lock.

Geary tilted his head, indicating the gate. "It was open when I got here—no sign of forced entry—but the owner claims he keeps it locked. Says he was gettin' his mornin' coffee when he looked out the window and noticed that the birds were peckin' at somethin'. When he realized what it was, he called the Met."

Williams took a step back to gauge how far away the house was. "Did he hear the shot?"

"Says he didn't." The other detective shrugged. "That's possible, I suppose—it's a big yard, and he's an older gentleman."

Doyle glanced over her shoulder at the posh neighborhood, where large homes were discreetly concealed behind high hedges, and well-tended circular driveways. "Mayhap there was a chase—a burglary gone awry?—and the victim got himself caught in this dead-end."

"Could be," Geary agreed. "But there've been no incident reports in the neighborhood. And it would mean that the owner is mistaken, and the gate must have been left unlocked."

"Any sign of a struggle?" asked Williams.

"Doesn't seem so, but I didn't get very far. As soon as the ID hit, I secured the scene and rang you up."

"Weapon on site?" Williams was asking as a matter of form; it seemed clear the other detective had already ruled out a possible suicide.

"No gun on site, and shot is to the back of the head."

Williams nodded, and rested his hands on his hips. "Let's see what DCI Acton wants to do, then—I've already called him in."

"I'll inform the field unit." Two uniformed police constables were guarding the perimeter, and the Irish detective walked over, no doubt to warn them that DCI Acton was on his way, and best look ship-shape.

Through the bars of the gate, Doyle gazed at the still figure who lay adjacent to the fountain located at the center of the garden—incongruously, the water was still warbling gently. "Chin up, Thomas; there may not be any connection to your case a'tall—this one doesn't look to be a spite-murder."

Her companion took a resigned breath. "Not my luck, Kath. The Council-murders case is already an epic wormhole, and so it only stands to reason."

The Met's CID was short-handed at present, and—aside from the other cases on his docket—Williams was the lead detective on the high-profile Cavanaugh case. Sir Cavanaugh had been a member of the now-notorious Health Professions Council, and recently he'd been brutally knifed to death, for his sins. In fact, he was the latest of three Council-members to be murdered, and all in a similar fashion.

To the horror of the general public, the respected Council had been exposed as running a sex-trafficking rig that preyed on young immigrants. The rig was very lucrative, and so—as an added bonus—the Council also had been heavily involved in corruption and money-laundering; said corruption having resulted in the arrests of several higher-echelon police personnel, who were now cooling their heels in prison.

The Met was therefore a bit short-handed at present, and—being as the Council-members tended to be very wealthy and high-profile individuals— the Public Corruption Department's investigation into their many misdeeds was going very slowly, and swathed in a veil of secrecy. The public could not be blamed for the general perception that the Crown Prosecutors were soft-footing their pursuit of these criminals, and so—as often happened when such was the perception—it appeared that one or more vigilantes had decided to mete out a rough justice. Three Council-members had now been brutally murdered in quick succession, and the sole survivor had fled the country rather than await his turn.

In detective parlance, they called the Council-murders "spite-murders" due to the obvious emotion that had triggered the homicide. Spite-murders tended to involve torture, or multiple, bloody wounds because the motivation was personal, and the killer was enraged beyond rational thought. They also tended to be easy to solve, since there was usually only a small universe of persons who were so passionately angry at the victim. In addition, due to the general bloodiness of the murder, there was usually lots of helpful forensic evidence left behind.

The Council-murders case, however, had proved to be a surprisingly tough nut to crack, and from what Doyle had gleaned from Williams, they'd few leads, which was one of the reasons he was being run ragged, and wouldn't welcome yet another case tossed atop his load. The poor man had already missed a few days, being as he was a diabetic, and was not taking care of himself properly amidst all the commotion. Doyle had already scolded him as much as she dared—she well-knew that his condition was a sensitive topic, and he didn't like discussing it.

With a practiced eye, Williams reviewed the area around the body as he bent to pull exam gloves from his rucksack. "It may not be a spite-murder, but it seems likely that there's a connection to the Cavanaugh case." With a tilt of his head, he gestured toward the body. "This victim was the Council's limo-driver. As far as we can tell, he wasn't directly involved in the sex-slavery rig, but he was a witness—knew a lot about who went where, and when."

Doyle lifted her brows in surprise. "A private driver who was willin' to grass—now, there's a rare bird." A detective quickly learned that professional drivers were usually deaf, blind and dumb to their employer's misdeeds, and tended to be very unhelpful as witnesses. "Mayhap that's the nub of this murder, then—mayhap someone was worried about what this fellow was goin' to tell the coppers."

With a shrug, Williams replied, "Too late for that, he'd already told us plenty—the case broke some time ago, remember? He came forward because he was worried about being charged with conspiracy, and so he was willing to cooperate."

Doyle made an impatient sound. "He needn't have worried; the Prosecutors are draggin' their feet about chargin' anyone for anythin'."

This said with some heat, because to Doyle, justice was supposed to be blind, and the Council's lofty public standing as wealthy do-gooders shouldn't matter—not to mention that vigilantism tended to raise its ugly head, when the public had the perception that law enforcement was choosing favorites. It seemed apparent in this case that someone—or multiple someones—had decided to take matters into their own hands, and now the Council-member corpses were stacking up.

Williams bent to take another long look at the victim. "I doubt someone was trying to keep him quiet—his testimony has already been buttoned-up, and if he's dead, it would still be admissible."

"Not to mention there's no one left to murder him," Doyle pointed out fairly. "The Council-members themselves have all been murdered. Mayhap it's truly just a coincidence, Thomas; the victim was havin' an affair with the lady of the house, and she found out he'd taken up with the maid, on the side."

He looked up at the road. "Hold that thought, Kath. Here's Acton."

They watched as Chief Inspector Acton parked his Range Rover behind the field car, and then stepped out to speak to the patrol officers at the perimeter for a few moments. Tall and lean, Acton was famous for his exceptional work in solving homicides—indeed, the younger detectives called him "Holmes" behind his back—and he was much-revered by the public, not only for solving thorny homicides, but also because he held a title, and the public always appreciated it when an aristocrat tried to make himself remotely useful.

Doyle had first met her husband when she was a nervous rookie; nervous, because for reasons unfathomable she'd been partnered with the great Chief Inspector Acton who was renowned for not suffering fools, and she was aware that she fell well-short in this qualification.

But—rather unexpectedly—they'd made a good team, and had solved more than a few high-profile homicides together until—one fine day—he'd bundled her straight from a crime scene to the altar, the operation planned-out to a nicety so that she wouldn't have any time to consider the enormity of her actions.

And so—just like that—an Irish working-class girl became Lady Acton, leaving everyone to shake their heads and wonder what had come over the famous Chief Inspector— there'd not been a hint that such a thing was in the offing.

Not even for me, Doyle thought fairly; Acton knew she'd balk if she'd been given any time to reconsider, and so he simply hadn't given her any. All in all, it had been the correct tack to take, and she was very happy he'd swept her away— neither one of them was what they seemed on the surface, and so they were kindred souls, in a strange way. And they loved each other, of course—had a sweet little baby boy, to show for it.

Despite this strange and unexpected pairing, the public quickly warmed to Acton's new bride—and thought him very discerning, indeed—because hard on the heels of their surprise wedding, Doyle had saved a colleague's life by jumping off a bridge into the Thames, even though she couldn't swim. She'd been awarded a commendation for bravery as a result, and—because the news media loved stories about death-defying female officers—she was now something of a local hero, and tended to be recognized everywhere she went. Little did she know that when she ventured forth from Dublin to London she'd wind up semi-famous for multiple reasons, and Doyle could only assume that God had a mighty dark sense of humor.

Geary had briefed Acton as they approached, and now he greeted Williams and Doyle at the garden gate, his gaze resting thoughtfully on the corpse, where it lay near the fountain. "The homeowner is within?"

"He is, sir—with his wife. I told them we'll be needin' a statement."

Acton contemplated the crime scene for a moment. "They are Spanish nationals?"

Geary nodded. "I believe so, sir—Hispanic, in any event."

"Spanish, I imagine. It is not easy to grow Seville oranges, in this climate. Let's go in, then, and have a look."

Carefully, Doyle followed after the other detectives as they stepped along the terra-cotta pavers toward the body, moving slowly and methodically as they observed the ground along the way.

"It doesn't look as though he was dragged here," Williams commented.

Doyle could only agree; the pathway—as well as the plants and flowers that bordered the pathway—appeared undisturbed. "Killed on site, then?"

"I didn't see a bullet casin'," Geary offered. "But I haven't done a thorough search as yet."

They came to the body of the middle-aged man, dressed in casual clothes and wearing a light jacket. The cause of death was evident; an entry wound in the back of the head and a messy exit wound near the victim's left temple—the extent of the damage indicating a large-caliber weapon.

"No indication of flight, or of a struggle," Williams offered as they all crouched down. "And his hands are clean."

"The wound almost looks execution-style, save for it bein' only the one shot," Geary added. This was true; underworld executions usually involved two shots to the back of the head as standard underworld procedure—the professionals had to make certain that the victim was good and dead.

"No—I do not believe it was a professional hit," Acton replied thoughtfully. "It would not be the usual weapon, and note that the victim's eyes are closed."

Much struck, they were all silent for a moment, contemplating the dead man. In a normal shot-to-the-back-of-the-head murder, the victim's eyes would be open, as there would have been no time to react to the devastating disruption to the brain. If the victim's eyes were closed, it usually meant they'd been closed for him after death.

Acton glanced at Williams. "Is it indeed your witness from the Cavanaugh case?"

"Yes, sir."

"He'd already told his tale, though?"

"Yes. I'd be surprised if someone was trying to silence him—it's a little late for that."

Doyle added, "Not to mention they'll soon be no cases left for the prosecution to slow-walk; every man-jack is gettin' themselves murdered."

Acton nodded thoughtfully. "Does Castellano remain at-large?"

"Yes," Williams nodded. "He's the only Council-member left alive, and he's fled—we traced him as far as Dover, and we assume he jumped a ferry under an assumed name—can't find him on CCTV. There's no indication he's back in the country, and we've an All Ports Warning out for him."

As Acton considered the corpse in silence, Williams offered, "DS Doyle and I were not certain there's any connection to the Council-murders, sir. We've this fellow's deposition testimony already nailed down, and if he's dead, the testimony would be admissible at a trial—there'd be nothing to gain by killing him."

Acton raised his impassive gaze to contemplate the house for a moment. "Have we managed to track down Sir Cavanaugh's Assistant?"

Williams glanced over at him in surprise. After Sir Cavanaugh was murdered, his Assistant had disappeared, and it was unclear whether she'd been killed also, or was simply afraid—like Castellano was—that she was the next murder-victim in line. "No—no trace of Martina Betancourt, and again, we've an All Ports Warning out for her." Watching Acton, he ventured, "This doesn't seem like a woman's crime, though."

This was true; women tended to shoot people in the chest, rather than the head, and when Doyle had first learned this at the Crime Academy she'd been skeptical until experience had borne it out—there did seem to be gender-specific preferences for murder.

"And Betancourt is only five feet two," Williams added. "This victim was tall and fit, and so it seems unlikely that the shooter was someone short, who held up a large-caliber hand-gun at an awkward angle."

"No—unlikely the killer is a woman," Acton agreed.

He rose, and they all followed suit, with Geary saying aloud what they were all thinking. "Nothin' seems to fit, yet it's hard to believe it's a coincidence, sir."

"Unlikely," Acton agreed. "I believe it would be best to transfer the matter to DI Williams, and if you will call for the SOCO team, I will go inside to interview the homeowner, along with DS Doyle."

The two men nodded, and Doyle turned to accompany Acton, a bit surprised, because if it was now Williams' case, he should be the one sitting in on the interview and not Doyle, who was only his assist. But there was no doubt a good reason, and that reason was that Acton had decided he needed a truth-detector.

Doyle had an extraordinary instinct when it came to reading the emotions of the people around her—fey, the Irish would have called it—and in particular, she could usually sense when someone was lying. This talent had come in handy many a time in her career as a detective, although few knew of it—they only knew that she tended to come up with case-breakers on a regular basis, despite not being the brightest detective at the CID.

Acton, however, was well-familiar with her perceptive ability—indeed, she'd trusted him with it almost immediately, and it was one of the reasons they'd solved so many cases when they'd first started together. Her husband must have decided that her truth-sorting abilities would be needful for this particular interview, which meant that he was expecting a fish-tale from the homeowners—not truly a surprise, their story wasn't adding up.

As they walked toward the house's front door, she eyed him speculatively, and asked in a low tone, "What is it you're thinkin', husband? The owner's guilty?"

"It is an unusual garden," was all he would say. "And for more reasons than one."

CHAPTER 2

Acton knocked at the house's front door—which was heavy, carved mahogany—and it was promptly opened by an older gentleman, who seemed surprised to discover Doyle and the Chief inspector standing on his doorstop. In an abrupt tone, he asked, "What is this? Where is the other man?"

"He is not here," Acton replied briefly—Acton never let the witness lead the interview. "May we come in?"

"Yes—I imagine I have little choice." With a gesture, the man turned and led them into the formal dining room, where a woman—presumably his wife—was seated at an impressively large table. She had a coffee-service tray set up before her, and viewed their entry with a dispassionate expression that gave nothing away.

She reminds me of someone, Doyle thought, trying to catch at the elusive memory. The Dowager, mayhap? Acton's mother, the Dowager Lady Acton, had a similar resting expression—that of a woman who was steeped in her own importance, and rather surprised that she'd been asked to endure the company of others.

"More police, *Señora*," the man announced to his wife, and she nodded once—rather regally— without rising.

Not a'tall happy to see us, thought Doyle; but small blame to them—there's nothing like finding an early-morning body in the garden to disrupt one's day.

Because there was a thinly-veiled insolence to the couple's attitude, Doyle mentally braced herself, because Acton was one who tended to put such witnesses back on their heels straight-out-of-the-gate; it was important to impress upon an insolent witness that this was serious business, and if the full force of the law was brought to bear, matters could become very unpleasant, very quickly.

But to her surprise, Acton only bowed deferentially, and offered in what Doyle privately characterized as his House-of-Lords voice, "I am most sorry to disturb you, but—as you know—I must ask some questions. Allow me to introduce myself; I am Chief Inspector Acton."

The result was immediate, as the gentleman first looked startled, and then waxed apologetic. "Forgive me, *Ilustrisimo Señor*—I am remiss. Will you sit, and have coffee?" He gave his wife a husbandly glance, and she rose to rather awkwardly lift the china coffee pot.

"The other man—the one who first came here—he was very rude," their host explained. "An Irishman, and difficult to understand."

Oh-oh, thought Doyle; but rather than defend her Irishness, Acton only smiled slightly, and made an apologetic gesture toward her with his elegant hands. "I must warn you, then; Detective Sergeant Doyle is also Irish."

But their reaction was not at all what Doyle had expected, as there was a sudden, still silence, and the woman put the coffee pot down on the table with a click.

"This—this is your wife, *Señor*?" Two pairs of eyes considered Doyle in reverent silence.

Acton turned to smile at Doyle. "Your fame precedes you, Sergeant."

"Yes, sir," Doyle replied, rather surprised that this particular couple were bridge-jumper fans. To cover the awkward moment, she gestured toward the coffee-pot, which was surely leaving a heat-mark on the fancy wooden table. "May I pour, ma'am?"

"Please," the woman replied, and as she stepped back, Doyle saw her direct a glance of uncertainty toward her husband.

"This regrettable business," Navarro offered, as Doyle poured out the coffee. "I am not myself."

"Then we will attempt to disrupt you as little as possible," Acton replied in a conciliatory tone, as they were all seated around the massive table. "If you would not mind, I would like to hear an account of your morning's activities." He pulled out a small notebook and a pencil, which was of interest, since the protocol demanded that interview notes were to be electronic, whenever possible. He's being old-school, Doyle decided, because these people are old-school.

"Of course, *Señor*," Navarro agreed, and then paused so as to gather his thoughts for a moment.

This is crackin' good coffee, thought Doyle with deep appreciation, but then Acton's gaze rested upon her for a meaningful moment, and she straightened-up to pay attention. So; something was up, and Acton's nice-and-noble act was just a sham to gain their trust, for some reason.

"I rose in the morning, *Señor*, and came downstairs to take my coffee."

"Do you and your wife live alone?"

"We do," the man replied.

Startled, Doyle casually brushed her hair back from her forehead. It was the signal she and Acton used between them, when Doyle knew that the witness was lying.

"I sit here, where I can look out over the garden, and make my plans for the day."

"An excellent way to clear the mind, first thing," Acton offered, looking up from his notes with a small smile.

In an ironic gesture, Doyle brushed her hair back; Acton's own clearing-of-the-mind routine was to jump his sleepy wife, first thing in the morning.

"Yes. This morning, however, the birds were very noisy, and—" he made a gesture with his hands, searching for the word "—grouped over something on the other side of the fountain. I went to investigate."

Doyle brushed her hair back.

"Quite a shock, I imagine," Acton offered with a show of sympathy.

"It was. I informed my wife that we must telephone the police."

"Did you recognize the man?"

"No, *Señor*."

Doyle brushed her hair back.

"Did you hear the shot—or hear any disturbance during the night?"

"I did not." He paused, and then offered, "My hearing is not what it was, though."

As Doyle dutifully brushed her hair back, Acton smiled at Mrs. Navarro, who'd been sitting very quietly, and trying—without much success—to keep her gaze from straying to Doyle. "And you, *Señora*? Did you hear anything unusual?"

"No, *Señor*."

Why, that's strange, Doyle realized; Acton should not be interviewing these two at the same time. Witnesses—especially allied witnesses, such as a husband and wife—were always interviewed separately, so that there was less chance of collaboration. For some reason, though, Acton had left these two together. And—come to think of it—she'd the impression that Acton was only asking his questions as a matter of form; he wasn't truly very interested in their answers.

I'm going to be that annoyed, she thought, if Acton's already figured it all out whilst I'm not yet away from the starting-gate. Although it does seem clear that there's a cover-up going on—so he doesn't get any points for figuring that out. Hard to imagine this fellow stooping to murder anyone, though; perhaps these two are covering for the real killer.

Doyle's scalp prickled, which was what it did when her intuition was making a leap. That must be it—they knew who done it, and they were—rather clumsily—trying to cover for the killer. Clumsy, because the current scenario made little sense.

Acton checked his notes. "The garden gate was locked, last night? You are certain?"

The witness bowed his head slightly. "I have been thinking on this, and I cannot be certain. It is my habit, though."

Ah, thought Doyle; not so clumsy, after all—he's realized this is one of those locked-room mystery things, and he has to give himself a little wiggle room.

"Would the gardener have a key?"

There was a small pause. "No—I am the only one with a key to the gate. These deplorable times—" Mr. Navarro's mouth thinned in anger. "It is not safe."

Acton bowed his head in commiseration. "As we see."

"Yes." The witness carefully unclenched his hands. "As we see."

"I am sorry for it," said Acton as he rose, "but we must have a team in the garden for a few hours. The Coroner will remove the victim, and so I suggest you stay within-doors until his team departs. Do we have your contact information, Mr. Navarro?"

"I gave it to the Irishman, but here is my card." He removed a billfold from within his jacket, and handed the card to Acton, laying it on his open palm, and bowing with a formal gesture.

"Thank you. Allow me to give you mine." Acton followed the same card-offering protocol.

How nice; now *everyone's* being old-school, Doyle thought a bit crossly. So grand it is, that the proprieties are all being observed whilst we've a body turning cold, outside.

But—as it turned out—she was not to be left out of the formalities, because the silent Mrs. Navarro glided over to walk beside her as they all made their way to the door. "*Señora,*" she whispered.

Oh-*ho*, thought Doyle, as she discreetly lowered her head to listen to the woman. Mayhap the missus was willing to grass on her husband—which only went to show that you never knew.

But instead, Mrs. Navarro lifted Doyle's hand, and pressed a rosary into it. "Please—please take this."

Startled, Doyle regarded the beautiful object—silver, with beads of lapis lazuli—and stammered, "Oh—oh I couldn't possibly—"

But the woman had already stepped back, and then stood quietly in the recesses of the foyer, while her husband ushered the detectives out the door.

CHAPTER 3

A cton had decided he'd accompany Doyle back to their flat for lunch—she tried to keep her lunch-times clear, so as to have a mid-day visit with baby Edward—and as a result, Williams was assigned to stay at the scene, and oversee the SOCOs as they went about their forensic work.

On the drive home, Acton was silent, as was his wont when he was thinking deeply about something, and as Doyle tended not to think deeply at all, she respected this process, and stayed silent.

After a space of time, he reached to take her hand. "Tell me your impressions."

"Well, they were both lyin' liars who lie, but on the upside, the coffee was amazin'."

"What did she give you?"

Another reminder that her husband was as sharp-eyed as they come. "Her rosary, of all things. It was so awkward, Michael—it must be her personal one, since she was carryin' it on her. I didn't know what to say."

He nodded, as though unsurprised. "They appreciate courage. They are Carlists, I believe."

"Ah," said Doyle. "Well, that explains it."

With a small smile, he explained, "There was a split in the Spanish nobility, hundreds of years ago, with regard to the succession to the throne. The Carlists lost the argument, but nonetheless have persisted as a minor political faction. They are considered staunch traditionalists."

18

"It did feel a bit like Trestles," she ventured. "What with all the formality, and such." Trestles was Acton's hereditary estate, and Doyle always felt as though she'd entered a time-warp, whenever they visited. "And you wheedled them nicely, I must say; playing the 'nobility' card to a fare-thee-well. I wasn't sure whether I should curtsy first, before speakin' to either one of you."

He admitted, "I thought it might help to penetrate their defenses."

She eyed his profile. "I'd the impression, husband, that you took the lay of the land in short order, regardless of any defenses they may have thrown up. Can you tell me what it is you're thinkin'?"

He replied, "I imagine the victim was their servant."

In complete astonishment, she stared at him for a few moments before she could find her voice. "Their *servant*? Whyever—for the love o' Mike—whyever would they try to hide such a thing?"

"Because I imagine Mr. Navarro killed him."

Bringing her brows together, she turned to gaze out the windscreen. "I can't say I'm truly surprised, but tell me how you twigged it, Michael."

"No doubt they have some claim to Spanish nobility— although nothing that would be recognized, if they are indeed Carlist. And in the traditional manner of Spanish nobility, they would have a manservant to see to them. Note that Mrs. Navarro wasn't certain how to handle a coffee-pot; I suspect she has never been called upon to do so."

Conceding this point, Doyle blew a tendril of hair from her forehead. "Holy saints, Michael—there's some cold-bloodedness for you."

"Not quite so cold-blooded, perhaps; it would also explain why the victim's eyes had been closed. I thought at first he may have been their gardener, but his hands were too well-manicured." He paused. "Once I saw they hadn't a servant to attend them, it was rather an easy conclusion to reach."

She glanced over at him. "So, do we have an 'easy-conclusion' as to motive? Mayhap the manservant was stealin' the silver?"

Her husband tilted his head. "You jest, but that may have been indeed the case; these people have their own set of values—rather rigid ones, in fact."

Suddenly, Doyle was reminded of where this case had started, and exclaimed, "Wait—wait just a blessed minute, Michael; Williams says the victim was the limo-driver for the Health Professions Council."

"Indeed."

Worried that she'd missed something, she ventured, "Does that make sense to you?"

"No."

Somewhat relieved that her husband wasn't ten steps ahead of her, she contemplated the passing scenery with a knit brow. "So; I suppose that means either he held two jobs, or that Williams is mistaken."

"I doubt Williams is mistaken."

Thoroughly flummoxed, she mulled over this strange series of events. "It *must* be connected, right? Mayhap Mr. Navarro found out that his servant—who was moonlightin' as a limo driver?—was involved in the sex-slavery rig, and so killed him out of sheer disgust, since he's all noble-Carlist, and such."

Acton nodded. "Yes. Or it could just as easily be that they discovered he was turning over evidence against his Council employers. They have a rigid code, remember, and turning evidence on your masters would be an unforgivable breach."

With a sense of wonder, Doyle shook her head slightly. "What a strange way of lookin' at things—as though you've your own set of rules, and no one else's matters."

"We see it, occasionally," he reminded her.

This was true; every once in a while, they'd handle a murder by a member of a prominent family who would express their deep astonishment that they would be subject to the same laws as everybody else. Such thinking was hard for Doyle to fathom, and she said aloud, "It's like one of those clast systems, where you think the only thing that matters is your bloodline."

He squeezed her hand. "You may mean 'caste'. And yes; very similar."

She quirked her mouth, being as Acton himself was a card-carrying member of the upper caste, here in these parts. "Such *nonsense*; it's all so—so *contrived*, if that's the right word. There must be just as many bad bloodlines as good ones—it only stands to reason."

"I cannot disagree."

With some fervor, she continued, "And no one *ever* thinks about that aspect of it—the bad bloodlines—mainly because they're too busy admirin' their betters."

"All too true."

A bit belatedly, she realized that this was—perhaps—not the best subject to discuss with her husband, being as he could stand as Exhibit A for a bad bloodline. His father had been a monster, and—perhaps as a consequence—Acton had a dark side that reared up and showed itself, on occasion. And—beneath the heroic face that the public so admired—Acton was actually something of a vigilante, often acting to manipulate evidence so as to obtain the result that he considered appropriate. Indeed, much to her extreme dismay, Doyle had come to realize that her husband would not shrink from committing a murder or two, if he thought it necessary, and the fact that he'd be the last person anyone would suspect of such dark doings only enabled him all the more.

Doyle had become aware of these alarming traits only after they'd married—small wonder, since she'd married in haste—and as a result, she was now embarked on a determined course to help him mend his ways. His immortal soul was at stake, after all—not to mention that it boggled the mind to think of Acton in prison; unlikely they'd allow him a manservant.

She didn't always succeed, in her attempts to curb his renegade ways, but it fell to her to try, because she was the only person on earth who had any influence whatsoever. As it turned out, her husband's rather dark and complicated nature also revealed itself in his obsessive love for his unlikely bride—indeed, her pairing-up as his rookie partner had been carefully planned-out by man who saw her as the center of his universe, and was dead-set on keeping her within arm's reach.

He was a complicated man, and so it was slow-going, but she felt she was making some headway in easing him away from his path of destruction. Knock wood, of course; he was a force unto himself, was Acton, and when he thought his methods might upset her, he simply didn't let her know what was going forward. In point of fact, he'd just recently recovered from a bout of mind-troubles, where he'd seemed almost paralyzed by an unknown fear, and what sleep he could catch had been plagued by nightmares.

He'd recovered, somewhat, but he wasn't completely recovered; not as yet. He'd buried it deep, but she knew him like no other, and hoped that whatever-it-was that was troubling him would eventually fade away.

After deciding she wanted to change the direction of her thoughts, she offered, "So—whatever the motive—we think Mr. Navarro's the killer. Do we take a discreet look at his electronics, or just go in with brute force—gatherin' up a field unit, and stormin' the castle?"

"I would be very surprised if he owned any electronics."

"Oh—good point. He's as old-school as old-school can be."

Acton nodded thoughtfully. "Instead, let's hold back—there's no hurry, if what we think is true, and I don't want to tip him off. We'll meet with Williams after lunch, and with any luck he'll have a preliminary report. I'd like more information, before we plot out a case-management plan."

Doyle offered, "I'll be happy to do the legwork, Michael—poor Williams is up to his neck in cases, what with Gabriel in rehab, and Munoz takin' her lumps."

Because the Met was already short-handed due to the corruption scandal, it could ill-afford losing Officer Gabriel to a thirty-day rehab stint, whilst Officer Isabella Munoz was also temporarily suspended for dereliction of duty. Unfortunately, the villains didn't much care about the Met's staffing problems, and so everyone who stood in the breach had been miserably slammed with an overload of work.

He nodded. "I've made a request for temporary Processors, to help with the paperwork and programming. I would rather not bring untrained personnel into the field, but having additional Processors should help to relieve the burden somewhat. I've also asked Inspector Geary to assist Williams whenever possible."

Doyle nodded. "Geary's a great help, I think—a shame, that he had to turn this Navarro case back over to poor Williams, although I suppose Geary's another one who's so busy he doesn't know whether he's afoot or on horseback. I heard that the brass has pulled him in to help with Commander Tasza's disappearance."

"Yes; because she disappeared in Ireland, it was thought he might have some helpful insights."

Curious, she glanced over at him. "*Have* they any helpful insights? Did they ever recover a body?" Tasza Kozlowski was an MI 5 Commander who'd mysteriously disappeared, recently. As part of her counter-terrorism work, she'd arranged to interview a prisoner in a remote area of Ireland, but—as it turned out—the prisoner in question didn't actually exist, and—even more ominously—the Commander had disappeared whilst on her way to speak with him.

Due to the nature of her counter-terrorism work, it could only be presumed that someone had decided to take her out, and the department was turning over every stone in an attempt to determine what had happened.

Acton replied, "No—no body as yet. And the investigation is further hindered because CCTV cameras are few and far between, in that area."

"Which is no doubt why she was lured there in the first place." Thinking on it, Doyle shook her head in wonder. "Faith, Michael, it's hard to believe that someone like Commander Tasza was so easily hoodwinked."

"Indeed."

She was quiet for a few moments as he navigated the traffic, and then was reminded of something he'd said that morning. "Why did you think the garden was unusual,

Michael? You knew somethin' was strange well-before you saw that their manservant was missin'."

"The plants were unusual. Many of them weren't thriving because they were more suited to a sunny climate, like Spain."

"The orange trees," she remembered.

"Yes; it seemed clear the owner was determined to have the same type of garden found in his homeland, but was experiencing difficulties in that aim."

"May as well bark at the moon," Doyle offered rather glumly. "It rains a lot, here."

"Very true. But it is of interest, because it also indicates he was not at all happy to be residing in London. And this would only make sense, if they considered themselves Carlist nobility; indeed, it is rather surprising that he was willing to live outside of Spain at all."

She nodded, thinking that the older couple did seem too top-lofty to be concerned with lesser beings, and therefore unlikely to be dwelling cheek-by-jowl with foreigners—especially foreigners of the dreaded peasant variety. She couldn't voice this thought aloud, however, because her wedded husband was cut from the same cloth.

Acton added, "And aside from the unsuitable plants, there was a freshly-turned area beneath the fountain's basin that looked to be grave-sized."

Astonished, she turned to stare at him. "There was a *grave* in the garden?"

He shook his head slightly. "No—only a shallow disturbance in the soil. I imagine Mr. Navarro started out with the object of burying the victim, and then abandoned the project as beyond his powers."

Thoroughly disapproving, Doyle observed, "There's some brass for you, Michael—thinkin' no one would notice if this poor fellow just up and disappeared. Not to mention the victim was a witness in an important homicide case—Navarro should have known that law enforcement would soon come knockin' at the garden gate."

Acton tilted his head. "Remember that Martina Betancourt has disappeared, and from the same case."

There was a small, surprised silence, and then Doyle ventured, "D'you think our Mr. Navarro may have murdered Cavanaugh's Assistant, too?"

"I don't have a working theory, as yet. I will need more information."

Doyle thought this over, as they pulled into the parking garage for their building. "It must be a containment murder, Michael—that's the only thing that makes sense. This servant-fellow knew somethin' about Navarro, and Navarro decided—apparently after ditherin' about it for a time—that he couldn't take the chance his servant might squeak to someone, and so he murdered him so as to contain the scandal."

"It is possible," Acton agreed.

She smiled as she glanced at him sidelong. "No need to humor me, Michael."

He parked the car, and reached to run a fond hand down her arm. "I doubt it was a containment murder. If the victim had been threatening to blackmail Navarro, his death would not have been so peaceful."

"Oh," said Doyle, much struck. "You're right; his death doesn't seem much like any kind of vengeance-murder."

"No, it doesn't," he agreed.

And you're the expert, she thought silently, then wondered why her scalp began to prickle.

CHAPTER 4

Reynolds served them lunch as Doyle held baby Edward on her lap—the baby slapping the table with the flats of his hands and thinking this a very enjoyable pastime, despite the fact it made eating a hit-or-miss endeavor.

Doyle noted that their very-correct butler was emanating a pleased satisfaction, which was due, no doubt, to the stupid Investiture ceremony that was fast approaching. Acton had inherited another title—because apparently, one could never have too many—and there was to be a formal ceremony in Parliament to officially bestow it upon him.

Unfortunately, Doyle was forced to go along with the whole holy-show because she was married to the main participant, and thus would wind up with another title, herself. Besides, Doyle knew that—beneath his indifferent posture—Acton was actually well-pleased with the aforesaid holy-show, and so she'd best quit being such a baby and try not to verify everyone's opinion about how things always went downhill as soon as you allowed the Irish in.

It's another one of those in-the-blood things, she thought a bit crossly, as she quickly moved her plate so that Edward couldn't reach it. The Navarros would fit right in—although on second thought, they'd probably think themselves too toplofty for the paltry House of Lords.

Reynolds related, "Hudson informs me that the arrangements are nearly complete, sir. Since Master Edward is so young, Hudson was wondering if perhaps he should wear his christening gown for the occasion."

Holy Mother, thought Doyle in extreme alarm; she'd already resolved to hide all photographs of Edward's Baptism—when he'd been required to wear the voluminous and ancient lace gown—because the poor boyo shouldn't be forced to lose every shred of self-respect at such a tender age.

"I think a simple suit-of-clothes, rather," Acton replied.

Gratefully, Doyle expressed her approval of this plan. "Much better—who thought to put boys in dresses, anyway? It's inhumane, is what it is."

"Yet the Irish do," her husband teased.

"Kilts are a completely different sort of thing," she replied, very much on her dignity. "It's a cultural heritage."

Acton reached to retrieve his fork from the baby's quick hands. "Perhaps Edward should wear a kilt, instead."

"You'd be drummed out of the place faster than the cat could lick its ear, Michael. Don't tempt me."

Smoothly, Reynolds intervened, "And Hudson has delivered the other item we spoke of, sir."

This said with a nuance which made Doyle instantly suspicious—Hudson was the Steward of Trestles, and she was aware that this was no idle remark, but that some plot had been carefully planned out between these two connivers. "Oh? What other item is this?"

"Your tiara," Acton replied in a mild tone, and Doyle could sense that both men steeled themselves for her reaction.

I can't be a baby, she reminded herself, as—with a mighty effort—she controlled her abject dismay. It's important to Acton, and it's not as though I'll ever have to do it again—they can't *possibly* keep handing him titles. "All right, then; let's have a look."

Hiding his relief, Reynolds went to fetch a small velvet bag, and then laid it reverently upon the kitchen table.

"There were several to choose from," Acton explained, "but I thought you might like this one, as it is not as ornate as the others."

Doyle opened the drawstring and removed the tiara, which was a half-circle made of silver-colored metal, with the crown part consisting of linked-filigree ovals, encrusted with diamonds and pearls. "*This* is the simpler one?" she asked in surprise, and quickly pulled it away from Edward's grasping hands.

"Very tasteful," Reynolds offered, in the tone of someone trying to coax a child. "Edwardian, perhaps?"

"A bit later," Acton explained. "I thought it best to have something more modern."

"It *is* lovely," Doyle said firmly, trying to convince herself.

"Will you try it on, madam?"

For reasons she could not name, Doyle found that she was reluctant to place the tiara on her head. Knocker—go on, with your foolish self, she self-scolded; this is every little girl's dream. Carefully, she placed it on her head.

"Very smart," Reynolds said in an encouraging tone. "Elegant."

"It does become you," Acton assured her. "Is it heavy?"

"No—not heavy." Faith, I don't like it at all, she thought, rather surprised at herself. There's something—something a bit *off* about it. Happy for the excuse, she removed it, and handed it over to Acton for his inspection.

"Platinum," Reynolds said with satisfaction. "A shame there is little occasion to wear such a thing, nowadays."

"I could wear it when I take the pram to the park," Doyle teased. "It might help—there was a woman yesterday who asked if I worked full-time, or was available for other families."

Rather than being amused upon hearing this anecdote, Reynolds was discreetly distressed. "Perhaps I should accompany you on your walks, madam."

"And ring a bell, to clear the way?" she laughed. "Faith, Reynolds, it was a natural assumption, all things considered; I wasn't insulted in the least."

"Very good madam," the servant replied, in a tone that made it clear this was not very good at all.

With a wry mouth, she observed, "You'd fit right in with the Navarros, Reynolds—and they're lookin' for a new manservant, I hear. You could moonlight for them, and I can moonlight as a nanny; it never hurts to have a bit of extra pocket-money."

"Do I know the Navarros, madam?"

"No, and I suppose that's just as well, my friend."

Acton met her eyes, briefly.

Oh, she thought, reminded; I shouldn't be discussing a pending case. A shame, it was, because Reynolds was mighty long-headed, and often had some good insights.

Acton excused himself to go raise Williams on the phone, and Doyle stood Edward up on her knees, to bounce him as he laughed with delight. "You'd best behave yourself for Reynolds, my boyo—he'll be busy as a fishwife at Lent, when Mary's on her honeymoon."

Reminded, Reynolds told her, "With your permission, madam, I told Miss Mary that I would mind Miss Gemma here at the flat today."

Doyle smiled her approval. "Good one, Reynolds—give the bride a few hours to dash about. It's a kind man, you are."

In actuality, this was no hardship for Reynolds, who was very fond of Mary-the- nanny's little girl. Doyle had first met Mary when the young woman was a witness in a homicide case, and had promptly hired her on as Edward's nanny, even though she'd no previous experience as such.

Mary was raising her stepdaughter, Gemma, who'd she'd taken-in when her husband had been killed, and as part of the nanny-hiring plan, Acton had arranged for the little girl to enroll in preschool at nearby St. Margaret's.

Thanks to the House of Acton, Mary and Gemma seemed to have landed on their feet, until it was revealed that Gemma was not Mary's late husband's daughter at all, but a Russian child, hidden away in England for her own safety because—in an astonishing turn of events—it was revealed that little Gemma was one of the last surviving members of the Romanovs, the royal family of Russia.

She was in danger because—as could be expected—those who currently ruled Russia were very much opposed to the restoration of a hereditary monarchy, and therefore anyone who carried the illustrious bloodline of the Romanovs was a flashpoint of contention amongst the various factions.

And so, Doyle thought, yet again we're back to that in-the-blood subject, where a small girl has to bear the burdens from centuries of warfare for no other reason than her bloodline, and with no one thinking that it's all a passel of nonsense, and instead *by their fruits shall you know them.*

Reynolds interrupted her thoughts. "This afternoon I plan to show Miss Gemma photographs of Paris, madam, and teach her a few French phrases."

Mary and her new husband had decided to take Gemma along with them on their honeymoon in Paris, and—as could be anticipated—this plan was met with grave uneasiness by

Colonel Kolchak, who was the Russian nobleman tasked with keeping Gemma secretly safe, here in England. Indeed, he'd nearly scotched the plan outright, until Acton had intervened to convince him otherwise—there was no better convincer than Acton, when all was said and done.

Doyle's gaze drifted over to watch her husband, who'd finished his phone conversation and was now taking a moment to check on something at his desk, reading the computer screen with what seemed to be mixed emotions, before he carefully logged out of his laptop.

With little success, she tried to tamp down a feeling of uneasiness; it was never a good omen, when Acton seemed to be monitoring something closely whilst trying to obscure the fact that he was doing so. I hope he's not planning on murdering his mother, she thought, only half-joking. A shame, it was, that no one ever explained to you that marriage involved so much murder and mayhem on a regular basis.

She shook herself out of her abstraction; Acton seemed much better, lately, and she was over-reacting, to think that he'd some project underway that would make her hair turn grey. He was getting better, and it was probably a good thing that they'd so many events lined up, what with all the weddings and Baptisms and Investitures; it was probably best to keep that mastermind of his distracted.

As her husband made his way into the kitchen, he dropped a casual kiss on the top of her head. "Leave in twenty minutes?"

"Yes, sir," she teased, and wished she could shake off her uneasiness.

CHAPTER 5

Doyle and Acton sat across the desk from Williams whilst the three detectives tried to brainstorm a working-theory on the Navarro case, although it seemed clear to Doyle that such a task was going to be tough-sledding.

Williams had been informed about the victim's apparent dual-identity and—since Acton famously didn't believe in coincidences—they were casting about for a connection—however tenuous—between the notorious Health Professions Council and the Navarros. Nothing was leaping to the fore, though; it was not an easy leap to make, after all.

It was also Acton's philosophy that whenever a working-theory did not present itself, it was best to follow the evidence wherever it led without the hindrance of a working-theory, and so they were now taking this tack in the hope that something of interest would eventually pop up. Unfortunately for law enforcement, having no working-theory meant a lot more legwork, since there wouldn't be an easy way to sort out priorities.

Acton instructed, "I'd like to know how long Navarro has been living in London, and whether it coincides with his servant's emergence as a witness in the Council's sex-trafficking cases."

Doyle informed Williams, "I was wonderin' if Navarro was involved in the sex-slavery rig, somehow, and he shot his servant because the man was blackmailin' him, or threatenin' to grass him out."

But Williams ducked his chin, and evidenced the same skepticism that Acton had. "I don't know, Kath; it doesn't add up, timing—wise. When he was giving us his testimony, the driver never made mention of Navarro, and we've rolled-up just about everyone who was involved. If Navarro was really worried about being exposed, the driver would have been killed long since."

Doyle had to reluctantly concede this point, and—aside from the timing problem—there was another reason it probably wasn't a containment murder, and that reason was because her illustrious husband would not have been as stymied as he was. Instead, Navarro would be in cuffs faster than you could say pedophile-going-to-prison.

Williams pulled-up the sex-trafficking case's timeline, and after reviewing it, noted, "The driver came forward in February, a year ago."

Thoughtfully, Acton turned to gaze out the window. "He came forward voluntarily?"

"Yes—almost immediately, as the case was breaking. He was worried he'd be tangled up in a conspiracy charge, and so he wanted to make a clean breast, and name names."

Acton seemed to find this of interest, and asked, "Has it been verified that he was actually the Council's limo-driver? Has anyone placed him in the car?"

There was a small silence, and Doyle could sense that Williams' surprise matched her own. He ventured, "Do you think he may have been an imposter?"

Acton continued to gaze out the windows. "I am wondering if there is anyone left at the Council's offices who could positively identify him as the driver."

Williams thought this over. "Unlikely. Castellano, perhaps, if we can find him, since he'd have been a passenger in the limo, but the other Council-members are all dead. I'm not sure that anyone on the administrative staff can make a positive ID, since the drivers were on-call."

Into the ensuing silence, Doyle ventured, "Are you thinkin' that this fellow may have actually been an informant, of some sort, and not the real driver? That he was planted as a witness, to grass everyone out to the police?"

This was actually not so very far-fetched; it would explain the private driver's unusual willingness to turn state's evidence on his clients—she could see why Acton's interest had been caught.

Acton replied, "Let us find out how he fits into the timeline, and see if anyone can positively place him as the driver in the car. But be discreet, please—there is something here that we do not understand."

"Yes, sir." Williams typed a note.

Acton added, "I would also like to know the courses Navarro teaches at the University, and when he began teaching there."

Doyle offered, "Should we see if any of Navarro's neighbors can positively ID the victim as his manservant? We can bring Navarro in for obstruction of justice, if he lied to the police about not knowin' who he was."

"Not as yet," Acton decided, as his mobile pinged, and he checked the message. "Let me have the other information, first; I don't want to tip-off Navarro that we are suspicious."

"Surveillance?" Williams suggested.

"I doubt he will go anywhere of interest," Acton replied, as he checked his watch and then rose. "But yes—let's put a man on him."

"Right, sir."

Acton paused at the door. "And if you would, please forward Castellano's file to me—everything we have, including background, and last known."

At this reference to the still-missing Council-member, there was another surprised silence, and Doyle ventured, "D'you think *that's* the connection? Mayhap Castellano's corpse is buried somewhere in Navarro's garden, and he's had to kill his servant, to cover it up? I suppose it would only make sense, since Castellano seems to have dropped off the face of the earth."

"On the contrary," said Acton as he left through the door. "I would not be surprised if Castellano is very much alive."

CHAPTER 6

"He's got some idea, percolatin' about," Doyle said into the silence. "I wonder what it is?"

"It seems fairly clear he thinks the driver's an imposter," Williams replied, as he pulled his laptop closer to him and started typing. "I didn't see that one coming."

"No—that's a wrinkle-and-a-half," she mused, thoughtfully eyeing the door her husband had closed behind him. "And he must think Castellano's involved in Navarro's murder, somehow. Interestin', that he doesn't want to move on it, and knock some heads together until he gets some answers."

"It's all speculation, Kath—he's right, we've got to find something solid, first."

Doyle bent her head to review her notes from their meeting. "Shall I start by showin' the driver's snap around at the Council's offices? I can see if anyone can positively ID him as the limo-driver—although it may be a sleeveless task, if Acton thinks he's an imposter."

"Sleeveless in more ways than one; there's hardly anyone left working there. The place is half-shuttered, now, and the Minister's trying to decide whether to shut it down completely. No one wants to be associated with the old Council, so most of the employees have quit."

Doyle made a face. "They should tear it down, stone by stone, and then salt the ground where it stood, Thomas. It's horrid, that these people did such despicable things, all the while thinkin' that they were untouchable."

"They were obviously wrong."

There was an edge of satisfaction to his tone, and Doyle was suddenly reminded that Williams had his own history of meting-out vigilante justice, when it came to pedophiles. Surely—*surely*, Williams wasn't involved in these Council-murders? On the other hand, they were having trouble getting hold of any evidence, considering the type of murders these were; despite the white-hot brutality of the murders, the killer—or killers—were very good at covering their tracks.

With some dismay, she lifted her face to gaze at the wall for a moment, wishing she hadn't held the thought. But there was no mistaking that Williams wasn't overly-dismayed that vigilantes had decided to take justice into their own hands. To be fair, though, everyone else felt the same way—the Crown Prosecutors had dropped the ball, and let this be a lesson to them not to shrink from pursuing justice, no matter how untouchable the suspect.

It's not Williams, who's doing these Council-murders, she assured herself; I would have got a glimpse, if it were. After all, I've been working cheek-by-jowl with the man and there hasn't been the slightest twitch-of-a-cat's-tail that he's involved in anything murky; I'd have caught a sense, like I've done with Acton, who's all on-end about something, and working like a journeyman to hide this fact from the wife of his bosom.

Williams interrupted these rather unsettling thoughts. "I don't think it will tip-off Navarro if we pay a visit to the University to check out his personnel records—we could say it was a routine background-check."

"And by 'we', you mean 'me'," she teased.

With a half-smile, he acknowledged, "If you wouldn't mind."

"How are you feelin'?" she asked, since this seemed the perfect opportunity.

"Better," he said briefly.

"Not true," she declared. Williams was the only other person—aside from Acton—who she'd told about her truth-detecting abilities.

He gave her a look. "They're having to adjust my insulin, is all. It tends to take a little while, to work itself out."

"Right. Let me know if you need help," she offered. "Don't be all stoic—faith, but I've had my fill of stoic men; if you or Acton were Irish, you'd belly up to the bar, announce your troubles to the world, engage in a bout of fisticuffs, and go home the better for it."

"It will work itself out," he said again, in a firmer tone.

Men, she thought; honestly. "Shall I show the driver's snap around at the University, too? Unlikely that Navarro drove himself anywhere, and someone may recognize the driver."

Williams thought about it, then nodded. "Just be discreet. Acton's worried about showing our hand, for some reason."

With a hint of exasperation, she replied, "He's definitely not showin' us *his* hand, even though it's clear as glass he got a workin'-theory."

"There must be a good reason, Kath."

Doyle paused, and slowly opined, "You know, Thomas, I think Acton's none-too-happy about his workin'-theory, and that's why he's holdin' his cards so close to the vest. Acton knows what makes him tick—Navarro, I mean; apparently he's from some old branch of Spanish nobility, and it makes

Acton—" she paused, trying to decide what it was that she was trying to say. "It makes him *wary*, for some reason."

Which didn't make much sense; Acton was wary about how he was going to handle the Navarros, but they didn't seem to warrant such concern—they were incapable of handling a simple coffee pot, for heaven's sake. Or a garden burial.

Williams shrugged. "I haven't come across anything in Navarro's background that would raise a flag."

Doyle quirked her mouth. "Aside from his bein' a murderer, and all."

He lifted his palms. "We don't know that as yet. But even so, he doesn't seem a likely suspect."

"Ach—you haven't yet met them, Thomas. Arrogance was oozin' from every pore until they realized Acton was noble, too, and then they unbent just the *tiniest* bit. Killin' people who needed killin' would be strictly routine, for someone like our Mr. Navarro—it runs in the blood."

He grimaced. "That's a scary take, Kath."

"It's true," she insisted. "They remind you of one of those portraits of the Spanish royal family—all haughty, and above-it-all."

"It's interesting they'd stoop to be here in London, then."

Reminded, Doyle nodded in agreement. "You know, Acton's thinkin' the same thing. He'd the impression that Navarro's not a'tall happy to be here—livin' amongst the no-account English—so why hasn't he taken a bunk back for Spain, if he's killed a man?"

"Flight is a pretty clear sign of guilt," Williams reminded her.

But Doyle only shook her head. "He's not one to allow a murder investigation to interfere with his wants—he's far too top-lofty for that. For some reason, he's stuck here and wishes that he weren't, and now they haven't a manservant to serve them their excellent coffee—I don't know as either one of them would know how to strike a match and light the stove-top."

Thinking this over, Williams leaned back in his chair. "Which must be why Acton wants to know what he's teaching at Winchester University, of all places."

This, because Winchester University tended to be a working-persons university, where the schedule of classes was flexible and intended for adults who were trying to better themselves—not at all a prestigious place, which would probably be more in keeping for someone like Navarro.

Doyle nodded thoughtfully. "Good point, Thomas. All the more reason for me to take a nose-around, and see what I can see." As she tucked her notepad in her rucksack, she added, "Although I suppose I shouldn't paint such a nasty picture of them—they were massive bridge-jumper fans, of all things. Faith, the wife gave me her very own rosary, and it was *ridiculously* uncomfortable."

He lifted his brows. "She did? Should we dust it for prints?"

Aghast, Doyle paused to stare at him for a long moment. "Holy saints, Thomas—that never even occurred to me. What was I *thinkin'*? I can't go about takin' gifts from suspects."

"No one will hear about it from me," he replied easily.

But Doyle had another protocol-skirting revelation, hard on the first one. "Acton saw it, but he didn't say anythin'. And—come to think of it—I shouldn't have been Acton's support officer in the first place—it's not allowed." While a husband and wife could work at the Met, neither one could have supervisory obligations over the other.

Williams pointed out the obvious. "He must have had good reason to want you in on the interview, Kath."

She conceded, "Indeed he did, since it turned out that Navarro was lyin' like a dog on the butcher's stoop." Frowning, she drew her finger along the edge of his desk as she thought about it. "But we're not movin' on it, for some reason. I wish I knew Acton's secret workin'-theory—I haven't a clue."

Williams put his hands on his desk so as to rise. "Let's get on it first thing tomorrow then, and see if we can give him the information that he needs. Be careful not to raise any alarms."

"Right-o; I'll be as subtle as a serpent." As she rose, she remembered to ask, "Are you comin' to Mary's weddin', this week-end?"

Williams had dated Doyle's nanny for a time, and Doyle had the sense that he'd been well-smitten, only to be disappointed when Mary met her Howard, and was in turn well-smitten, herself.

"No," he replied in a casual tone. "I wasn't planning on it."

She caught a nuance in his tone, and with a grimace, offered, "Sorry, if it's a sore subject—I speak before I think, sometimes."

But he chuckled, unoffended, and rose to open the door for her. "No one knows this better than me, Kath."

As she lifted her rucksack onto her shoulder, she admitted, "I almost wish I weren't going to the weddin', myself; I'm not one for public ceremonies, and I've got two comin' up, between Mary's weddin', and Sofia's Baptism. Three, if you count the stupid Investiture."

"The rituals of life," he conceded. "You can't avoid them. I've had to go to a lot of weddings myself, recently— everyone's getting to be that age."

"I bet no one is forcin' you to wear a tiara."

He grinned. "I would pay good money, Kath. Make sure someone takes a snap."

"Done," said Doyle easily, and privately vowed that any photographic evidence of the newly-minted Countess of Aldwych would be given the same treatment as Edward's Baptism photos.

CHAPTER 7

He was having trouble sleeping.More so than the usual; he'd lie awake, keeping his eyes closed and trying to fight the urge to go over the protocol one more time, to make certain that he hadn't missed anything. If he started down that path—thinking about the protocol—sleep would become impossible.

It helped to listen to her breathe; she tended to breathe rather loudly, for such a small person, and when they'd first married it had kept him awake, because he was so conscious of it. Now, he couldn't imagine sleeping apart from it—and there was a motivator like no other.

Normally, if he was having trouble sleeping he'd have a drink, or work until he was tired, but he couldn't risk it—not now. He couldn't risk her knowing that he was restless; she's start probing for the cause and she was remarkably good at seeing beyond what he wanted her to see.

Her intuitive sense was extraordinary, really, and somewhat of a mixed blessing since he'd been walking a tightrope, carefully guarding his reactions in light of the current situation. He wouldn't have it any other way, of course; it was part and parcel of who she was. She was utterly perfect, and he was fortunate beyond measure.

The dreams, however; the dreams gave him pause. Presumably, her subconscious was gathering information without her realizing it, and was then delivering the information to her conscious mind in the guise of a dream—

44

such a transference was well-recognized, in the circles of neurophysiology.

And this theory only made sense, based upon what he himself had observed, firsthand. She was not the most careful of detectives, and oftentimes she'd miss the significance of an important clue, but—presumably, thanks to her intuitive sense—the information would be nevertheless retained, processed, and then emerge as a dramatic revelation in a dream.

Indeed, it was the only explanation available, since the conclusions she reached in the dreams seemed extraordinarily on-point, for a person who didn't pay very close attention in her day-to-day life.

And after all, the only other alternative was as she believed; that she was some sort of conduit for information—information which, in large part, seemed to consist of a call-to-action directed at himself.

He opened his eyes to consider the ceiling for a moment, before closing them again. That was highly unlikely, of course, as it spoke of unknown-and-unknowable forces at work. Instead, it was much more likely that her dreams were a subconscious-to-conscious transfer; a manifestation of her extraordinary intuitive abilities, revealed in a comfortable narrative that was rooted in her religious heritage.

He listened to her even breathing for a moment, and congratulated himself; he was almost certain that she hadn't any suspicions about the protocol. It was fortunate they had several social events lined up as a distraction—there would never be a better time. 'If it were done when 'tis done, then 'twere well it were done quickly', after all.

It would be best if he could arrange for them to be out of the country, of course; unlikely, that she'd ever guess, but she was who she was, and he didn't want to risk it.

Listening to her breaths, he tried to calm himself, and sleep. It was no easy thing, to be the keeper of secrets.

CHAPTER 8

A s Williams had predicted, Doyle did not experience much luck when she visited what remained of the notorious Council's offices the following morning. Only a skeleton crew manned the desks so as to answer the phones and deflect all inquiries elsewhere, and none of the personnel recognized the snap of the limo-driver.

One young woman was in the process of methodically varnishing her nails, but nonetheless took a moment to explain to Doyle that it was usually the Council-member's Assistant who called for the limo, since they'd be the ones who knew when it would be needed.

"Like Martina Betancourt?" asked Doyle, thinking of Sir Cavanaugh's missing Assistant.

At the mention of the name, the girl immediately perked up, and lifted her head to ask in a ghoulish whisper, "Has she been murdered, yet?"

"No," said Doyle, and then hurriedly added, "Not to my knowledge, leastways," because her instinct was telling her that her first answer was indeed true; Martina was very much alive.

This was of interest, and as the driving service ferried her over to Winchester University, Doyle tried to decide what it meant—that Sir Cavanaugh's missing Assistant was apparently alive and well, somewhere. There'd been no evidence that the young woman was involved in the Council's many crimes, so it didn't appear that she was fleeing law enforcement. Had she disappeared because she held dangerous knowledge, and feared for her life? But—as was the case with the limo-driver's murder—it didn't make a lot of sense; the timing was off, since the case had broken quite some time ago. That, and there was no one left to threaten her; all the blacklegs on the Council were getting themselves murdered, save for Castellano, who—whom?—Acton seemed to suspect was still alive. Mayhap Martina was afraid of Castellano?

With an effort, she tried to remember what she knew of Castellano—no easy feat, since it hadn't been her case, and she never paid much attention if it wasn't her case. She seemed to recall that Castellano wasn't one of the original Council-members—he took the position just before the massive scandal broke, which was poor timing on his part, especially if he wasn't involved in all the dark doings. But he was obviously worried enough to flee the scene, and—as Williams had noted—flight was a pretty clear sign of guilt.

It *is* strange, she decided; the whole thing doesn't make much sense, which is probably why Acton is stewing like a barleycorn—although I'll bet my teeth he has a glimmer. He has a glimmer, but doesn't want to share his theory, just yet.

She gave up on trying to come up with her own theory, but reminded herself that she needed to tell Acton about Martina—about how she was still alive. It was important, for some reason.

Winchester University was in Midtown London, fronted on a busy street and very much no-nonsense—not one of your fancy-gardens-and-archives sort of universities, in keeping with its premise of serving the working-class. As she considered the weather-worn façade, Doyle was again struck by the feeling that it didn't fit, somehow; Mr. Navarro was not the sort of person to dip his fingertips into such an institution, no matter the incentive. Acton must have had the same thought, since he wanted them to have a long look into the suspect's teaching stint, here. Something wasn't adding up.

Once inside, Doyle crossed the linoleum-floored lobby to explain to the person at the front desk that she was on police business, doing a routine background-check on one of their adjunct professors. After showing her warrant card, she was escorted back into the administrative offices, where she was then steered through the crowded, busy room to the Human Resources Administrator, an earnest, middle-aged woman who wore dark-framed glasses and worked with a dog at her feet.

Immediately, the small beast leapt up and began growling at Doyle, his hackles raised. This was not a surprise to Doyle, because dogs didn't much like her and in turn, she didn't much like dogs.

"Bertie," the woman scolded, embarrassed. "Down, now."

But Bertie wasn't having it, and only continued hostile, lifting his lip to bare his teeth.

The woman tugged rather ineffectively on his leash. "My therapy dog," she explained. "He wouldn't hurt a fly."

"I'll just come over on this side," Doyle offered, and squeezed between her desk and the desk of a heavy-set, swarthy man who sat back to regard Doyle with unabashed masculine interest.

The man shrugged his massive shoulders in a derisive manner. "She must have the dog with her."

He'd an accent, and Doyle decided it might be Russian; not a surprise, since much of the clientele for this type of institution tended to be new immigrants.

Doyle discerned an aura of long-established hostility between these two, and was reminded why she hated interviewing fellow office-workers, who could never seem to resist the urge to backbite. "Yes, well, I have a few routine questions—"

"Bertie has saved my life, many a time," the woman defended herself to the heavy-set man. "You will do well to mind your own business, Mr. Sergius."

With an amused, superior glance at Doyle, the man went back to his computer screen.

Ignoring the dog—who continued with his low-voiced growling whenever she spoke—Doyle explained, "I need to have a look at Professor Navarro's records, if you don't mind. He's a witness on a case, and it's a routine background-check."

"That one—he is a *pakhan*," Mr. Sergius piped up, unabashedly eavesdropping.

Bertie's owner pointedly turned a shoulder to her neighbor. "I haven't much—Professor Navarro taught an evening class last term, but it's over, now." She squinted at the screen. "*History of the Battle of Cartagena de Indias, and the War of Jenkins' Ear.*"

Doyle blinked in disbelief. "Is that a made-up name?"

With a hint of censure, the Administrator replied, "No; a very crucial battle, in terms of South American history."

But Doyle could not hide her incredulity. "And people *signed-up* for it?"

"Many people are interested in other country's histories," the woman explained, trying without much success to hide a superior tone. "And in addition, the class would fulfill the general history requirement."

But Mr. Sergius chimed in, yet again. "He needed an excuse to meet with his *ptitsy*." He then smacked his lips in masculine appreciation.

"That's *so* rude," the administrator scolded, turning a bit pink. "You'd best beware, or I'll have you written-up."

But Doyle had found this tidbit extremely interesting, and asked the Russian man in a casual, amused tone, "He was datin' one of his students, then?"

"His *ptitsy*," Again, he made an exaggerated smacking sound, trying to provoke his office-mate.

"I wouldn't know," the woman said firmly. "It would be against the rules, though; professors are not supposed to date students—even adjunct professors."

But Doyle's scalp was prickling, and she was trying to decide why this would be. That arrogant, wealthy men felt they were entitled to feminine attention went without saying, and indeed, here would be the likely reason Mr. Navarro had gone slumming in Midtown to teach a class that no one would want to sign up for; he wanted cover so as to conduct an affair. And if this were the case, the girlfriend might be a valuable asset—especially if he'd broken it off, and she felt slighted; slighted girlfriends were a detective's best friend.

"If this woman was enrolled in his class, would you have her information?"

"Of course," the Administrator replied punctuously. "We are very careful about security at the University, and you must have a photo-pass around your neck at all times whilst on premises. During night classes, such as this one, we're doubly-careful; we have only the one access door, with a doorman posted."

She turned to pull up the roster for Navarro's class, but when Doyle leaned to look over her shoulder, Bertie took great exception to this, and began barking again.

"Hush," the woman insisted in an ineffectual manner. "I'm so very sorry, officer, I don't know what's got into him."

"He protects you," the Russian man pronounced, as he shifted his bulk in his chair. "He is a dog."

"No matter, ma'am," Doyle said, trying to ignore the commotion.

"Fah—I will take him," the man offered, and reached for the leash. "Come, little dog."

"Oh—" the woman exclaimed in mild protest, but to everyone's surprise, Bertie meekly allowed the Russian man to bring him around to the other side of his desk.

Turning her attention back to the task at hand, the woman pulled up the class list—seven people, in all, and began methodically clicking on each enrollee's name to bring up their ID card information. "This one," Doyle indicated with a finger. "There's only one woman."

"We mustn't make assumptions about gender," the woman cautioned in a prim tone. Her cheeks then flushed with anger as her office-mate made a derisive sound.

Doyle decided to stay out of the hostilities, and so patiently waited until the Administrator came to the student identified as Judith Bethulia. The ID photograph flashed up on the screen, and Doyle was hard-pressed not to gasp aloud, because the face presented to her was that of Martina Betancourt, Cavanaugh's missing Assistant.

CHAPTER 9

After thanking the Administrator for the information—and once again assuring her that it was strictly a routine background-check—Doyle could hardly wait to ring up Williams as soon as she was outside on the pavement. "I've got somethin' important on the Council cases—can we meet-up?"

"Is it exigent?" she could hear background noise and other voices; it sounded as though he was outside, somewhere.

"Remind me what that means, Thomas."

"Is it an emergency? I've my hands full for the next hour or so."

She checked the time. "Can you break for a quick lunch, later? I'll have Reynolds cook you up a brisket, or something." Since Williams was a bachelor, this was a tried-and-true method of bringing him to heel—not to mention that he was looking a bit peaked lately, and should probably eat something hearty. "Acton should hear it, too—I'll check-in to see if he's free."

"Acton is here."

"Oh—oh, ask if that's agreeable, then." This was of interest; as a Chief Inspector, Acton tended not to go out into the field unless there was something unusual at play. Of course, they were so short-handed that it was all hands to the pump, nowadays.

After a murmured conversation, Williams reported that the lunch plan was agreeable.

"Fine; I'll go home and crack the whip over Reynolds whilst I start on my report. Unless you need my help with your case—I can come over straightaway, if you'd like me to." This said with a hopeful air, since for Doyle, field-work was infinitely preferable to paper-work.

"You wouldn't like this one, Kath. See you later."

Hope it's not a dead baby, she thought with a grimace, as she rang off. Ever since she'd become a mother, she'd turned very sensitive on the subject.

She'd forgot that Reynolds was minding Gemma today, and so upon her arrival she was treated to the sight of the butler sitting at the kitchen table, assiduously bent over a project with the little girl—one that involved sequins and glue, from what Doyle could see.

"Look, Lady Acton," the little girl exclaimed with much excitement as she indicated the object on the table. "It's a photo frame."

"Now, there's a crackin' wonderment," said Doyle diplomatically, since personally she didn't care for purple glitter and unicorn stickers.

"It's a wedding present for my mum and Mr. Howard," she said proudly.

"Perfect," Doyle assured her. "Up on their mantel it shall go."

Reynolds hid his dismay at this suggestion with only limited success. "Actually, madam, you and Lord Acton are gifting the couple a sterling silver picture frame for their wedding photograph. This one is for a photograph with Gemma, while they are visiting Paris."

"Even better," said Doyle immediately. "If the Eiffel Tower isn't purple, it should be."

Gemma held her hands over her mouth and giggled as Doyle explained, "We're havin' a workin' lunch, Reynolds; Williams is comin' over, and so we should try to feed him somethin' substantial."

Reynolds perked up, as he always did when he was asked to cook something for a more appreciative audience. "Just so, madam."

After she'd ducked into the baby's room to watch little Edward's sleeping form for a minute, Doyle then wandered over to sit at Acton's desk in the bedroom, thinking over how best to frame her report. The morning visit to the Council's office was easy, because there wasn't much to report—no one recognized the driver, and no one seemed much interested in doing anything other than marking time. But the Martina Betancourt information was big news, and so she had to write it down in an orderly fashion, which wasn't exactly her strong suit.

Dawdling, she looked out the window for a minute, and then she lifted Acton's framed picture of herself, which was the only item on his immaculate desk since he was one of those ODV people—or whatever you called it—where everything had to be just-so. A wonder, it was, that the man had chosen a raging bundle of disorder as his wife, and now that she'd promptly produced a baby, he'd a three-ring circus going on in the midst of his formerly just-so life. The spare bedroom was now a nursery, and he'd been forced to move his desk into their bedroom, since it held the only semi-quiet corner.

Doyle had been carefully avoiding the subject, but it seemed clear they'd have to move someplace with more room, especially if they were to have more children, which was likely, due to their sex-at-the-drop-of-a-hat habit. That Acton wouldn't like having to move from his penthouse sanctuary, here on the seventh floor, was a given, and so she was putting off the discussion as long as she could.

Her thoughts were interrupted by a ping on her private mobile—which wasn't much of a surprise; Acton must wonder what she'd discovered, and he was not one to be too busy working on the current case to hear about it, like Williams was. A multi-tasker, was our Acton.

Without preamble, she announced into the mobile, "Martina Betancourt was takin' Mr. Navarro's class under a different name."

"That," he said, "is very interesting."

With some surprise, she observed, "You're not half as shocked as you should be."

"I do have a theory," he admitted. "But it is rather far-fetched."

She quirked her mouth into the phone. "I'll remind you that you're speakin' to the Queen of Far-fetched-land, my friend."

"That is true."

"Well, I'm not goin' to go about droppin' bombshells if you don't give me a proper reaction."

"I do beg your pardon. Shall we start over again?"

"No point—that ship has sailed. What are you workin' on, that Williams thinks would make me squeamish?"

"A dead priest," he replied.

"Who?" she asked, sitting upright in surprise. Roman Catholic priests were as rare as hen's teeth, here in the land of the bog-proddies.

"Father Ambrose, formerly of St. Cecelia's."

She frowned. "Can't say as I know that one."

"I am not surprised; he is quite elderly, and has been living out his retirement in the parish rectory."

Suddenly, Doyle realized that she was missing the main point. "And he was *murdered*?"

"It does seem that way."

With a knit brow, she asked, "Who'd murder someone that old? And a priest, for heaven's sake—it's not like he'd have anythin' worth stealin'. Was he wanderin' about in the wrong part of town?"

"No; he was found in the rectory garden."

Doyle raised her brows. "Mother a' mercy, Michael—that's alarmin'. And it must be why Father John phoned me up this mornin'; he left a message, but I haven't had a chance to ring him back." Father John was the pastor at St. Michael's Church, their own parish, and as such he could be forgiven for being a bit anxious to hear details, if priests were getting themselves murdered, hereabouts.

"I must go, I'm afraid."

"Cheers. See you soon."

Doyle rang off, and then rather guiltily scrolled so as to return Father John's call straightway, so that she wouldn't forget yet again.

"Hello, lass; are you ready to go off to your fancy-dancy weddin'?"

Doyle gently scolded, "I hope you're not castin' aspersions on people of other faiths, Father." Due to the constraints of having secret-Russian-royalty as a stepdaughter, the powers-that-be had insisted that Mary marry Howard in the Russian Orthodox Church. Mary had little choice in the matter, since her claim to Gemma was tenuous at best; indeed, the powers-that-be had only allowed the girl to stay with Mary because they were both living under Acton's auspices, and no one had tighter security than Acton.

"Best pack a lunch, lass." Father John had warned Doyle that the ceremony would take the better portion of two hours, being as he knew the fair Doyle tended to be a bit restless.

"You're cold comfort, Father. Were you callin' to tell me about Father Ambrose?"

With some surprise, the priest asked, "Now, how on earth did you know that?"

She blinked. "How did *you* know that?"

"He told me."

She frowned in confusion. "He *told* you he was murdered?"

There was a small, alarmed pause. "Was he *murdered*, lass?"

Oh-oh, thought Doyle. "Forget I said anythin', Father; there's a pendin' investigation, and I'm not at liberty to say. But if you know somethin' that would be helpful to the police, I'm all ears."

Slowly, the priest said, "Then we're at a standstill, I'm afraid. There's a confessional seal involved, so I'm not at liberty, either."

Doyle raised her brows in surprise. "Is there still a seal, even if he's been murdered?"

"There is. But I did want a bit of advice from you, when you have a moment to visit."

This suggestion was carefully posited, and—coming as it did upon the heels of the revelation about the priest's murder—it led Doyle to conclude that Father John must have information he wanted to drop without being obvious about it. Doyle gladly shoved aside all report-making obligations, and told him, "Right then; I can come by after lunch—will you be at the Church?"

"I will—I'll be in my office. Come in the back way, to avoid the construction."

"I will see you then."

"Thank you, lass."

Now, here's a wrinkle, she thought, as she rang off. And it must be something mighty troubling, if Father John is trying to figure out how to work around the seal of the confessional—she was a bit hazy on the protocol, but she knew it must be very serious indeed, if such were the case.

Since Edward very much wanted his mother to be made aware that he'd awakened from his nap, she rose to go fetch him, hoping that Father John had a case-breaker, and thinking that it would be quite the feather in her cap, if she were to stumble on two different body-in-the-garden case-breakers on the same day.

CHAPTER 10

Although he hadn't time to make a brisket, Reynolds had managed to pull together some sort of pasta concoction with a hearty meat sauce that Williams was consuming with much appreciation as the three detectives sat at the kitchen table.

Doyle had finished reciting her adventures at Winchester University, and now Acton was asking a few follow-up questions, which is what he tended to do to make her report a bit more cohesive, since she tended to jump to the good bits and gloss over the basics.

Even so, his first follow-up question was a bit surprising. "Did you recognize anyone else who was taking the class?"

Thinking about it, she admitted, "I wasn't paying close attention, because I was waiting to see the girlfriend's snap. But I think I would have noticed, if I recognized anyone else— I saw them all go by."

Acton's next question seemed equally surprising. "Why did you think that Martina Betancourt was Navarro's girlfriend?"

She blinked. "I just assumed that she was—why else would she have used a false name? In fact, the only reason I thought to look her up at all was because one of the people working in administration thought that was the case—that she was his girlfriend, on the side." With a mighty effort, she tried to recall the term. "He called her Navarro's '*ptitsy*'."

To her surprise, this remark garnered her husband's full and immediate attention. "Who said this, Kathleen?"

Willingly, she recited, "There was a Russian fellow at the next desk—or at least, I assumed he was Russian—and he was needlin' our Records Administrator like a Job's comforter. And in turn, she was all offended that he'd make such an assumption about one of their professors, and tell tales." She paused, watching him. "Why—what's it mean?"

Acton said slowly, "The term has a specialized meaning, in Russian. It means the same as 'honeypot', in English."

"A'course, it does," she agreed. "Never doubt it."

As Williams hid a smile behind his hand, Acton explained, "It describes a woman who is a lure—who is sent out to gather information from unsuspecting men."

She considered this, frowning. "Like a *spy*?"

He nodded. "Like a spy. Did the Russian man make any other remarks?"

Doyle closed her eyes, trying to remember. "When Mr. Navarro's name was first mentioned, Mr. Sergius called him a "*pick-on*" —or somethin' like that."

"*Pakhan*," Acton corrected, and there followed a small silence, whilst he gazed out the window thoughtfully. "We may have to have a follow-up conversation with Mr. Sergius, you and I."

But Doyle was at sea. "I don't understand, Michael—Mr. Navarro's not Russian. Faith, he'd probably stab you through the heart at the very suggestion."

"No," he agreed. "But Mr. Sergius must believe that he plays a role similar to that of a *pakhan*, which refers to—" here, he paused and it seemed that he was trying to decide what she'd understand easiest. "A position similar to a mafia leader. It would also explain his reference to Martina

61

Betancourt as a *ptitsy*." He paused, then added, "And note well that her assumed name is 'Judith'."

"Oh," said Doyle, in dawning realization. "The Judith from the Bible."

Thomas spoke up. "I'll bite. Who was Judith from the Bible?"

Doyle explained, "She seduced an enemy general, and then cut off his head. A true honey-jar."

"Honeypot," corrected Williams.

"Honeypot," she agreed. Mulling this over, she sought to understand Acton's theory. "So—you think Martina wasn't Navarro's girlfriend a'tall, but was double-crossin' him, in some way?"

Acton tilted his head slightly. "No—I believe the opposite. I believe this group—the class, headed by Navarro—may have been the ones who were orchestrating all the Council-murders."

This was unexpected, and both Doyle and Williams stared at him in the silence that this revelation deserved. Williams finally said, "If that's true, then we should award them all the George."

Doyle gave him an admonishing look, and ventured, "I don't know, Michael; if that's your workin'-theory, then it *does* seem a bit far-fetched. You're goin' to have a hard time convincin' me that our Mr. Navarro bestirs himself enough to be a vigilante, so as to avenge mistreated immigrants. And mistreated immigrants in London, at that."

Acton bowed his head in acknowledgment. "I would tend to agree. But, on the other hand, note that he was willing to teach a night class at a Midtown university."

"Not a'tall in keepin'," she agreed. "You're right—it must have been a cover. Not to mention the class subject was so ridiculous that no one would want to sign up—some battle, somewhere in South America, that no one would give two pins about."

"No doubt the subject was specifically chosen to discourage the interest of others."

Doyle nodded. "Aye, that. So—we think Navarro's the one who's givin' the orders for the Council-murders? Faith—he doesn't seem like the mastermind-type, to me."

With a knit brow, Williams leaned back, and crossed his arms. "Why? I haven't had a lot of time to look into his background, but so far, there's not a lot to raise a flag. Wealthy Spanish family, he's here on a short-term visa."

Acton replied, "I suppose we could presume, as a working-theory, that he is here in London for the express purpose of overseeing the Council-murders."

Williams considered this. "Again, why?"

"That remains to be seen."

"But you don't think he's necessarily the perp?"

Acton shook his head, slightly. "No; unlikely he'd wield a knife, and besides, the perpetrator would have to be a strong man—or men. These victims did not die immediately, and presumably were constrained, while they bled out." He paused, and then added, "Which I think was rather the point. These murders were brutal, and drawn-out for maximum misery."

Doyle offered, "If vengeance was the motivator, then I suppose that's not a surprise—that the victims were made to suffer."

But Williams continued skeptical, and shook his head slightly. "I still don't get it. We think this was a conspiracy, then? A gang of vigilantes, working within a sophisticated and well-coordinated rig, and—save for Doyle's twigging onto

Martina's photograph—they probably would have got clean away. Why would such a conspiracy be murdering their victims with spite-murder-type knifings? It doesn't add up, to me."

This was indeed a good point; usually, multiple-wound stabbings were intensely personal, and committed by a perpetrator who was enraged beyond all rational thought. Indeed, it was why the CID was taking a careful look at the families of the sex-slavery victims for potential suspects; ordinarily, this type of vengeance-murder was committed by a spouse, or a distraught relative.

"The gang wanted to disguise the motive?" Doyle suggested. "Although you'd be takin' a chance, since a bloody homicide leaves buckets of evidence behind."

Acton nodded. "All good points. There is something here we do not understand, as yet. Do we have Martina Betancourt's date-of-hire in the timeline?"

"I'll double-check, but if I remember correctly it was one year ago February," Williams replied. "I remember it, because Sir Cavanaugh's previous Assistant quit when the original pedophile scandal broke—when Severon was murdered."

At the mention of this subject, Acton's gaze drifted over to the window again. "Is Severon's murder in the timeline?"

Surprised yet again, Doyle and Williams regarded him for a moment, before Williams ventured, "Do you think there is a connection, sir? We know Severon was murdered by another actor—we had a full confession, after all."

This seemed irrefutable; the first Council-member to be murdered was a pedophile, abusing the boys who participated in a youth sports group that he'd founded himself. His murderer, however, had been caught and had confessed, so that Severon's murder would appear to be unrelated to the current ones—save for the fact that all Council-members were shown to have been despicable and corrupt blacklegs, through-and-though.

"It seems an extraordinary coincidence."

In Acton-speak, this meant that he didn't think it was a coincidence at all, and so Williams offered up, "If Severon's murder started this chain of events, then its possible these subsequent murders are shadow-murders."

This seemed a good thought; a shadow-murder was one committed in the hopes that it would be pinned on another murderer, and it could very well explain the wholesale slaughter of Council-members, once Severon had been killed.

But Acton shook his head. "Unlikely. Severon's killer was dead before these murders were committed—there was no one left to lay-off blame."

"And the m.o. is different," Doyle reluctantly conceded. "These are face-to-face knifin's, whereas Severon was shot from behind, unawares."

"Severon's death was more humane," Acton agreed. "Whereas these deaths are not humane at all. A different mode, a different motivator."

"Bloody vengeance," Williams agreed. "But we still want to include Severon's murder on the timeline?"

"Yes," Acton replied. "Severon's murder may have inspired these others, somehow." He then glanced at his watch. "I'm afraid I am due at Headquarters. Please have the team take a careful look at the secondary people around Severon's original molestation victims—let's see if there is a relative, or anyone else with a vengeance motive who has a connection to Navarro's night-class. And in the same way, let's have another look at the secondary people around the Council's sex-trafficking victims; look for possible connections to these night-class participants." He paused. "Take special note of anyone with a Spanish surname."

Williams nodded, as he typed an entry. "We think it may be a blood-feud, then? It shouldn't be too hard to find a connection, in that case."

But Acton was not as optimistic. "Unfortunately, many of the sex-trafficking victims have not been identified. Therefore, the connection may be to an unknown."

This was a sad byproduct of the sex-trafficking trade; oftentimes, the victims were reluctant to come forward, which made the CID's work that much harder.

Acton loaded his electronics into his valise, and closed it up. "What has Navarro done, in the past day?"

Williams checked his tablet. "Surveillance says he hasn't gone anywhere."

Doyle said in a dry tone, "No need to; the class is over, and everybody's dead."

"Except Castellano," Williams reminded her.

She made a wry mouth. "Don't be so sure, my friend. I told Acton that Castellano was probably buried in the garden, and if that's truly the case, Navarro's work here is done."

But Acton offered, "I don't believe Castellano is necessarily a target, as he came onto the Council after the sex-trafficking rig was exposed, and doesn't appear to have been connected to it. I also think it is significant that he is the only member to have escaped, and that we can find no trace of him."

Doyle raised her brows in surprise. "You think he may have been part of Navarro's vigilante-gang—an inside-man?"

"We will take a look, when we visit the University," Acton said. "You may have missed his photograph."

But Doyle was confused about this latest glimpse into Acton's theory, and ventured to express her doubts. "But there's somethin' here that's not addin' up, Michael. The class is over, and its object's been achieved in spades—the Council has been well-and-thoroughly murdered. We think that Martina Betancourt—and Castellano, perhaps—are part of it, and they've gone to ground so that we can't find them. If that's the case, why hasn't Navarro gone to ground, too?"

"I imagine," said Acton, "it is because he is not quite finished."

CHAPTER 11

T heir lunch-meeting concluded, Williams was now driving Doyle to her meeting with Father John at the Church, so that on the way over they could take the opportunity to divide-up their duties on the Council-murders case.

Williams said, "I'll have a Processor amend the timeline to add the other potential players, and also set up a program to cross-check the night-class personnel with everyone who's ever crossed our radar as a potential suspect; we'll focus on relatives of the sex-trafficking victims in particular. I'll need a class list, though, and I don't want to stir the pot by asking for one—did Acton say when you were going back to the University?"

Doyle was thoughtfully reviewing the scenery that passed by her window. "No, Thomas, he didn't; mainly because he's slow-footin' this whole thing."

There was a small pause. Williams did not refute this observation—Williams was no fool—and instead, he offered, "Can you blame him? These people in the night-class—whoever they are—are more heroes than villains."

Exasperated, she turned to him. "That's not our call, DI Williams; *someone's* supposed to uphold the law, and it falls to us."

This was familiar ground, and often a source of friction between them; Doyle held on to the staunch belief that the justice system—despite its flaws—had to be respected, whilst Williams tended to share Acton's view that the justice system was often an annoyance and should be circumvented whenever necessary.

He lifted his thumbs from the steering wheel. "Let's pretend we say the same things we always say, and no one changes the other's mind."

"Done," she promptly agreed. She wasn't in the mood, just now, because there was something here that was bothering her; something about Acton's night-class theory—

"Where's your security?" Williams asked, glancing in his rear-view mirror. "He's usually hovering around, off-screen."

"His name's Trenton, and shame on you, for pretendin' you don't know it," she replied in a tart tone—Williams tended to be rather territorial about her, and didn't appreciate the fact that Acton had a private security man assigned to keep track of the fair Doyle. "Trenton may have been switched over to Edward—I haven't seen much of him, lately, ever since he's come back from his holiday." Reminded, she turned to him. "Did you know that Trenton and Lizzy Mathis are cousins?"

"I did not," he replied, in the manner of someone who did not wish to discuss this particular topic. It had become clear—judging from past adventures—that Lizzy Mathis harbored a crush on the worthy DI Williams, which was interesting in that she was not the sort of girl to harbor crushes—she was all efficiency, was Lizzy Mathis.

Doyle had originally met Lizzy as a result of the girl's work in the Met's forensics lab, but soon discovered that she had an ancestral connection to Acton's estate—Lizzy was Hudson-the-Steward's grand-niece. Once Doyle learned of it, she was almost unsurprised by the discovery because *of course* someone like Acton was going to have a loyal source in the forensics lab, and Lizzy Mathis was entirely loyal to the House of Acton.

And— because her family had been serving Acton's family for many generations—Mathis was also distantly related to the ghost of a medieval knight who haunted Trestles—a knight who'd been pestering Doyle, recently, to find a husband for the fair Lizzy. This seemed a daunting task, considering Lizzy's personality, and Doyle's small circle of acquaintances.

And so—despite all indications that her companion didn't wish to discuss this subject—Doyle persevered. "Well, Trenton and Lizzy are indeed cousins, and they even went on holiday together, of all things. I was sorely disappointed to hear that Trenton was her cousin, because I was thinkin' he might be a good candidate to marry her."

"Oh-oh," Williams said, joking. "Here comes the pitch."

Blowing out a breath, she conceded, "I know you're not Lizzy-husband material, Thomas—and more's the pity, since she can cook like nobody's business—but I've been tasked with findin' her a husband, and I haven't a *clue* who'd be willin'."

"I'll ask around," he offered.

She smiled her appreciation, even though she suspected he offered as a means to close down the subject, more than anything else. "That's grand of you, Thomas—thanks. I'm not one to know any men who aren't on the fast-track to prison."

"How about Geary? Or is he going back to Ireland, soon?"

Doyle pondered what to say, and then decided to reveal, "I think our Inspector Geary is head-over-heels smitten with Izzy Munoz."

This revelation engendered exactly the sort of reaction it called for, and Williams turned to stare at her in abject surprise.

"Mind the road, Thomas."

"Are you *sure*?"

"I am. I think that's the main reason we're not hearin' much from that quarter, lately." Detective Sergeant Isabella Munoz had been placed on a thirty-day suspension for dereliction of duty, but Doyle had the sneaking suspicion that she wasn't suffering much with it, but was instead spending all her spare time with Inspector Geary so as to decide whether they should make a go of it, despite their differences.

"What about Gabriel?"

This was a good question, as Officer Gabriel was ostensibly Munoz's beau. Gabriel, however, was doing a Met-ordered stint in rehab to clear up an addiction problem, which happily coincided with Munoz's opportunity to spend more time with Geary.

She cautioned, "I can't say for certain, one way or the other, Thomas. Keep it under your hat, if you would."

"Of course, Kath. Although if Gabriel is the loser, we could always set him up with Lizzy Mathis."

She laughed, as he'd intended. "Now, there would be an answer to all lovelorn loose-ends, wouldn't it? I'll have to throw those two together, somehow. Mayhap I can convince them both to come to Sofia's Baptism."

He said dryly, "I don't know as Habib and Elena need any more drama."

"Point taken, Thomas." Munoz's sister Elena had a baby girl who was to be baptized in two weeks, but the story was an unusual one; in fact, Elena had been an intern at the notorious Health Professions Council before she was abducted, and became one of its victims. After Acton set-up a sting operation, the girl had been dramatically rescued by Inspector Habib, Doyle's supervisor at the Met.

Elena had fallen pregnant as a result of her ordeal, and Habib had promptly offered to marry her, and raise the baby as his own. Sweet little Sofia was the result, and Doyle could only marvel as Habib had shown the new baby's snap around at Headquarters, proud as any other new parent.

"Habib's a wonder," Doyle remarked.

Williams nodded. "I don't know as I could have done what he did."

She made a wry mouth. "Whist, Thomas; I seem to remember that you'd have done the same for me." This was actually true; before Edward was conceived, Acton and Williams had concocted a scheme to allow Williams to pose as Acton's heir, so as to stymie Acton's true heir, who was a viper of the first order. The extant plan, if Acton had died, was for Williams to then marry Doyle without missing a beat. It went without saying that neither man had consulted with the fair Doyle about this plan because they knew that she would have taken the rough end of a jacksaw to the both of them.

"That's different; I already knew you."

"No more schemin' behind my back," she teased.

"Thankfully, there's no more need."

"No—Edward's all ready to be the next Lord Acton, once he figures out how to feed himself. Not to mention there's already enough schemin' goin' on as it is, which brings us back to the original topic, and why Acton is slow-walkin' this investigation."

Williams reminded her, "You did say that you thought he was wary, for some reason."

Nodding thoughtfully, she said, "Yes—mayhap because—in light of what we're findin' out—this Navarro person seems to be another Acton-style schemer. Faith, when you think about it, he and Acton are peas in a pod—small wonder he's wary."

Williams offered, "In the end, I think your working-theory is the right one, though; they're conducting an efficient vigilante operation, but in order to disguise the motive, they're making it look like disorganized spite-murders."

But Doyle knit her brow. "I don't know, Thomas; Acton seems to think it's a blood-feud of some sort, what with his focus on the Spanish-surnames."

Her companion considered this. "Was everyone in the class Spanish? Did you notice?"

"I didn't notice, but I'm not sure that's it. These people aren't just Spanish, they think they're in an entirely different—canst? Is that the word? I always mix it up."

"Caste, maybe?"

"Yes, thank you. They're top-o'-the-trees—or at least, they think they are—and not subject to the ordinary rules."

But Williams didn't seem to think the suspect's status in life was significant, and he shrugged, slightly. "Not a news-flash, that aristocrats think they're better than everyone else, Kath. No offense, of course."

But she frowned, trying to decide what she was trying to say, and wondering why she felt it was so important. "It's not that they think they're *better*, necessarily; it's more that they think they've established themselves as beyond the regular rules. This vigilante-gang thinks they've got the solution to the evil-Council-problem, and if anyone dares to disagree, it hardly matters." She thought of Acton, and added somberly, "It's a dangerous way of thinkin'."

"Oh-oh," he said. "I thought we'd agreed to disagree, on this topic."

She lifted the corner of her mouth. "Knocker. I'm not talkin' about our usual topic—although you're wrong, wrong, wrong on that, and I'll just slip that in, as an aside. Instead, I'm talkin' about the—the 'caste' thing. I think Acton is wary because he's spotted a fellow-member of the no-rules caste, and so he's got to be very careful about how to proceed."

But Williams came back to the nub of their problem. "What's the motive, then? It seems a bit strange, for someone like Navarro to come to a different country and deliberately skirt the law so as to punish some bad actors, a thousand miles away. Why?"

Doyle, of course, wished she knew the answer, and she imagined that Acton wished he knew, too. "Let's see what Acton's suggestion about the Spanish surnames comes up with. We may find Navarro's motivation there."

He glanced at her. "'Castellano' sounds Spanish."

She nodded. "But if it's a blood-feud, then why would Navarro's gang succeed in killin' everyone on the Council *except* Castellano?"

Williams guessed, "To cover-up his motive? An ABC murder?" This, in reference to the Agatha Christie story, where the murderer killed a random variety of victims to obscure his motive for killing the true intended victim.

"Mayhap," Doyle mused. "To someone like him, the fact that innocent people might have to be killed would be like brushin' off a fly." Her scalp prickled, but she'd no idea why, and so she ignored it.

"I'll get a Processor to create a search program—that sounds like a priority."

Doyle nodded. "Good. And don't forget we have an in-house witness, so to speak; mayhap we should ask Munoz's sister Elena whether she recognizes any of the people in the night-class."

But Williams was skeptical. "Elena's already been debriefed pretty thoroughly, Kath."

Doyle glanced at him. "She's got a Spanish surname."

"Not any more she doesn't, after she's married Habib. I think she was just an intern at the Council who got caught up in the web, Kath—she's a pretty girl, and you can see how it would happen. And besides, if she knew anything that would help us on these Council-murders, Acton—or Munoz, or even Habib—would have jumped on it."

"True," Doyle conceded. "And I suppose I can't very well buttonhole her at Sofia's Baptism, and ask her about that time when she was kidnapped."

He smiled. "Probably not."

He pulled the car in front of St. Michael's Church, which was partially obscured by construction scaffolding, liberally swathed with tarps. Leaning in to look up at the façade, he asked, "Is that a new bell tower?"

"'Tis, and one fine day they'll finally be done with all the renovations—it always seems to take forever."

"Will you need a ride back? Shall I wait?"

"Thanks, but no; Father John's bein' a bit mysterious, and I've no idea what I'm in for."

"All right; keep me posted."

Before closing the car door, she leaned in to say, "Thanks for the lift, Thomas, and thanks for helpin' out with Lizzy. In return, I'll see if I can nose-out another case-breaker for you; I'm a giver, that way."

"Always appreciated, Kath." Lifting a hand, he drove away.

CHAPTER 12

Father John drummed his fingers on the edge of his battered wooden desk, apparently trying to decide what he could say to Doyle in good conscience.

This was rather a surprise, because—in the usual course of events—the Irish priest was rarely at a loss for words. He was a slightly stooped, kindly man who'd been minding his own business and managing a small-but-hardy parish in an obscure corner of London until the day that the famous Lord Acton had taken a fancy to one of his parishioners, and as a result of this unlooked-for occurrence, his flock had nearly doubled, renovation money was pouring in, and he was now tasked with having to decide between marble and terrazzo tile flooring. Fortunately, Nellie, his assistant, came from a long line of people who had excellent taste in churches, and tended to prod him firmly in the right direction.

As she sat in the silence, Doyle resisted the urge to glance at the clock and instead prompted, "Someone told you somethin' in Confession, Father?" Best cut to the nub, here; she'd a night-class vengeance-gang to investigate, after all.

The priest sighed mightily. "No, lass; instead it was in reference to another's Confession."

"Oh," she said, trying to follow. "So, a Confession-once-removed?"

"Yes," he agreed. "A Confession-once-removed." He then fell silent again.

"Was it Father Ambrose, who heard this other Confession?" This seemed a logical leap, since the elderly priest had been murdered, and Father John seemed to think it was somehow connected.

"Aye, that." He sighed again, and glanced up at her. "Father Ambrose was hisself givin' me hints of what had been said to him—I had to admonish him, of course; the seal of the confessional is absolute."

"Oh," said Doyle again, and wondered what it was going to take to get the ball rolling, here. "Why would he tell you anythin', then? Is he so old that he's forgot what's-what?"

Father John raised his chin to contemplate the far corner of the ceiling, and carefully said, "I'd hate to think that he was bein' prideful, Kathleen. Instead, I'd like to think he sought my opinion as to how he'd handled Church doctrine."

"Better you than me," said Doyle, and then asked in a delicate manner, "What was the doctrine he wanted to discuss? Can you tell me that, at least?"

Slowly, her companion revealed, "It has to do with absolution, lass. There's a Church doctrine that allows for absolution if it is determined—well, if it is determined that the takin' of another person's life was justified."

Surprised, Doyle straightened up. "Oh—oh, I've heard of this. 'Just cause', we call it, in police work." She paused, and then confessed, "I wasn't sure I believed that the Church had such a thing; it all sounds a bit smoky, to me."

The priest shot her a look from beneath bushy brows. "'Tis true enough. The Church believes if the killin' is done to protect innocent life—and there is no other way to protect it—then the penitent is absolved of any sin."

Thinking this over, Doyle offered, "So—Father Ambrose was troubled about a Confession he was hearin', and he was seekin' your advice, even though he couldn't tell you the particulars."

But Father John grimaced, slightly. "No—he wasn't troubled, lass. He was rather pleased, in fact—so pleased that he was willin' to skirt around the seal of the confessional to let me know what he'd done."

Surprised, Doyle seized on what seemed to her detective-self like a clear case of motive. "If Father Ambrose was speakin' out of turn, mayhap that's why he was killed? Someone didn't want their murder-secrets to be bandied about by a gabblin' priest?"

Thinking this over, Father John shook his head. "That seems unlikely, lass. No one would know that he'd spoken of it to me—and I can't imagine he'd tell anyone else; he knew he shouldn't have told even me, but it seemed he couldn't resist."

"How can we know for certain, Father?" she ventured. "If he's such an old man, I mean. Mayhap he did say the wrong thing to the wrong person."

But the priest assured her, "Oh, no—Father Ambrose had a keen mind, despite his age, and he was a practical, hard-headed priest. He'd lived a challengin' life, lass; during the Nazi occupation, his father worked with St. Maximillian Kolbe on the underground printin' press. The entire family was arrested when Ambrose was just a lad, and they were all taken to the camps. He wound up as the sole survivor."

Much struck, Doyle pointed out, "So—Father Ambrose was the perfect candidate to hear a Confession about justified murder. After all, he'd have welcomed such a thing, himself."

"We all have our own perspective, based on our own experiences," Father John conceded.

But Doyle had taken hold of a working-theory, and offered, "I think you are troubled, Father, because you're afraid that someone is gamin' the system—so to speak—and choosin' a priest who's goin' to be a little more lenient about absolution, when it comes to murder."

Considering this, the priest shook his head. "I'm afraid I can't say more."

Pausing, Doyle had to reluctantly acknowledge the logical hitch in her working-theory. "But—if we assume the penitent is the one who up and killed poor Father Ambrose—why would he do such a thing? He's managed to get himself a pocket-priest who's willin' to absolve him for murder, and that's no easy feat."

"I suppose that's a good point, lass."

"It might be unconnected—the Confession, and his murder," Doyle mused. "But I doubt Acton would think so— and besides, you wanted to speak to me before you knew Father Ambrose had been killed, so you were worried enough about whatever-was-confessed to drop hints to the police."

"I'm not droppin' hints," Father John insisted, much affronted.

"You'll be needin' your own Confession, to sort it out," she replied in an absent tone. "But I'll agree that there's somethin' here, and I'll consult with Acton about it straightaway."

The priest nodded with relief, since it was apparent that he was stepping carefully, with his goal to have Doyle mention the matter to Acton without jeopardizing any immortal souls in the process. Which could only mean that he was very troubled, indeed.

A loud crash reverberated through the stone walls, and they both jumped.

"Holy St. Brigid's *shoe*," groused Father John. "When will there be an end to it?"

"Soon enough," Doyle soothed. "Surely, it can't be much longer, now."

But the priest revealed in a sour tone, "There's troubles with the builder, lass. That fellow who's big in construction offered to take the project at a discount—bein' as he's RC— but he's havin' money troubles, I think." Leaning forward, the priest revealed in a low tone. "I think he has a gamblin' problem."

Doyle offered, "Want me to have a look? I can ask Acton to give him a bit of a push."

But Father John waved his hands at her. "Oh, no; no, lass—I don't want to rock the boat. He's got a connection to the Kingsmen, and so I don't want to ruffle 'im."

"Oh," said Doyle. And then, after wracking her brain, she ventured, "D'you mean the football team?"

Father John's expression evidenced his deep surprise that she was so ill-informed. "Haven't you heard, lass? They've acquired Rizzo."

"Have they? That is excellent."

Father John leaned back in his chair, and contemplated the ceiling with great satisfaction. "He may be the greatest ever. Faith, I'd love to see him play, but ticket-prices will go through the roof."

Doyle offered in a cynical tone, "Best curry some favor with the builder, then; the Church will have to wait."

But the priest was unrepentant. "Now, lass, things have already ground to a standstill, in any case. They've found some strongboxes, hidden beneath the basement floor, and Nellie's not sure if we should call in the English Heritage people, since they look to be quite old."

Doyle found this to be of great interest. "Truly? Were they full of pirate's treasure?"

"Ach—would that it were so, lass. Documents, mainly, and hard to make heads or tails of them, because they all seem to be written in cypher. There are references to a 'gypsy queen', though."

Doyle raised her brows. "Mayhap she was a sorceress, or somethin'. I hope she wasn't burned at the stake, poor thing." This, because such a thought hit very close to home for the fair Doyle, who would probably have met a similar fate, back in the day.

"Lost to time, I'm afraid." He blew out a breath. "But if the historical people come in, it would slow things down considerably, so I wish there was a way to determine whether the documents were important, without tippin' them off. Does your husband speak Spanish? Some of the correspondence seems to contain references to a Spanish woman and a falcon, but I can't make heads nor tails of it."

Doubtfully, Doyle offered, "I don't know—Acton speaks French, but I don't know about Spanish. He could probably find someone discreet, though."

The priest made a sound of impatience. "A shame, it is, that Father Ambrose has been gathered-up; he spoke fluent Spanish."

Doyle stared at him, her scalp prickling like a live thing, and managed to say, "Did he indeed?"

The priest nodded. "Indeed, he did. He attended seminary in Castile, at the Order of St. James."

CHAPTER 13

Acton had picked-up Doyle so they could drive together to the University, and she could hardly wait for him to open her door before she launched into her working-theory.

"And—since the murdered priest spoke fluent Spanish, and he was hearin' a Confession about justified murder—a penny to a pound says it was Navarro himself, seekin' absolution."

"Very likely," Acton agreed, as he took his seat behind the wheel.

She eyed him, her antenna quivering. "Tell me, husband, that you didn't already know this."

"I didn't," he disclaimed, glancing her way as he watched for an opening in the traffic. "On my honor."

"Yet you don't seem very surprised that this is all tied together."

"No," he admitted. "I am not surprised."

Letting out a pent-up breath, she turned to gaze out the windscreen so as to think over this latest revelation. "A shame, it is, that I didn't know about the Father Ambrose angle when we were havin' our little coffee-time at the Navarro's house—I could have tested it out."

He tilted his head. "By asking the suspect whether he'd been to Confession, lately?"

Stubbornly, Doyle insisted, "I would have thought of somethin' less obvious, Michael. Or, more correctly, you would have thought of somethin'—you're the one who's the wilier, between us."

But his answer rather surprised her. "I would ask that you make no such attempts, absent my go-ahead, Kathleen."

This was said in what was for him a firm tone, and so she turned to eye him yet again. "I'm wonderin' what it is that's makin' you step so carefully, husband. Can you give me a hint?"

Slowly, he revealed, "I believe Betancourt and Castellano may be at-risk. Indeed, they may be dead, already."

She stared at him in surprise. "I thought you thought they were on team-vengeance, with Navarro."

"I still do."

At sea, Doyle tried to make sense of it. "So, Navarro's killin' his own team?"

"Regrettable, but necessary."

The words were said in a matter-of-fact tone that made the hairs on the back of her neck stand up, and crossly, she retorted, "For heaven's sake, Michael—it gives me the shivers when you say things like that."

He glanced at her. "I beg your pardon. But I do believe it is Navarro's mindset; he has succeeded with his object, and now he has no compunction in sacrificing those who might implicate him."

"Like his manservant, who posed as the limo-driver," she realized. "That's why it was such a humane death, with the eyes closed. He's that sorry he has to kill 'im, but kill 'im he does."

"Yes," Acton agreed. "I would not be surprised if everyone in the night-class is slated to be eliminated." He paused. "If they haven't been already."

"Well, just so you know, Martina's alive," she informed him. "I've one of my feelin's, I do."

He raised his brows. "That is of interest."

Doyle watched him. "So—what do we think? She's hidin' from Navarro because she's wise to him, with his regrettable-but-necessary murders? Or mayhap he still needs her, for some reason?" She paused, thinking about it. "Mayhap she truly is his girlfriend."

He nodded. "Any are possible. We should find her as quickly as possible, though, since I do believe she is at-risk. I will ask Williams to send out another APW."

Reminded, she asked, "Should I report-in to Williams about my Father Ambrose theory, or should we wait to see whether it's ruled-out by the evidence?"

"Report, by all means. But it is important that Navarro not be made aware how much we know, or have guessed. We want to protect the other participants, and we have yet to understand the motivation behind this night-class."

"Saints," Doyle observed in wonder, "his motivation must be a doozy, if he's been compelled to go to all this trouble. He didn't strike me as one who would bother to bestir himself."

But Acton only noted, "He did kill his servant."

"Oh—oh, I suppose that did take some bestirrin'; can't imagine killin' our Reynolds, no matter how regrettable-but-necessary."

Suddenly struck, she observed, "You know, Michael, that may be why Navarro's still here in London—you were wonderin' why he hasn't shaken the dust of this place off his sandals, and that could be the reason why; he's tidyin' up the loose ends by disposin' of everyone else on his team. And poor Father Ambrose, for good measure."

"Very plausible," he agreed.

Doyle nodded. "All the more need to identify who was in the class—it's like a handy list of potential murder victims."

"Indeed. So we will proceed carefully; if it is discovered we are suspicious, I imagine the deaths will accelerate."

She nodded. "So, what's our story, for comin' back to the University to take another gander at the list? Last time, I said I was just doin' a routine background-check, so my administrative lady is goin' to think it very strange that a Chief Inspector has now come to call."

But as always, Acton had already considered this aspect. "On the contrary; Mr. Sergius made a reference about the Russian mafia, and you thought you'd best mention it to your higher-ups."

She smiled. "And it will all be cleared-up as a misunderstandin'. Good one, Michael; my hat's off to you. Although yet again, I think we're skirtin' around the 'no marrieds workin' together' rule."

"It's not an official matter, per se," he replied, unruffled. "You wanted me to hear what Sergius had to say before you raised such a serious subject in your report."

Laughing, she teased, "And there you go. You're definitely the wilier, between the two of us; I can't hold a candle."

"I will disagree; I am not the one who is pulling multiple case-breakers out of thin air."

Making a face, she looked out her window. "I've an unfair advantage—it's a blessin' and a curse, it is."

He lifted her hand to kiss its back. "No—not a curse by any means. But I will remind you that it is very important no one else knows of your—your advantage, Kathleen. No single case is more important than keeping your secret, and if we have to err on the side of allowing a murderer to go free, then that is what we must do."

She nodded, because she knew he fretted about it—faith, he was not at all happy that she'd told even Williams. "I know, Michael. And—considerin' how I'm such a dim-bulb—I think I've done a fair job of keepin' it under wraps."

Gently, he shook the hand he held in his. "Yes. But often you speak without thinking."

While this observation was unfortunately true, nonetheless she reminded him, "Whist, I did a bang-up job of throwin' up dust, during Tasza's stupid task-force. No one was the wiser, and I pretended it was all a big lark."

Commander Tasza Kozwalski—the self-same MI 5 Commander who'd disappeared—had created a task-force for officers who seemed to have an intuitive knack with respect to detective work. Doyle had been put forth as a potential candidate, and she'd been forced to go along with it, since even the mighty Acton couldn't refuse an MI 5 Commander.

Doyle had attended a single session and had hated every moment, since she'd spent the entire time pretending to cooperate even though her instinct was doing the equivalent of flashing red warning lights in her face.

Fortunately—although it was not a very nice thing to think—the task-force had been abandoned when the Commander had disappeared, and thank God fastin'; it was one of the rare times that her high-ranking husband hadn't been able to cover for her, and—although she felt confident that she could have navigated those particular rough waters— it was a relief not to have to try, owing to the aforementioned dim-bulb lack of wiliness.

Casting her mind back to the original subject, she asked, "And speakin' of which, how come you interviewed the Navarros together, instead of separately?"

"I didn't want him to be made aware that he is the prime suspect."

She nodded. "Good one, Michael. I noticed you didn't ask him any probin' questions—even though he did his locked-gate backtrack."

"No. No need."

Thinking of this, she bent to pull Mrs. Navarro's rosary out of her rucksack, and then frowned as she considered the beautiful object, absently winding it around her fingers. "You should have reminded me that I mustn't take gifts from suspects, Michael. Williams joked that I should have dusted it for prints."

"Not at all necessary. It was clearly spur-of-the-moment generosity."

She glanced over at him, teasing. "Are you goin' to write me up?"

"Williams has disciplinary authority over you," he countered mildly. "I was present solely to make a case-management decision."

"And to butter-up the suspect."

He smiled his half-smile. "Yes."

Doyle frowned, as she fingered the vivid blue beads. "Do Russian Orthodox people use rosaries? I could give it to Gemma, mayhap."

He glanced over at her. "You don't want to keep it? I believe it is rather valuable."

Slowly, she replied, "Mayhap that's why I don't like it, Michael. Rosaries should be humble things, and a fittin' tribute to the Blessed Mother, who was the humblest of the humble."

"By all means, then."

She packed the rosary away, and after they'd driven for a few minutes, she noted aloud, "You know, Michael, I got a funny feelin' from Williams, when I asked if he was goin' to Mary's weddin'."

But her husband only shrugged, slightly. "To be expected, surely?"

She lifted her face to contemplate the buildings, passing by. "I don't know—I think he's disappointed it didn't work out between them, but I don't have the sense he's pinin' for her. It seems a little out of keepin', that he'd be all melodramatic, and avoid her weddin'."

Her husband reached to take her hand. "We should visit Paris, ourselves."

She grimaced. "No thank you—I'm still recoverin' from Dublin; I don't travel well." She turned to eye him. "Neither do you, my friend."

He conceded this point with a tilt of his head—she would know if he was lying, after all. "I will be happy to go if you'd like, though."

Fondly, she rested a hand on his shoulder. "Let's stay home, and pull up the ladder, instead."

"No argument, here."

Idly, she watched the traffic in front of them and thought it a shame that home was no longer a sanctuary for him—what with babies and nannies, not to mention nannies' children, piled atop the babies and the nannies.

With a smile, she offered, "Since this is our big chance to be alone, let's go 'round the block once more."

"Certainly," he agreed, and made the turn.

CHAPTER 14

Once again, Doyle stood squeezed-in between the desks as she spoke to the HR Administrator at the University, and once again, Bertie had taken up the cudgels and was barking at her with all the gusto he could muster, which did not sit well with the illustrious Chief Inspector, who did not hesitate to ask Mr. Sergius to take the animal away, and immediately.

"I'm so sorry; he's usually such a kind little soul," the woman apologized, as she ineffectually pulled at the outraged dog. "Do take him outside, Mr. Sergius; and remember that you'll need those walking shoes by tomorrow."

As the man willingly lumbered away with the dog in tow, the woman confided to Doyle, "It's not healthy for him to be carrying so much weight, so I've managed to convince him to come along when I walk Bertie at my lunch-breaks."

Doyle hid a smile and agreed in a grave tone, "I do think Mr. Sergius may need some lookin' after."

"Now, how may I help you?" the woman asked, in the tone of someone who had complete certainty that all matters within her control were above-board and by-the-book.

Doyle, who'd rehearsed her lines, replied, "When last we spoke, I was doin' a background-check on one of your adjunct professors, and you may remember that Mr. Sergius made some reference about the professor's bein' in the Russian mafia. Since I wasn't certain whether he was jokin' or serious, I thought I'd best call in my boss, just to make sure."

As such a passing-of-the-buck was completely understandable to any bureaucrat worth her salt, the woman nodded in agreement. "Certainly. Would you like to see Mr. Sergius' personnel records, Chief Inspector?"

Acton bowed his head. "If you would. I am curious as to whether there appeared to be any connection between Mr. Sergius and Mr. Navarro."

"*Professor* Navarro," the woman corrected. "And it didn't seem to me as though they knew each other—although Professor Navarro was not one to socialize. But let me pull up the record."

She did so, and Acton bent and pretended to scrutinize Mr. Sergius' information for a long moment. "Thank you. In an excess of caution, would you mind if I also reviewed Professor Navarro's class members?"

"Of course," she replied, and began typing the prompt. "His was not one of our more popular classes, so we'd only had a handful of students. Our students tend to gravitate toward history classes that focus on Europe or Asia, to fulfill their general education requirements."

Doyle watched as the woman pulled up the class list, and again, Acton bent to scrutinize the names—eight in all. Doyle wondered if she should try to take a snap of the screen, but decided that if Acton was playing it off as a cursory once-over, she shouldn't raise any alarm bells.

Her husband was the picture of polite unconcern as he straightened up and said mildly, "I see nothing to merit further investigation, Sergeant, but you were right to double-check."

"I do think Mr. Sergius was just jokin', sir," Doyle admitted. "I'm sorry for the inconvenience."

"You can never be too careful," the Administrator replied with approval, since this was probably her personal motto. "And although the attendance sheet says eight, in reality there were only seven." She pointed to one of the names on the list. "This man came to just one class, and then dropped out." Reviewing the readout, she frowned slightly. "He hasn't contacted me to claim his credit, though; if you drop out after one class, we will credit your enrollment fee towards another class—the University wants to make sure everyone enjoys their experience."

"Laudatory," said Acton. "The class was Friday evenings at seven?"

"Yes," the woman nodded. "One of the few we've offered on a Friday evening—attendance tends to be too low, so we try to avoid it. Professor Navarro could find no other convenient time, though, and so we made an exception."

"And we are certain that everyone who attended was registered?"

"Oh, yes," she nodded vigorously. "You can't be too careful, nowadays—although I suppose none knows this better than the police. I explained to Sergeant Doyle that everyone must wear a photo passkey when on campus, and at night we've only a single-entry door, with a doorman stationed to check all entries."

Reminded, she made a sound of impatience. "We've just had to replace the night doorman—such an inconvenience; the old one just stopped showing up, and we haven't been able to raise him—we still owe him a paycheck."

Doyle could sense Acton's surge of interest. "Perhaps I could take his name?" he asked. "If you'd like, I can try to trace him."

"Oh, please—if you would," the woman readily agreed. "I hate to think we owe him money." She typed in the prompt, and the doorman's personnel photograph was dutifully displayed on her screen.

"Ah," said Acton, and even Doyle recognized Castellano; after all, the missing Council-member's photograph had been spread far and wide, in the All Ports Warning.

CHAPTER 15

"I feel as though I've gone down the rabbit-hole," Doyle said in wonder, once they were back in the Range Rover. "It all gets curiouser and curiouser."

"Yes," Acton said thoughtfully, as he pulled into traffic. "Or you might say that the players become more and more defined."

She raised her brows. "More *defined*? I'm not sure that's the right word, Michael, and comin' from me, that's truly sayin' somethin'. We've a servant who was doublin' as a limo driver, and a Council-member who was doubling as a *doorman*—of all things. Everyone's playing multiple parts."

"True," he agreed. "I meant only that it all comes back to a single plan, with the night-class serving as the meeting place for a small group of players."

Doyle nodded in agreement. "So; Castellano was in on it, and was probably stationed at the door to keep an eye on the comin's and goin's."

"And he may have been the muscle," Acton added. "They would have need of someone fairly strong, for this type of murder."

He glanced at her and asked, "Would you mind taking down the class names for me? I'd rather not include them in a report, as yet."

Willingly, Doyle jotted down the names that Acton had apparently memorized, and—just so that she didn't seem completely useless—she noted, "And now that we've the class

93

time and dates, we can check for CCTV film of each of them as they came and went."

He nodded. "Yes; it will be helpful, if it comes to a conspiracy charge."

Doyle eyed him in surprise. "You don't think it will? There doesn't seem to be much doubt that there's a conspiracy, afoot."

"I would agree with that assessment."

Wondering at his hesitation, Doyle noted fairly, "Although there may be no one left to charge, if all the conspirators are gettin' themselves killed—save for Navarro, of course. Mayhap that's his grand plan—to be the last man standin'; regrettable-but-necessary, since dead men tell no tales."

But to her surprise, Acton asked, "What was your impression of Navarro?"

"Full of himself," she said promptly. "Made your teeth stand on edge."

"How capable, do you think he is?"

"Not very," she answered immediately. "He couldn't handle a simple body-disposal, for the love o' Mike. Nor a simple coffee pot, for that matter."

"That was my impression, also."

The penny dropped, and Doyle ventured, "He's not the mastermind, then?"

"I would doubt it, very much."

After deciding she was a dim-bulb for not coming to the same conclusion, herself, Doyle offered, "So that explains why you're soft-footin' this; you'd like to snare whoever's behind it all."

"No simple thing," he agreed. "This plan is very well thought-out, and I imagine the perpetrator has carefully covered his tracks." Thoughtfully, he added, "I will be interested to see what Williams has discovered about Castellano."

Since she hadn't yet considered this aspect, Doyle was much struck. "Faith, now, there's a question-and-a-half—how did Castellano wind up on the Health Professions Council? He can't have been plucked off the street."

"I imagine he posed as a fellow sex-trafficker, and was well-connected, in some way."

Doyle could only agree. "There had to be good reason, for the other blacklegs to welcome him into their bosom. I'll bet that's it—he was posin' as a fellow blackleg. And if he's posin' as a fellow blackleg, he must have had some money to throw around."

He nodded, watching the traffic. "Yes; this was an expensive proposition. Of course, Navarro is possessed of a fortune—many of the Carlists are very wealthy."

Doyle ventured, "So—are you thinkin' that Castellano's another Carlist, then? All the Spanish-surname people are Carlists, and that's the connection betwixt them?"

"I would not be surprised. The exception is the man who dropped out, after the first class. He was the Council's original limousine driver."

She looked over at him in surprise. "Was he indeed? They must have killed him, then; they drew him in somehow, killed him, and switched him out for Navarro's manservant."

He nodded. "Yes. They wanted their own people in place, so as to orchestrate the murders. Which is why Castellano became a Council-member in the first place, I imagine; he was their insider, to set-up the victims."

Doyle thought about this. "Do we think Castellano's dead, too?"

Acton glanced at her. "Do you have a sense?"

She shook her head. "I do not, I'm afraid. But Martina Betancourt—" she frowned, trying to decide what it was she was thinking. "Martina's the exception, or somethin'. She's still alive, and safe as houses. She's not at-risk, for some reason."

"Then perhaps she is indeed related to Navarro. Or is his girlfriend."

They sat in silence for a few minutes as they rounded the park, and headed toward their building. Musing over what they'd learned, thus far, Doyle finally shook her head. "I'm not gettin' it, Michael; the plan is startin' to take shape—and it's a crackin' good plan—but we haven't a *clue* yet as to motive. Why go to all this trouble and expense, to kill-off a bunch of foreigners?"

"There is a motive," he said. "We have only to discern it."

Taking a cast, she ventured, "Mayhap they're a band rovin' vigilantes?"

He tilted his head. "That seems unlikely, given the personalities involved. And if they were all Carlists, they'd have little interest in righting English wrongs."

Glancing over at him, she suggested, "I suppose we could throw up our hands, and just haul-in Navarro for questionin' on a twenty-four hour hold. He did have a body in his garden, and a very sketchy story."

"Monday, perhaps," he suggested. "I'd like to see what I can discover about the class attendees, first. Again, I would not be surprised if we have not yet seen the person who is behind the plan."

She gave him an admonishing look. "As long as we're not coverin'-up for the perpetrators, Michael. A lot of people may think they're on the side of the angels, but that's not our call."

He offered in a mild tone, "Understood."

Not quite convinced that he agreed, she reminded him firmly, "Murder is murder, Michael."

"Not always; recall that Navarro was granted absolution."

"Only after some priest-shoppin', and sleight-of-hand," she retorted crossly. "But I suppose that little factor sums up our problem in a nutshell; the Met doesn't need another public-relations nightmare, and it would only be more grist for the mill if the coppers come down hard on the vigilantes who are only doin' the job that the coppers themselves are sidesteppin'."

"We may need a nuanced approach," he agreed. "It can wait until Monday."

She saw a silver lining in this cloud, and asked hopefully, "Then does my report wait 'till Monday, too?"

"If you would."

Reminded, she asked, "You never managed to speak to our Mr. Sergius; did you decide it wasn't needful?"

"I doubt he is involved with Navarro, but if he is, it is best that he is not tipped-off that our true object is not the Russian mafia."

She could only agree with this reasoning. "Yes—I didn't get the sense that he was hidin' anythin', and he was kind enough to take wretched Bertie away—thank heaven for small favors."

"The dog was a distraction."

She could feel his surge of annoyance on her behalf, and sighed. "Dogs don't like me. Cats are indifferent, but dogs are very much opposed."

"Then we will return the favor," he said, and nodded to the security officer as they pulled into their parking garage.

Always her champion, was Acton, and she fondly leaned her head on his arm. "But what if Edward wants one, Michael? Little boys are hard-wired to long for a puppy."

"Then he will have to be content with a pony."

She teased, "Of course he will—what was I thinkin'?"

He smiled, as she'd intended, and as he pulled into their parking slot she decided to venture into dangerous waters—Acton didn't like to speak of his childhood. "Did you have a dog?""

"I did not."

"How 'bout a pony?"

"There were no animals at Trestles, when I lived there as a boy."

She raised her brows. "You'd no pets? Faith, Michael; we've somethin' in common—*finally.*"

After turning off the engine, he kissed her head, where it rested on his arm. "I must disagree. We have much in common."

But she only quirked her mouth, as she fingered his sleeve fondly. "We're chalk and cheese, my friend, and we've only to wander back into the murder-is-murder discussion for proof-positive. Lucky, it is, that we manage to manage it, somehow."

"Nonsense; I think we are very compatible."

She laughed. "That's exactly what you said when you proposed—if you could call it a proposal. Mayhap we do have somethin' in common—romance is not our strong suit."

"Perhaps not," he conceded.

She lifted her head to look at him. "Sex, on the other hand, *is* our strong suit, so at least we have that goin' for us."

Inspired by this accolade, he bent to kiss her soundly. "I cannot disagree."

"A shame we can't be spontaneous like the old days—I do miss bein' thrown down on the entry-way rug. Mayhap we can sneak out, after everyone's asleep tonight, so as to take a visit down memory-lane."

"You'd have to stay quiet," he teased.

"I can be quiet, if it's needful," she declared, very much on her dignity.

He smiled as he unbuckled his seat-belt. "I will call your bluff, you know."

"Not a bluff a'tall," she declared wickedly. "Gird your loins, husband."

CHAPTER 16

Reynolds took Acton's coat at the door, but Doyle kept hers, explaining that she'd like to whisk Edward away for his walk before the light faded.

"I shall accompany you then, madam," the servant said in a firm tone.

"They're still goin' to think I'm a nanny," Doyle warned. "I suppose we could jerry-rig the tiara, so that it glows in the dark."

But the servant did not find this a joking matter, and did not deign to offer a reply as he rang-up the concierge to bring out the pram.

Gemma was coloring at the kitchen table, and Doyle was reminded that, with Reynolds coming on her walk, her husband would be saddled with babysitting duties when he was no doubt itching to delve into his Navarro-class research. She asked Reynolds, "Could we sneak Gemma along, d'you think? If Colonel K finds out, we can say Acton needed some quiet—and besides, the poor lass is due to have a runabout, after bein' cooped up like a prisoner at the gate."

"I'm afraid I have strict instructions, madam," Reynolds apologized. "Gemma is to remain within doors until after the wedding tomorrow."

But Doyle only scoffed. "Strict instructions are made to be disobeyed, my friend—have you learned *nothin'* from your stint alongside the likes of me? And speakin' of which, I don't see why Colonel K gets to be in charge, any more than me or you."

The servant looked a bit dubious. "I can inquire as to Lord Acton's wishes, if you'd like, although—"

"No—allow me," Doyle cut him off, and then called out to her husband, who was bent over, with his head in the fridge. "Michael, we're takin' Gemma along with us to the park, and if you bar the door I will shoot you dead."

"Very well," came his muffled reply.

"You see?" Doyle explained with some satisfaction. "You have to know how to handle these things, Reynolds."

"Very good, madam."

Fairly, she added, "Although I suppose Colonel K can be forgiven for bein' all cautious-like; he's another one who thinks that bloodlines are more important than the people who carry them."

But Reynolds could not allow such heresy to go unchallenged, and offered, "I believe the Colonel is genuinely concerned, madam, and with good reason."

Doyle hoisted up Edward—who was delighted to recognize the signs of an impending walk—and rested him on her hip as she headed toward the door. "No one's stealin' Gemma on our watch, Reynolds—they haven't got a chance. And Gemma herself comes from a long line of murder-in-the-blood, so truly, we're only comin' along to provide her with a back-up."

Unable to hide his profound distaste at this characterization, the servant said with some repression, "I don't know as I would phrase it quite that way, madam."

But Doyle only teased, "Faith, Reynolds; it's the only reason us peasants allow the nobs to rule over us—they've got murder-in-the-blood, and so we've got to watch our step."

This said a bit loudly, because Acton was walking past them, on his way to the bedroom desk.

Alive to the fact that the master could overhear, Reynolds offered, "Surely, there is something to be said for inherited leadership, madam. Especially amongst fair and like-minded people."

Dryly, Doyle observed, "It's more like inherited ruthlessness, my friend. That's what convinces everyone that they should be like-minded, in the first place." Expanding on this theme, she added, "Take Acton, here. When we were talkin' about people who would be willin' to kill their own servants, Acton thought you were expendable, but I stood up for you."

"Then I am grateful, madam."

"It was a near thing," Acton observed, as he settled into his desk.

Since Reynolds knew better than to be joking-about with the master of the house, he refrained from comment. "I will fetch Gemma's coat, then."

"Edward's too; it's a bit cold outside, and the blanket may not be enough."

"Do not forget your mobile, Kathleen," Acton reminded her, and then he bent to examine his screen.

CHAPTER 17

They went downstairs to the lobby, where Reynolds rather fussily organized Edward's blankets in his pram before allowing the doorman to usher them out the door and in the direction of the park, with Gemma skipping alongside in her excitement.

Doyle breathed in the evening air, privately thinking that it would have been nice to have a spot of alone-time with Edward, but this was the price one paid for living with servants, not to mention Romanov royalty. Not that she would ever have anticipated that such was to be her lot in life, but it only went to show you that God had a wicked sense of humor. The nuns would have been aghast to hear her say such a thing, but the nuns weren't the ones who'd gone from working in a fish-market to having to deal with a flippin' entourage.

Speaking of which, she took a quick look behind her and saw what she was expecting; Trenton, Acton's private security man, was keeping a watchful eye from the flank, about twenty paces back.

Because it was clear he wished to remain unnoticed, she immediately called out, "Ho, there; how are you, Trenton?"

"Good, ma'am," the man replied, ably hiding his dismay that she was blowing his cover.

She paused for a moment so as to allow him to approach closer, and then smiled. "Did you have a good holiday, you and Lizzy?"

"We did, ma'am." Not a chit-chatter, was our Trenton—not to mention that he was unhappy she was skirting security protocols by addressing him thus. Tiresome, it was; between Trenton and Reynolds, everyone needed to stop clutching at their pearls and just calm down—she'd bet her teeth that they were both armed, courtesy of Acton, who tended to pass out small-arm weapons like candy.

After deciding it would be best to have pity on the poor man—faith, you wouldn't think that Trenton would be such a bundle of nerves—Doyle concluded the conversation by remarking, "Well, I hope you stayed away from the bogs, my friend; we lost a perfectly good Commander to them."

As they resumed their walk, she explained in an aside to the servant, "He'd gone on holiday to Ireland, with his cousin Lizzy Mathis."

Reynolds raised his brows. "I was not aware Mr. Trenton and Miss Mathis were cousins, madam."

"Me, neither. But it turns out they're distantly related to Acton himself—I forget exactly how—from some unholy alliance, way back when."

"Is that so, madam?"

"Never doubt it," she replied. "So you'd best watch yourself, Reynolds, since they've got murder-in-the-blood, too—although I suppose it's a more dilute version; can't see Trenton pushin' you out the window, after all."

Reynolds, as could be anticipated, made no reply to her teasing, but she was rather surprised to find that her scalp began to prickle. What? she thought, caught off-guard. The familial relationship twixt those two truly shouldn't come as any revelation; it only explained their out-sized devotion to the House of Acton—not to mention that Acton was not one to trust just anyone, in the first place. That he trusted

Reynolds was a near-miracle, but Acton had married his very own truth-detector, which was a great help to the man in sorting such things out.

Her scalp prickled yet again, and she frowned slightly, wondering what it was that she was supposed to be understanding.

Reynolds ventured, "If I might suggest, madam, in the future it may be best if you did not distract Trenton from his duties."

With a rueful smile, Doyle acknowledged the justice of this. "I know—but I couldn't resist, Reynolds, the man's been avoidin' me like Adam in the Garden. I've probably offended him, all unknowin', and now he's got a bone to pick, and mutters beneath his breath."

"That seems very unlikely, madam," the servant replied, with a tinge of disapproval.

"Well—speakin' of pickin' bones—d'you know of any butlers who'd like to marry Lizzy Mathis? I'm on a mission to match her up, and I'm runnin' out of presentable candidates."

Raising his brows, the servant offered, "I would think Miss Mathis would have no difficulties in attracting a mate, madam, particularly if it is revealed that she is related to Lord Acton."

"She's very clever," Doyle mused, "and a lot of men don't like 'clever'."

Reynolds suggested, "There are dating services, madam—they abound, I understand, and are often successful."

Doyle made a face. "Hard to imagine our Lizzy doin' such a thing. I signed up for one, myself, through the Church, and thank all available saints I managed to marry Acton before I had to show up for the first meetin'."

105

Carefully, the servant avoided asking for clarification, and instead offered, "I could pass the word discreetly."

She turned to him in gratitude. "Would you? That would be grand—Williams said he would, too. I'm not one to know any eligible men, and although I think Savoie rather likes her, I doubt he's marriage-material. The knight wants her married as soon as may be, since that's all he thinks women are fit for."

At sea, Reynolds asked, "Which knight is this, madam?"

"Oh—oh, you know; one of those knights that you run across," Doyle said vaguely. "Bein' a nob, and all." Talk about murder-in-the-blood, she thought; the ghost-knight at Trestles had it in *spades*. There was nothing he'd like better, one would think, than to be able to push people out a window from seven stories up.

Gemma had spotted a likely dog to pet, and—cognizant of the nervous Nellies who surrounded her—Doyle called out to the girl to say a quick hello, but that then they should be on their way.

"He's a spaniel," the little girl reported, as she ran back to them. "His name's Toby."

"That is excellent," said Doyle. "There could be no finer name for such a beast."

Giggling, Gemma skipped ahead, and Doyle cautioned her not to stray too far. They continued along the pathway as the shadows lengthened, and—since Reynolds was not one to initiate idle conversation—Doyle cast about for a topic to discuss.

"You know, Reynolds, there aren't any dogs at Trestles, and you'd think that would go along with the whole goin'-out-to-shoot-peasants sort of thing."

"I believe you mean pheasants, madam."

106

"Either one, my friend," she declared, unrepentant. "I never thought about it—the dearth of dogs, I mean—but it does seem a bit strange, and out-o'-keepin'."

"Perhaps the Dowager has allergies."

"Mayhap," she agreed, and then shivered a bit, as a cool wind blew past.

Suddenly Gemma called out, "Mama!" and then ran toward the couple who were approaching them along the path.

"Is it?" Doyle asked in surprise, peering through the dim light; they were in a fairly deserted area, and the torch lights hadn't yet come on.

"Gemma, my darling!" Mary crouched to gather her daughter in a hug, as Howard, her fiancé, regarded them fondly.

"What a happy coincidence," said Doyle with a smile. "We were just breakin' her out for a walkabout."

"And we were headed over to fetch her," Howard said. "We've just come from the final rehearsal at the Church, and we were worried it would be too late."

He's nervous, Doyle thought, hiding a smile. Nervous, but putting up a good front. Small blame to him, to have pre-weddin' jitters—although I suppose technically, I was one who had post-weddin' jitters, which were probably very similar but included plenty of sex, as a sweetener.

"Not too late at all," she assured him. "Come on then, and we'll convince Reynolds, here, to cook us up a pre-weddin' scramble."

"Please excuse me, Lady Acton, but I'm exhausted," Mary confessed with a smile. "If it's all the same to you, we'll just take Gemma with us."

Doyle could discern an underlying current of emotion in the woman's words, and surmised that she was having her own set of jitters, too. Nothing like turning one's world upside-down, no matter the affection one had for one's intended. Not to mention their life ahead appeared to be one of constant constraint, due to her adopted daughter's exalted status—a shame, it was, that Mary and Howard would never be able to make their own choices, like ordinary parents do. But Mary loved Gemma, and love called for sacrifices—some bigger than others, and some positively cataclysmic, as Doyle well-knew.

"Right then," Doyle said cheerfully. "I will see you at the altar, tomorrow—bright as a new penny."

They said their goodbyes, and Doyle turned back toward home, since Reynolds was worried that the evening was becoming too cool for Edward, who had no mittens.

"He shall have no pie, then," Doyle remarked with a smile, as they retraced their steps on the pathway.

"I beg your pardon, madam?"

"The three little kittens," she explained. "Who lost their mittens."

The servant looked a bit puzzled. "Surely, madam, Master Edward is not to blame?"

"No, I suppose not," she admitted with an inward sigh, and sorely missed her mother, yet again.

As they came in through the flat's entry door, Doyle called out to Acton, "We've off-loaded Gemma, Michael. I'm sick to death of the whole Russian-infightin' rigmarole, and so I gave her to the first person who offered a good home."

"Did you?" asked Acton, as he rose from his desk to take Edward from her. "I cannot say I am surprised."

As Reynolds retreated to prepare the baby's room for the night, Doyle confessed, "We ran into Mary and Howard, who were on their way over to pick her up. It was rather sweet; they were nervous, although the both of them combined didn't amount to one hair's-breadth as nervous as I was, at our own weddin'."

He acknowledged the fairness of this observation. "I had to step carefully, so as not to overset your fragile state."

She stood on tip-toe to invite his kiss around Edward, who was clinging like a barnacle to his father's neck. "If by 'stepping carefully' you mean that you rushed me off to bed, quick as a cat, I will agree."

"It did seem the best course."

"*So* kind of you," she teased. "Such heroic sacrifice."

"Nonsense; I was only happy to be of service," he replied, and as he freed an arm to include her in a family embrace, she decided with some relief that she'd been over-fanciful, to be so worried about his current frame of mind. He seemed perfectly normal—well, normal for him, leastways—and she should not go about borrowing trouble where there was none to be had.

"I'll make his bottle," she said, and lifted up on tiptoe to kiss them both.

CHAPTER 18

That night, Doyle had one of her dreams.She had them occasionally, and—as they usually featured a person who was no longer alive—in her own mind, she deemed them 'ghost-visits' although the people who visited didn't truly seem very ghostly. They seemed more like messengers—but not scary messengers, like the ones in that famous story where the dead partner came in chains to issue dire warnings. Instead, the visitors seemed to be much as they were when they were alive, with the exception that their message never seemed to be very straightforward, as though normal channels of communication were too primitive.

But Doyle had learned to take the vaguely-delivered messages very seriously, because the ghosts tended to warn her of trouble on the horizon—trouble that oftentimes could be laid directly at the door of her renegade husband.

Indeed, it was the main reason the fair Doyle was willing to tolerate the ghosts in the first place, instead of pulling the covers tightly over her head and plugging her fingers in her ears; she was being prodded with a call-to-action, and she'd learned from past experience that it behooved her to figure out what it meant, rather than ignore it. After all, if she was supposed to be steering Acton toward a better path, it would be best to pay attention for both their sakes.

In light of recent events—and because she'd entertained a dead-priest ghost on a previous occasion—Doyle was half-expecting the late Father Ambrose to show up, so as to shed some light on all the murky goings-on surrounding his murder. To her disappointment, however, the spectre who appeared before her was as unexpected as she was unwelcome.

"I don't have to say 'ma'am' to you," the ghost began with a touch of defiance. "You don't out-rank me."

"Full of pride, you are," Doyle observed in a tart tone. "And look where it's got you."

They were standing on a rocky outcrop, dark and dim, with a persistent wind that silently swirled around them, even though Doyle couldn't feel it against her skin. It was not a good place to be.

"I'm that sorry for you," Doyle continued. "You're all bound up in this honor-above-all-else thing, and it's ended up twisted back on itself."

"I'm a Peterson," retorted the late Claudia Peterson. "It's in the blood."

"Well, I may have lowly Doyle-blood, but I know better than to go about killin' people. Or to kill myself, for that matter." The ghost had been a Sergeant with the Metropolitan Police Force, until a shameful scandal had inspired her suicide.

"You can't know," the woman returned in an angry tone. "And you'd never understand."

But Doyle wasn't having it, and fired back, "I understand enough not to defy God. We're supposed to 'give thanks in all things', and the Apostle wouldn't have put it quite that way unless the 'all things' included some lumps and nasty surprises."

In an impatient gesture, the irritated woman standing before her crossed her arms. "I'm not here to argue with you, I'm here to warn you that he's going to kill the baby."

There was a long moment of stunned silence. Incredibly, the words were completely true, and—shocked to the core—Doyle could only gape in disbelief until, with a mighty effort, she found her voice. "*What*?"

"He's going to kill the baby." With some impatience, the ghost watched Doyle's reaction and added, "You can't be so surprised; it's just like he's killed all the others."

"Holy *Mother*—no; no, I'll not believe you."

But the ghost only added, "He'll kill the baby, but you won't be able to tell that it was him. It's how he does things."

Again, the words were true as true could be, and—completely taken-aback—Doyle couldn't muster up a response for a moment. "It *can't* be," she finally whispered, but found that she was speaking to empty space, as the touchless wind blew around her.

"Are you quite all right?"

Blinking, Doyle found that she was now being addressed by a rather thin young woman, who languidly held a long cigarette holder balanced between her pretty fingers.

"No—no, I'm not," Doyle exclaimed, thoroughly alarmed. "She said that Acton's goin' to kill the baby."

The young woman chuckled and drew on her cigarette. "Oh—*please* don't pay her any mind; she hates you for spoiling everything."

Doyle teetered on the edge of explaining her truth-detecting abilities, but instead drew back, and then was almost surprised by her next words. "I wouldn't think you'd be allowed to smoke."

Amused, the woman dropped the cigarette holder, and it immediately disappeared. "Frightfully sorry; it was all the thing, back then."

Still struggling to make sense of the previous ghost's revelations, Doyle tried to take a deep breath, despite the miserable, frozen feeling in her chest. "Saints and holy angels—it *can't* be true; I'm that flummoxed."

"Don't be," the woman soothed. "Everything will turn out just fine."

To Doyle's great relief, this also rang true, and with some gratitude, she was able let go of her horror long enough to focus on this latest visitor. "How—who are you, if you don't mind my askin'?"

The ghost spread her slender hands in an ironic gesture, and bowed her head slightly. "I'm Lady Acton, same as you. Although you're to be a Countess now, lucky thing—all thanks to me."

"Oh," said Doyle, trying to remember the history—Acton had explained it all once, but she hadn't been paying much attention. "You're the heiress. You're the heiress who married Acton's grandfather, and saved Trestles."

"That's me." Ruefully, she drew down her red mouth into an attractive pout. "Not that it was appreciated much. And then my miserable son did his best to squander it all."

"Not a nice man," Doyle ventured. She'd the dubious pleasure of meeting Acton's father's ghost on a best-be-forgotten occasion, but she didn't want to hurt his mother's feelings by making a disparaging remark.

However, the ghost had moved on, and she knit her pretty brow in chagrin. "It isn't fair that I didn't get to be a Countess, at the very least, with the kind of money Papa had. He should have held out for a better title, but *oh, no*—he was in *such* a hurry to see me married off."

"Oh," Doyle remembered, "Lord Aldwych was your Papa. Well, I suppose men of that stripe don't want to worry about such things, overmuch." Indeed, the knight at Trestles came to mind, with his insistence that the fair Doyle marry off Lizzy Mathis as soon as may be, as though she could conjure up a willing suitor out of thin air.

With a laughing toss of her head, her visitor continued, "I will be at the ceremony in spirit, at least; the tiara was originally mine, you know." Pursing her lips, she gazed off into the distance. "I wanted sapphires, instead of pearls, but Papa wouldn't hear of it—said I wasn't old enough."

"It's lovely," Doyle assured her. "I've never seen a better."

"I should have been a Countess," the ghost repeated wistfully. "At the very least."

Doyle offered, "The irony's thick on the ground, then, because I think bein' a Baroness is a tough enough row to hoe."

"You'll do fine," the woman assured her in a kindly tone. "Don't listen to that policewoman—she's only trying to stir up trouble."

"I suppose," Doyle agreed doubtfully, since it seemed very unlikely that Sergeant Peterson had been sent for no good reason—although it was true that she's caused a lot of misery, when she was alive. And surely, the woman who now stood before her would only have Doyle's best interests in mind— Edward was her great-grandson, after all, and one would think she'd offer her own warning, if Acton were truly planning on doing harm to the child. Suddenly, Doyle could feel a cool breeze, and shivered slightly.

"Good girl," said the ghost, with a nod of approval. "All will be well. Ta for now." She smiled over her shoulder as she turned away, and then disappeared.

As was always the case after her dreams, Doyle awoke with a start—her heart pounding and her eyes open wide—and made a mighty effort to temper her reaction so as not to wake Acton, but in this she was unsuccessful, being as she'd a husband who was very much attuned to the wife who slept beside him.

"Kathleen?" Sleepily, he reached to pull her close. "Did you have a dream?"

He'd been witness to more than a few of her dreams—and their aftermath—and sometimes she thought he respected their importance more than she did.

"I did," she admitted, trying to decide what to say. "A strange one, it was."

He held her against his chest, and she could feel his breath on her hair. "Can you tell me?"

"I-I don't think so," she stammered.

"Right, then," he said in a soothing tone, and asked no further questions.

In the dimness, she lay awake, trying to make sense of it as she stared at the bedroom wall, knowing that he lay awake, also.

Claudia Peterson—of *all* people— had given her a warning—of *all* things—that Acton was going to kill Edward. It was impossible to even *consider*, that Acton would do such a thing. And besides, the heiress—the other Lady Acton—had assured her that such was not the case. Except—except that Doyle's formidable instinct was telling her to be wary of the heiress; there was something—something a bit *off* about her.

Thoroughly bewildered, Doyle wondered what it could possibly mean; who was right? And how could she even give it any credence in the first place—Claudia Peterson had an axe to grind like no other, and she was obviously bent on causing trouble. Except—except that she'd been telling the truth.

But *was* she—was she truly? Perhaps she'd found a way to fool Doyle, somehow, now that she'd lots of time on her hands. And it was *nonsense,* of course; Acton had turned a corner, and was no longer going about killing people, willy-nilly. And he loved little Edward—*loved* him; she was certain of it. Not as much as he loved the fair Doyle, of course, but that was a whole 'nother level of craziness.

This last thought, unfortunately, did not exactly calm her fears. What if Acton didn't want to share her with the baby, any more? What if he was pig-sick of the three-ring circus? What if—

Stop thinking about it, she commanded herself in alarm; get along with you, Doyle. Sergeant Peterson's up to no good— which is a first, for a ghost—but there's a first time for everything, and for reasons that are not clear she's decided to torment you.

"All right?" Acton asked softly.

"Yes, Michael; please don't worry—all's well," she replied, and fervently hoped it was true.

CHAPTER 19

T he next morning, they prepared to attend Mary's wedding, and Doyle had to resist the urge to snatch-up Edward every time Acton entered the room.

Despite her self-assurances the night before, she couldn't help but be alarmed by Claudia Peterson's warning, particularly because the police officer had so casually mentioned Acton's m.o., which was to pull the levers from behind the scenes so that no one was aware that he was pulling the levers—a wily one, was Acton, and he never left any tracks. It only added to Doyle's general level of concern— that Claudia Peterson knew how Acton operated; no one knew how Acton operated, save Doyle, and even at that, she was certain there was much that she did not know.

For example, despite her best efforts to wish it all away the previous night, she knew—in the way that she knew things— that Acton hadn't yet fully recovered from the mind-troubles he'd experienced after Edward was born. He wasn't quite his old self—not as yet—and he had an aura of—of *graveness* about him, if that was a word—although he was carefully trying to hide it from his wedded wife.

Could it be, that he was longing for the more-peaceful times, before the baby turned everything upside-down? He was not one to tolerate a situation not to his liking, was Acton, and he *had* to be unhappy, what with all the constant commotion.

And so, she found herself scrutinizing her husband very carefully whenever he interacted with the baby, and—unfortunately—what she saw was not exactly reassuring.

Edward was old enough to recognize the signs that indicated his parents were going somewhere interesting without him, and so he whined and clung, with Reynolds trying to keep him from doing any real damage whilst attending to Acton at the same time.

"I will need another tie, when you have a moment," her husband announced to Reynolds in a clipped tone.

"I'll hold him, Reynolds," Doyle offered rather anxiously. "But let me take my earrin's off, first."

"I think not, madam; you are wearing silk. I shall put him in his crib for a few minutes."

As could be expected, this plan did not meet with the baby's approval, and his protests were loud and unrelenting as his parents hurriedly worked to extricate themselves from the din.

"Have you your clutch-purse, madam?"

"Oh," said Doyle. "I don't know as I need one."

Reynolds tried to hide his dismay with only limited success "To hold your handkerchief, madam. And your gloves."

"Oh," said Doyle.

"I shall fetch it for you," said the butler in a firm tone.

"I won't wear the tiara, Reynolds," she called after him, over the baby's wails. "That's a bridge too far."

"Are you ready?" asked Acton, in the tone that husbands used when they very much feared that such was not the case.

"Two shakes, Michael, let me see if I can quieten Edward—I hate to leave him in such a state."

A bit anxiously, she leaned into the shrieking baby's crib to kiss him goodbye, only to find that this was a tactical mistake, as Edward took the opportunity to pull off one of her earrings with crowing triumph.

Ouch, you miserable blackguard, Doyle thought in extreme annoyance; I'm a pig's whisper away from murdering you, myself. She called out, "Can you rescue my earrin', Reynolds? I don't want him to swallow it, but I don't want to give him a shot at the other one."

This feat accomplished, Doyle hurried to the door, re-applying the slightly slimy earring and saying in a bright tone, "Here we go, Michael—no harm done."

"With the exception of my tie," he half-joked, as Reynolds shut the door behind them. "We certainly felt Mary's absence, this morning."

"Sorry, Michael; mayhap I should ask Lizzy Mathis if she could come in to lend a hand till Mary's back."

"No matter—we'll manage," he said, as they headed toward the lift. "And Mathis is at Trestles, helping Hudson prepare for the fête."

There was a nuance to his tone that made her antenna quiver, for some reason, and she wondered if perhaps Acton wasn't happy with Lizzy Mathis. Half-teasing, she asked, "Well, is Trenton any good with babies?"

With a hand to her back, he steered her down the hallway. "I'd prefer that we have no one else underfoot, just now; we are a bit overcrowded."

Again, her antenna quivered, and she wondered nervously if this was a veiled reference to a nefarious plan to solve this particular problem by eliminating the culprit who was most underfoot.

"You didn't realize that marriage required such a cast of supportin' characters, did you?" she offered with forced heartiness. "But it's no hardship *a'tall.*"

"Are you all right?" he asked, and took her hand as they waited for the lift. "You seem a bit on-end."

"Nothing to signify," she replied, trying to calm herself. "Truly, Michael."

"Was it the dream?" he ventured, watching her with concern.

"Whist, not a'tall," she assured him brightly. "And besides, the dream made no sense, remember?"

"Let me know if you need help sorting it out," he offered as they stepped into the lift, and Doyle was reminded that her husband knew her very well, indeed.

CHAPTER 20

D oyle had never found occasion to venture within a
Russian Orthodox Church, and so she looked about her
with a great deal of interest, as she sat beside Acton in the
front pew. Although Mary and Howard had planned a simple,
private ceremony, she recalled Father's John's warning, and
was therefore reconciled to sitting through a lengthy ritual.

And I thought a Wedding Mass was over-long, she
thought; these Orthodox people take the cake—it must be a
test of sorts; if you're willin' to profess yourselves in front of
God and everyone for two hours straight, then it *must* be true
love.

Doyle had asked Mary if she should mind Gemma during
the ceremony, but had been assured that it wouldn't be
necessary, and so she resigned herself to having to sit quietly,
which also meant she'd not be able to avoid thinking about
the upsetting message delivered by Claudia Peterson the
night before.

But as she gazed upon the faces of the various saints,
featured on the icons that lined the walls, she suddenly
realized she was being beyond foolish, and immediately
righted her ship—there was nothing like the interior of a
church to encourage logical thought.

And the logic was obvious—so obvious that she was
ashamed she hadn't realized it immediately. The baby might
be a pain-in-the-neck, sometimes, but Acton was not going to
jeopardize his marriage to the fair Doyle over a fussy baby.

Instead, he'd move heaven and earth to keep her happy—
indeed, he'd already done so, on certain memorable
occasions—and he wouldn't—*wouldn't* take a step that was
certain to drown her in utter misery, even if he thought he
could get away with it.

She'd been foolish to even consider such a thing, in light
of his—his whatever-you-might-call-it; "obsession" might be
the appropriate word, but she didn't like the way her scalp
prickled when she said it, and so she corrected it to "over-
devoted," and hoped she wasn't being over-foolish. He'd an
out-sized devotion to his red-headed wife, but there was no
malice in it—as had been well-demonstrated, time and again.
Instead, he wanted nothing more than to keep her happy, and
such an object would not be served if he up and murdered
baby Edward; she'd been a gobbin' fool to even hold the
thought.

Much relieved, she glanced at her over-devoted husband,
seated beside her, and thought he looked very handsome in
his dark suit—even though he was wearing his second-
favorite tie. Rather ashamed that she'd even entertained the
horrible   thought-that-should-not-have-been-thought-for-
even-a-moment, she slipped a fond hand in the crook of his
arm. He seemed a bit preoccupied, and she teased, "Why so
grim, husband? Are you thinkin' on our own weddin', and of
your many regrets?"

With a small smile, he covered her hand with his own.
"The finest day of my life."

"Aside from Edward's being born, mayhap," she ventured,
tamping down a stubborn twinge of anxiety.

He tilted his head in disagreement. "Edward's birth was
not exactly my finest day."

This was only true, and she took herself in hand, thinking that she couldn't keep second-guessing everything he said on account of some stupid ghost's being stupid and spiteful.

She shifted in the pew a little, because it seemed as though they were waiting a bit over-long for the ceremony to commence, and it also seemed a little strange to Doyle that the altar remained empty—one would think in a respectable marble-and-icons church like this one, the priest and the altar servers would have put in a solemn appearance, by now. After deciding it would be bad manners to openly check the time, she whispered to Acton, "D'you suppose Mary's got a case of cold feet, or somethin'?"

"I doubt it," he whispered back.

Startled, she turned to stare at him. "What is it?" she whispered in alarm.

"What is what?" he said.

"You will tell me what's afoot, husband," she continued in an ominous tone, "and immediately."

But there was no time for Acton to prepare his reply, because Colonel Kolchak had come down the aisle in a series of furious strides to halt beside Acton, his face like a thundercloud. "This is your doing, no doubt," he ground out between clenched teeth.

Acton raised his eyes to the other, and in an even tone that was nonetheless as hard as steel, asked, "Do you threaten me?"

For a long moment, neither man moved. A face-off, Doyle thought in astonishment; and one with a thousand-years-bloodline on either side—I wish there was a way to sell tickets.

With an effort, the other man was seen to control himself. "Where is the child?"

In a cold voice, Acton replied, "The child is with her parents. They did not feel as though their wishes were being properly consulted, and so they have married elsewhere."

Furiously, the man's right hand twitched.

Don't hit Acton, Doyle thought in alarm; it's the last thing you'll ever do, fancy church or no.

For his part, Acton sat still and silent, his level gaze never leaving the other's.

With a visible effort to calm himself, the other man gritted out, "What is it you hope to achieve?"

"A negotiation," Acton said.

"*Surely* you must see that she cannot simply disappear."

"No. But she will go on as before, and be protected, here. You planned to spirit her away to St. Petersburg, where she would not be as safe."

This was of interest, and Doyle hid her surprise.

The Colonel did not deny it, but paused for a moment, as he bent his head, thinking. "You are well-informed."

"It is my business to be. And I might also mention there are questionable funds, being funneled through St. Petersburg."

There was a significant pause, and Doyle could feel the other man's alarm. In a more conciliatory tone, he said, "But—but you must see that she cannot be left in England, to become English."

"She will not; you will continue with her lessons, and you will be consulted on all day-to-day decisions. But she is too young to become a rallying-point; not without placing her in grave danger."

Lifting his head, the other man regarded the altar a bit bleakly. "My people—those who back me—will be outraged."

But Acton tilted his head. "Perhaps not. Her new stepfather is not only an MP, but he is also a scion of the House of Khilkov."

The other man turned to regard him in astonishment. "This is so?"

"Indeed," Acton lied. "His family were White Russians, who fled Belarus. The connection has been obscured, but I will provide the records, if you'd like."

Very believable, thought Doyle with approval; it's a good thing Acton's had plenty of practice in spinning a decent fish-tale.

She had the impression that the Colonel might not actually believe the claim, but definitely recognized its usefulness. "Yes; well—" he nodded, thinking. "This will placate many."

"Perhaps," Acton ventured, "it could be suggested that the couple's flight was your doing, to circumvent a plot to seize the child."

"No," the other man said firmly. "I cannot take such unearned credit. But you are correct; we mustn't be too hasty, if Her Serene Highness is vulnerable."

"My thoughts, exactly."

The Colonel offered Acton his hand. "I will smooth down their feathers, although I could wish for your coolness."

"Not at all," said Acton, and Doyle solemnly brushed back her hair.

With a small bow, the man turned to leave, and in an unhurried manner, Acton stood and offered his hand to Doyle. "Shall we go?"

"We should," she agreed, gathering up her neglected clutch purse. "Nothin' left to see—it's all over but the shoutin'."

"Just so," he agreed.

On their way out, they shook hands with the Orthodox priest, who waxed philosophical about the runaways. "It happens," the man observed with a small shrug. "I will be pleased to bless their marriage any time they wish, when they return to London."

Doyle thanked him, but before she could turn away, the priest added, "I will admit I was hoping for a photograph, Officer Doyle, to include in the parish bulletin this week."

Apparently, there were bridge-jumper fans to be found in the unlikeliest of places, and Doyle could sense Acton's amusement. "By all means, Father—it's the least I can do, since the altar's turned-up empty for you."

And so, she took her place beside the full-bearded Orthodox priest, and pinned on a smile that was more sincere than her usual. As the church secretary carefully took several snaps of them, the priest ventured, "If I may ask, Officer Doyle, what were you thinking, when you jumped?"

For the first time, Doyle answered the question honestly. "I wasn't thinkin', Father. I was pullin' up a bucketful of faith, and hopin' it would be enough."

"Ah," he observed, turning to bid her farewell. "And we see that it was."

As they walked out the Church's entry, Doyle took Acton's arm and lifted her face to the bright sunlight. "Tell me about the funneled funds, husband. That's what turned the trick, with Colonel Kolchak."

"Do you think so?" Acton asked innocently.

"Someone's launderin' money?" she guessed.

He thought about it. "I'd rather not say," he decided.

She eyed him. "Is it a pendin' case?"

"No," he said. "At least, not as yet."

"Fine," she said a bit crossly. "Keep your precious funneled-money secrets to yourself."

He promptly dangled a change of subject before her, which was what he tended to do when he wanted to distract her from the subject at hand. "You've not asked where Mary and Gemma have gone."

She decided she was willing to take the bait—she probably didn't want to know how Acton knew about illegal money sloshing around in Russia, anyway. "There's no need to wonder, my friend; they've gone where everyone goes to hide out—St. Brigid's, in Dublin."

He smiled in confirmation, amused that she'd guessed. "Mary and Howard were married there this morning, with Gemma as flower-girl."

Recalled to the fact that she shouldn't be annoyed with someone who—despite his questionable methods—had come to the rescue in such a spectacular fashion, she offered in all sincerity, "Thank you, a million times over, Michael. You're a wonder—what with arrangin' for Gemma's switch-off last night whilst no one was the wiser, and then whiskin' everyone away. And that explains why you sent Lizzy and Trenton to Ireland—you wanted them to prepare the ground."

"In a manner of speaking," he agreed smoothly. "I am sorry I didn't tell you ahead of time, Kathleen, but secrecy was imperative."

"And I'm not so good at secrets-keepin'," she conceded. "Especially the imperative sort."

With a fond gesture, he tucked her under his arm, as they walked along. "No. You tend to be rather transparent." To take the sting from the words, he bent to bestow a kiss on her head. "Not that it isn't charming."

She made a wry mouth. "You should try it yourself, sometime."

"I should," he agreed in a mild tone, and it wasn't exactly true.

CHAPTER 21

B ack at the flat, Doyle sat on the floor with Edward, entertaining Reynolds with a dramatic re-telling of the events at the Church as she and the baby played with the wooden ark animals. "I was half-expectin' a duel to break out on the high altar, Reynolds; it was somethin' like."

"That is indeed alarming, madam." Reynolds was preoccupied, though, and voiced his main concern. "Are we certain that Miss Gemma will be kept safe?"

"Nary a doubt, Reynolds—you can trust Acton to see to it."

She then stilled her hands, much struck, being as she wasn't taking her own advice, and shame on her.

On the car-ride back from the church, she'd been preoccupied, thinking about how timid, sweet Mary—of all people—had been willing to take such a bold course of action because nothing was more important to her than her daughter's safety. Doyle couldn't help but compare Mary's situation to her own dire-ghost-warnings one, and wondered if perhaps she was being foolhardy not to flee, herself. Or at the very least, take Edward and find a safe haven, somewhere, until she'd a chance to think it all through—after all, the ghosts hadn't been wrong, yet.

But now—in the clear light of babies, and servants, and wooden toys, Doyle knew that she did trust Acton—she trusted him to move heaven and earth to help her, as he always had, and he always would.

Therefore, she rose, asked Reynolds to supervise the menagerie-playing and then wandered into the bedroom, where her husband was seated at his desk, going through the latest reports on his case files.

Sinking down on the foot of the bed, she pulled a leg up beneath her, and addressed him. "I need you to help me with my dream, Michael, but first I have to ask you somethin'."

Willingly, he paused and turned in his chair to face her. "I stand ready."

She considered how to best broach the subject, and then decided that it was too important to beat about the bush. "You must tell me that you don't plan to kill Edward."

He stared at her in surprise. "Our Edward?"

"Yes."

With genuine puzzlement, he reached to take her hands in his. "Why would you think such a thing, Kathleen?"

Her mouth dry, she insisted, "You have to say the words, Michael."

"I am not going to kill Edward."

"Of course not," she agreed, and then frowned slightly. "It makes no sense a'tall."

He contemplated the hands he held in his own for a long moment. "Tell me."

"It was the dream." Immediately, she gritted her teeth against the almost overwhelming desire not to speak of it. "A ghost warned me that you would. And the wretched ghosts haven't yet been wrong."

But his focus was elsewhere, and she could feel his sudden leap of concern. "Do you believe Edward is in danger?"

She stared at him. "No. No, he's not. Which seems strange, now that you mention it."

"Can you tell me more?" he probed gently, gazing up into her face. "It may be important."

Steeling herself to say the words aloud, she revealed, "It was Claudia Peterson. She—she warned me that you were going to kill Edward, but then said—she said that I wouldn't realize you'd done it."

Being Acton, he immediately focused on the most important part of this alarming and rather disjointed story. "And she was telling the truth?"

Doyle nodded. "Yes. But then, so are you."

He released her hands and sank back into his chair, thinking this over. "Why Claudia Peterson? Do you know?"

"No. Except that she's in trouble, and tryin' to make amends." She almost added that Dr. Harding was in the same boat, but then remembered that Acton didn't know about Dr. Harding's ghost in the first place, and therefore the least said, the better.

Slowly, Acton offered, "Could it be possible she spoke of Gemma, and not Edward?"

Doyle raised her brows in alarmed astonishment. "Never say you're goin' to kill Gemma?"

"Of course not, but Gemma is already under threat."

Much struck by this interpretation, Doyle fingered the coverlet on the bed and thought it over. "Gemma's not a baby—but since Claudia's never met Gemma, mayhap she didn't know any better. I'm certain she said "He's going to kill the baby." She paused, struggling against the powerful urge to stop speaking about it. "And then—when I was that horrified—she said somethin' about he'll do it so that I can't tell who did it, like he always does."

This was, of course, a rather damning indictment, and Acton made no comment but again appeared to be deep in thought. After a moment, he asked, "She doesn't know that you can sense the truth?"

"No. But she wasn't lyin', Michael. She was that upset that she had to speak to me at all. Holds a grudge, she does."

He met her eyes with all sincerity. "I'm not going to hurt Edward. Not in the slightest."

"I know. It makes no sense."

"It may be," he said slowly, "that your subconscious mind has transferred assimilated fears into your conscious mind, by way of dreams about death; disturbing dreams, about what you would fear the most."

She knit her brow, trying to follow, and then gave up. "Not a *clue*, Michael."

He leaned forward to take her hands again, and frowned slightly, as he played with her fingers. "Your subconscious mind processes so much—especially when you are surrounded by multiple other people. It may be—it may be overwhelming for you, on some level, and those repressed feelings reveal themselves in Claudia Peterson, a determined, ruthless woman, who represents everything that you are not."

Doyle blinked. "I think she's just a ghost with an axe to grind."

With a small smile, he looked up into her face again. "Or certainly it could be that, too."

She nodded, watching him. "So, we think Edward's safe."

"Edward is safe," he emphasized. "Although it may not hurt to be extra-cautious, until the dreams subside—your subconscious may be aware of something we haven't noticed, and I have great respect for your subconscious mind."

She gazed out the window, and saw the streetlights, lighting up one at a time. "I'm sorry I doubted you, Michael. I feel that foolish."

He rose to place a hand on either side of her so as to lower his head and kiss her, and then climbed over the foot of the bed to pull her with him, so that she settled in his arms as they lay back. Stroking her back in a soothing manner, he said, "You need a little break, perhaps. We should go away on a holiday, again—just the three of us."

"We've a lot goin' on, just now," she reminded him.

"When all our obligations are finished, then," he amended.

"That would be grand, Michael," she replied, and they lay together, unmoving, as the room gradually grew dark.

CHAPTER 22

Somethin's up," Doyle admitted. "I wish I knew what it was." "Didn't you hear what he said?" asked the heiress in surprise. With a negligent gesture, she paused to draw on her cigarette holder. "You're worried about *nothing,* silly you."

"It's not *nothing,*" Claudia Peterson chimed-in with a scowl. "He's going to kill the baby."

But Doyle was distracted, thinking about the conversation she'd just held with her husband. "He truly doesn't want to go on a trip—he's not one who likes to go anywhere. It's crackin' strange that he keeps suggestin' it."

The heiress laughed lightly. "If I had *your* money, I'd never stay home."

"Whatever it is," Doyle mused, "its buried deep. He's that worried I'll catch a glimpse."

"*Why* aren't you listening to me?" asked Peterson in exasperation.

But Doyle ignored her. "He can't get any—any *peace.* He's that fashed, poor man."

"Not poor at all," the heiress offered fairly, and took another puff.

"You're not much of a copper."

"Hush, you," Doyle snapped back at the deceased police officer. "You're not one to talk, after all. And why are you bein' so nasty, sayin' all these terrible things? Crackin' vengeful, is what you are."

"I am *not*," Peterson retorted in outrage. "He'll say its regrettable-but-necessary."

Brought up short, Doyle stared at the woman in alarm. "Holy *Mother*—that's exactly what Acton said about Navarro, murderin' his own team."

The ghost nodded emphatically. "That's how they think—all those nobs. They don't care; they're ruthless."

"I beg your pardon?" asked the heiress, amused. "Take your class-warfare elsewhere, if you please."

"You were ruthless, yourself," Doyle pointed out to Claudia. "So, I'm not so certain that I should be listenin' to the likes of you; Acton says you're just my subconscious-somethin'-or-other."

"You see?" said the heiress, waving the cigarette lighter in a casual arc. "You should listen to the man—you're working yourself up over *nothing*."

"It's not nothing," Claudia retorted. "Don't listen to her, she's a creep."

The heiress eyed the police officer with a playful touch of scorn. "Well, aren't *you* the vulgar one?"

"Everyone should just leave me alone," Doyle declared crossly, and wished she could hold her palms to her eyes. "I can't think, with the two of you bickerin' like a pair of jackdaws."

"No—you've got to pay attention, Sergeant," Claudia fired back.

But Doyle snapped back at her. "Don't you be givin' me orders—you don't out-rank me."

"You'll soon out-rank *me*," the heiress interjected wistfully. "I should have been a Countess, at the very least."

"There's somethin' here that I'm missin'," Doyle admitted. "And I've a feelin' it's somethin' obvious, somethin' in plain sight."

"I don't know how it could be *more* obvious," Claudia retorted. "He's going to kill the baby."

"No, he's *not*—for the love o' Mike, stop sayin' it."

"A strange sort of subconscious, you're got," the heiress offered in an amused tone.

"Oh," Claudia said in a fury. "If *only* I still had my Glock."

"No violence," Doyle admonished in alarm. "Please, ladies."

"Too late," said the heiress, and then chuckled as though at a private joke.

With a gasp, Doyle started awake, and lay for a moment, waiting for her heart to stop pounding. She knew immediately that Acton wasn't next to her, and—lifting her head to review his desk in the dimness—she realized he'd taken his laptop into the main room, which is what he did, sometimes, when he was having trouble sleeping.

Rubbing her eyes, she laid back down and tried to decide what it all meant—the dreams were always important, but this time it looked to be a crackin' ball of snakes, and she couldn't make heads nor tails of it. She'd two ghosts, for a change— who didn't get along—and one of them kept accusing Acton of wanting to do terrible things. The other one—and here, she frowned at the ceiling—the other one was trouble, in her own right; Doyle could sense it.

So; what was the point of having to deal with these two troublesome ghosts? Acton was not going to kill Edward, and even if that was his plan—which she didn't believe for a moment, mind you—he certainly wouldn't try to do such a thing now, after she'd raised the subject.

I'm not getting it, she thought in resigned frustration. But I always do, sooner or later, so I suppose I've no choice but to possess my soul in patience, and try to stay sharp; although I haven't the first clue what it is that I should be watching for.

Listening to the faint clicking of Acton's fingers on his keyboard, she drifted back to sleep.

CHAPTER 23

To Doyle's great surprise, the face that appeared over the wall of her cubicle on Monday morning was that of Detective Sergeant Isabel Munoz, who was supposedly on suspension for dereliction of duty.

"Faith, Munoz; what are *you* doin' here? Aren't they supposed to sound some= sort of alarm, if you darken the door?"

With a casual hand, the other girl smoothed back her long dark hair. "I'm still suspended from official duties, but I've been brought in as a temporary Processor to give support to Williams and Geary."

Doyle leaned back to consider this. "Well, there's a crackin' punishment. Which is the handsomer?"

"Williams," Munoz answered without hesitation, and sipped her coffee.

Doyle could not disagree with this assessment. "What if we added Gabriel into the mix?"

"Still Williams," Munoz decided. "Strictly based on appearance."

Doyle made a face. "Small good it does me; he won't marry Lizzy Mathis, no matter how much I beg and plead."

The other girl rolled her eyes. "You mustn't match-make, Doyle. You're not good at it."

Doyle sighed. "No, I suppose not."

"And why would you be matching-up Lizzy Mathis in the first place? She's got all the sex-appeal of a picket fence."

Hastily, Doyle retreated from any inadvertent disclosures about medieval ghosts—lesson learned. "She's pretty enough, Munoz—and she's smart as a whip, which surely must appeal to *someone*. It's just a project—I'm in need of a decent project."

After throwing a skeptical glance Doyle's way, Munoz pulled her mobile and checked the time. "You'll soon have projects enough; you're due in Williams' office for a case management meeting. I'm to come along."

Since Doyle had forgot about this appointment, she made a show of being annoyed as she pushed back her chair to stand. "I know, I *know*—I'm just gettin' organized. I was busy, over the week-end, what with the weddin', and—and such." It suddenly occurred to her that she'd best button her lip about the Gemma situation—or at least until she'd Acton's say-so to speak about it. Circumspect, I'm being, she thought with no small pride; which is a first for me—give the girl another medal.

Hoisting her rucksack, she turned down the aisle-way as Munoz reminded her, "Next week's the Baptism; don't forget about that, too."

This, in reference to Sofia, Munoz's new niece, and Doyle replied in a breezy tone, "Oh, we'll be there, with bells on. Wouldn't miss it for the world."

Curious, she slowed down, and lowered her voice. "What's Habib think about all this?" As Habib was Pakistani, it could be presumed that he wasn't necessarily a big fan of the Seven Blessed Sacraments.

The other girl shrugged. "Who knows? I've given up trying to read him. But my parents insisted on a traditional Baptism because Elena needs to placate all the relatives—they've been on a collective freak-out, ever since she married Habib."

Stoutly, Doyle insisted, "He's a good man, and I'll not hear a word against him." Being circumspect yet again, she refrained from mentioning that Habib was not disinclined to commit a murder or two himself, for just-cause purposes, since making such a disclosure might confuse the issue. Very difficult, it was, to keep track of all this "being circumspect" business and it was a wonder Acton managed it; her hat was off to him.

Suddenly, her scalp prickled, and she frowned, wondering why it would. Acton was a crackin' mastermind with many an iron in the fire—no news flash, there. Faith, she couldn't hold a candle to the man in terms of circumspect-ness, and there was no pretense in claiming otherwise.

From behind her, Munoz's voice interrupted her thoughts. "Habib's not exactly what they were hoping for, of course. They're all pretty hard-core RC."

"So are you," Doyle observed fairly. "You're pretty hard-core RC, Munoz, despite your best efforts to stifle it—just look at your artwork. Mayhap it's in the blood."

Annoyed, Munoz retorted, "Well, you're Irish, so you're not one to talk."

"Pot, meet kettle," Doyle conceded. "For the sake of peace, I will agree that both of us come from a long line of equally hard-core religious nuts. Faith, but you'd argue the hind leg off a donkey, Munoz; no need to give me the snash."

The other girl sighed, as they paused before the lift. "Sorry. I'm in a bad mood because the Baptism is bound to be an ordeal, not to mention I'll have to buy a demure dress."

"That's the only kind I own," Doyle admitted as the doors slid open. Then—hoping to hear the latest on the other's romantic dilemma—she ventured, "Will you bring a date?"

With some vehemence, Munoz retorted, "No, I won't. In fact, I should start a rumor that I'm taking the veil, just to make everyone feel better about Elena."

"You'd not make a good nun," Doyle said doubtfully. "I've known many a nun, and you're not cut from that cloth."

"Just a joke, Doyle," the other girl said crossly, and then pointedly sipped her coffee.

Doyle decided that she couldn't resist laying another twig upon the fire, and asked in an innocent tone, "What excuse will you give Gabriel? Surely, he's expectin' to meet the relatives?"

But instead of firing off a smart remark, Munoz suddenly sobered. "He wouldn't be able to come anyway; he'll be in the facility at least another week." She paused. "He's had a little setback."

Officer Gabriel, Munoz's supposed beau, had been enrolled in a thirty-day rehabilitation program at the local clinic, due to an unfortunate dependency on drugs. With a twinge of guilt, Doyle realized she hadn't given him much thought, lately, and shame on her, since presumably he would need all the support his friends could muster. "I'm that sorry for it; what's happened?"

Her companion sighed. "It's not clear, but he's not showing the progress he should be, so they're doing more tests. I'm going over to visit over lunch, want to come?"

"I will," Doyle hedged, "dependin' on what Williams has in store for me." Judging from the eagerness of the invitation, she had the uneasy suspicion that Munoz wanted a third person present so that she could avoid a personal discussion with poor officer Gabriel, who no doubt would be promptly dumped in favor of Officer Geary as soon as he was well enough to take the bad news.

"You should come—you always cheer him up. Speaking of which, he says Acton was surprisingly kind, when he came to visit."

Doyle blinked, because these words, put together in this particular order, didn't make much sense. "Was he indeed?"

The other girl lifted a dark brow. "You didn't know? Well, maybe they want to keep it quiet—Acton told him he'd be getting a commendation, even though he wasn't shot in the line of duty. They decided to make an exception, in his case."

"That *is* very kind." Especially since that particular adjective was the last one anyone would ever use to describe Acton. Something was strange, here, Doyle thought; a ministering hospital-visit to Gabriel seemed very un-Acton-like, not to mention he'd not said a word to her about it. Of course, he was always close-lipped about his goings-on with the CID brass, being as the poor man's wife was a gabbler of the first order. And perhaps he'd heard that Gabriel was suffering a setback, and wanted to cheer him up by throwing a medal or two his way.

Doubtfully, she considered this potential theory as Munoz cautioned, "I haven't mentioned to Gabriel that I've been taken-on as a temporary Processor, so try not to say anything to him about it."

No explanation was offered for this subterfuge, and Doyle drew the obvious conclusion; Gabriel was nobody's fool, and no doubt was already suspicious about having a rival in the worthy Officer Geary, who would now be seeing the fair Munoz on a daily basis.

Interesting, Doyle thought, as they made their way toward Williams' office; if I didn't know better, I'd think Acton was trying to throw Geary and Munoz together. And if Acton's decided to try his hand at matchmaking, Katy bar the door;

Doyle had been a front-row witness to his only other attempt, and in two shakes she'd been bundled off to the altar in a cloud of bewilderment.

Although if this were indeed Acton's latest project, it seemed as though the skids were already greased, because even though they were entering the handsomer-Williams' office, the Spanish beauty cautioned, "I can't stay too long, Geary wants to meet on a project."

"Understood," Doyle replied gravely.

CHAPTER 24

Doyle and Munoz sat across the desk from Williams, listening as he went over the latest developments in the limo-driver's murder, which had now been combined with the Health Council-murders, and would presumably soon be combined with Father Ambrose's murder.

Williams turned around his laptop so that they could read along with him. "Munoz has updated the timeline, and—much as we suspected—Castellano took his position on the Health Professions Council the same month that Martina Betancourt became Sir Cavanaugh's Administrative Assistant, which was about the same time Navarro's servant took over the job as the Council's limo-driver."

"That's got to be enough to bring Navarro in on a twenty-four-hour hold," Doyle noted a bit impatiently. "Acton said he might do it today, and I would think that some pointed questionin' would be in order. If nothing else, we should ask whether he knows where Betancourt and Castellano are—the fact we're on to him may shake him off his high horse."

But Williams reminded her, "Acton's reluctant to move in, because he thinks there's another murder on his list, and he'd like to catch him at it."

More like Acton's probably jealous, and wants to crib the stupid list, Doyle thought uncharitably, and then cautioned herself not to voice such thoughts aloud.

"So, we're in a holding pattern, sticking with the surveillance and hoping he'll make a move. We've probably got enough to bring him in, but it would be nice to have something more concrete to lay before the Prosecutors, since the Prosecutors won't be very eager to move on it—these Council-murders make them look bad. Meanwhile, the passport authorities are alerted, should any of them try to leave the country."

Doyle observed, "You'd almost hope they try to flee; at least we'd know where Betancourt and Castellano were, if the Port Authorities nabbed 'em."

Munoz, who'd already forgot that she was supposed to have on her processor-hat and not her detective-hat, asked, "Has there been any attempt at contact between them?"

Williams leaned back in his chair. "That's the puzzling thing—surveillance says Navarro hasn't called anyone, or gone anywhere—at least, as far as we can tell. Acton thinks it strange that he hasn't even gone to church."

"That *is* strange," Doyle mused. Presumably, anyone who'd go priest-shopping for murder-absolution wasn't going to miss a Sabbath obligation. "So—Navarro's got somethin' else in the hopper—else he wouldn't be stayin' in London—and Acton's waitin', hopin' he'll make a move. But—contrary to all expectations—he just he mopes around in his garden, and longs for Spain."

Williams cocked his head. "That about sums it up."

Munoz said to Williams, "Since we believe this is a conspiracy, I've mapped out other significant events that you may or may not want placed in the timeline for consideration."

This was standard procedure, especially when they had a suspect who may have committed multiple murders; the CID would start looking at all the unsolved crimes in the same time-frame, hoping for a lead.

"Right," said Williams, and scrolled to open the "Contemporary Significant Events" folder Munoz had created.

Munoz leaned forward to indicate, "I listed them in order of most interest, although nothing really jumped out."

"D'Angelo," said Williams, and made a note. "It's worth taking a look; he's high-profile."

"Who's he?" asked Doyle, who was not ashamed to expose her ignorance.

"He's a construction magnate," Munoz explained. "The rumor is he was involved in shady doings—international shady doings, which is a correlating point for the Navarro case—and he disappeared under suspicious circumstances, the same day as the limo-driver. They haven't found a body, yet."

Doyle raised her brows. "That's the name on all the construction signs at St. Michael's—small wonder, that the work's slowed down."

Munoz had moved on, and indicated another name. There's Chadway, as well."

Williams tilted his head with some skepticism. "That may be a stretch, Munoz. Unlikely there's any connection."

"Who's that?" asked Doyle again, who felt as though she were a child being allowed to sit at the adult table.

"She's the intern from forensic-psych," Munoz informed her a bit impatiently. "Didn't you see the funeral announcement?"

Doyle raised her brows again. "Someone from forensic-psych was murdered?" This was a surprise, although since the Met employed many people in many different capacities, it stood to reason that some of them got themselves killed, from time to time.

"It may have been an accident," Williams explained. "An overdose of insulin."

Doyle nodded in agreement—any unexpected death was automatically considered a homicide until the Coroner could pronounce it an accident or suicide, and sometimes there wasn't much in the way of evidence to make that determination.

Munoz explained, "It's still pending, mainly because no one seems to have been aware she was diabetic."

"Kept it well-hidden, mayhap," said Doyle, who carefully didn't look at Williams, who was also a diabetic, and kept it well-hidden. "I wonder if it's someone I met durin' the task-force—do we a snap?"

Doyle had attended a single session of the psychology task-force before it was abruptly cancelled, and she wondered if the decedent was the unpleasant intern who'd been a bit sneer-y when she'd administered one of the tests. Not that she'd wish death on anyone, of course—her wretched husband was rubbing off on her, and she should repent fasting—but it wouldn't have surprised her if the girl had met a bad end; she was the bad-ending sort.

But when the personnel photo popped up on the screen, she saw that the decedent wasn't the tech she'd been thinking of, but a different familiar face. "Oh—oh, I did meet her, poor thing; she administered one of the tests." With an effort, she knit her brows, trying to remember. "Somethin' about elephants."

"What happened to that task-force?" Munoz asked, as she closed the photo. "Is it still happening?"

"No—I think Commander Tasza was the movin' force behind it, and no one else thinks the game is worth the candle." Again, Doyle chastised herself for being relieved that some poor soul had been gathered up before her time—honestly, she was such a baby, to be judging terrible events only in terms of how it affected her.

"Anything new on the Commander's case?" Munoz asked Williams. "I've been out of the loop."

"I can't tell you officially, since you're on suspension," Williams replied as he pulled his laptop back 'round. "But unofficially, the answer is no. They have a ten-mile target area where she was last seen, but nothing has turned up. It's a remote area, and we can't even find a decent CCTV feed."

"I bet she's in the bog," Doyle offered in a knowing fashion. "Bogs are a murderer's best friend, and with her line o' work, there'd be a lot of enemies who wanted to see her gone."

"Probably not a personal crime," Munoz agreed. "As far as anyone knew, she'd no personal life to speak of."

"They're looking carefully at her current caseload, and the people she was monitoring," Williams offered. "It does seem unlikely that it was an accident, or a case of mistaken identity. Hopefully, a lead will turn up."

Doyle shivered slightly. "Another reason not to dance wi' the devil; sooner or later you're goin' to pay the piper."

Williams, being Williams, mildly remonstrated, "There's no indication that the Commander was corrupt, Doyle."

But Doyle wasn't having it, and made a derisive sound. "It's too much of a coincidence—that she mysteriously disappeared right as the Met's drug-runnin' scandal was breakin'. I may have been born at night, Thomas, but it wasn't last night."

"But if that's the case, then she might have orchestrated her own disappearance," Munoz pointed out. "She may not be dead—it's something they should consider."

Oh, she's well-and-truly dead, Doyle thought immediately, and then wondered why she was so certain. After all, Munoz was right—it was entirely possible the good Commander had chosen to drop out of sight, given the trouble she might have been in.

The three detectives got back to business, going through Munoz's other significant events—as always, the list of unsolved homicides was depressingly long—and at its conclusion, Williams had added three more open cases for further consideration, asking Munoz to take a deep dive for any possible correlations to the present case.

He was typing a note to document their conclusions when Doyle asked suddenly, "What about Elena?"

The others looked at her for a moment, and Williams paused in his typing. "What *about* Elena?"

Frowning, Doyle gazed out the window. "Wasn't she abducted from the Council around this same time frame?"

Whilst Munoz rolled her eyes, Williams explained almost kindly, "You've got hold of the wrong end of the stick, Doyle. We're looking for possible Navarro *victims* for the same time period. If the working-theory holds, then he—and his night-class—would be responsible for murdering everyone who was *behind* Elena's abduction—not responsible for arranging to have her abducted."

Hastily, Doyle demurred, "Oh—oh, of course. Sorry; I think with the Baptism comin' up, I've got Elena on the brain."

"Me, too," said Munoz a bit sourly. "I can't wait for it to be over."

"Sorry I'm going to miss it," Williams said ironically as he checked the time. "Got to go; I've got a witness interview in

Detention. Let me know if you find anything by end-of-day, Munoz."

Munoz rose to her feet. "I'll get right on it, but first I'm due for a meeting with Inspector Geary." Smoothing her hair back, the Spanish girl then rapidly departed from the room without a backward glance.

CHAPTER 25

Into the ensuing silence, Doyle gave Williams a significant look. "Told you so."But he wasn't one to gossip, was DI Williams, and so he only offered a half-smile as he snapped his laptop shut.

But Doyle suffered from no such compunction, and reported, "She said Gabriel's had a set-back of some sort, which is only adding insult to the poor man's injury."

Williams glanced up at her as he packed up his rucksack. "Has he? I was wondering why he wasn't back on the roster yet—we could definitely use another hand."

"We're supposed to visit Gabriel at lunch, if Munoz can tear herself away from makin' sheep's eyes at Geary." Eying her companion, she added, "I don't mind goin' to visit, but I should go home to spell Reynolds for an hour—bein' as we don't have a nanny, at present. Mayhap you should go spell Reynolds instead, since it's by your connivance that my nanny has fled the scene."

He smiled as he held the door for her. "No comment."

She teased, "You'll wear a rut in the road to Dublin, at this rate."

"I was happy to drive them to the ferry, Kath. Sorry I couldn't tell you."

But Doyle waxed philosophical, as they made their way toward the lift. "I'm a weak link when there's a scheme afoot— no question—but you're a good man, Thomas Williams. I hope your heart's not broken."

"Nothing I'm not used to," he teased, with a significant glance her way.

She laughed aloud, as they paused before the lift. "Faith, Thomas; at this rate you'll wind up a monk, livin' in a moated grange."

"That doesn't sound remotely inviting."

Doyle nodded thoughtfully. "Acton, on the other hand, would like nothin' better, but instead he's hip-deep in babies, with people constantly comin' and goin'. He'd love to live alone somewhere on a remote mountaintop; he'd probably have a stillroom, and keep bees."

They stepped into the lift, and Williams pressed the button. "I don't think you can have a moat on a mountaintop. Kath."

"He'd figure out how to manage it," she insisted. "He's Acton, after all, and if he decides he wants a moat, nothin' would dare stand in his way."

As they descended to the lobby, Williams offered, "I don't know, Kath; I think he enjoys doing exactly what he does."

Doyle had to acknowledge the truth of this. "You're a wise man, Thomas, and I stand corrected; Acton likes to have a finger in every imaginable pie, and there's no better place than the Met for havin' the opportunity to do just that. Although he does manage the occasional off-campus project, and let Mary's weddin' serve as an excellent example."

As they started across the lobby, she ventured in a casual tone, "In fact, he's got another project that's takin' up a bit of his time, but I haven't a clue what it is. Any guesses?"

But Williams knew her too well, and therefore was not fooled by the casualness of the question. With a small frown between his brows, he glanced down at her. "Are you worried? I can honestly say I've no idea."

"It makes me uneasy," she admitted slowly. "Not to know."

"You *are* the weak link," he reminded her, gently teasing.

"Aye, that," she acknowledged. "No argument, here."

"You should trust him, Kath. Only see how well Mary's situation has turned out, when she thought it was hopeless."

She made a wry mouth. "Everyone's tellin' me to trust Acton, but you've all forgot that my job is to throw a spanner into his wheel-of-many-schemes every once in a while, just to gum up the works." She paused, thinking about this with no small satisfaction. "No one can gum up the works like I can."

"I think that's a fair assessment," he agreed, amused.

"Well, will you tell me if you hear anythin'?"

"That depends," he replied, suddenly wary, "on the project."

She sighed, as she truly couldn't expect much more—Williams was Acton's henchman, after all, and whilst he was very fond of the fair Doyle, he knew better than to try and second-guess the illustrious Chief Inspector. Besides, on the whole, Williams was wholeheartedly in agreement with her husband's alarming philosophy of knocking the heads together that most deserved knocking, regardless of paltry considerations like the common law, and a jury of one's peers.

Overall, she should be relieved, because Williams was telling the truth, when he'd said he didn't know what Acton was up to, but—strangely enough—that was the very thing that made her uneasy.

They walked by the Desk Sergeant's desk—a new fellow, and very conscientious—and then Doyle was surprised to be hailed by the woman who was standing at his input counter. "Oh—there you are, Officer Doyle; what a happy coincidence. I was just leaving a note for you, since I imagine you are kept very busy."

Doyle beheld the HR Administrator from Winchester University —no dog with her, this time—and so she approached with a smile. "Oh—oh hallo, again." Small wonder she hadn't recognized the woman at first, she looked quite a bit different from the last time they'd met; aside from not having the dog at her side, her hair had been bobbed into a more flattering style and her dark-framed glasses had been replaced by updated pink ones.

In her efficient manner, the woman smiled a perfunctory greeting upon being introduced to Williams, but then got down to business. "After you'd come in to do the background check on Professor Navarro, I went through his file—you can never be too careful, you know—and I thought I should let you know that I found a mistake in his personal information. His permanent address had been crossed-up with the address for the University of Salamanca, which was where he'd studied for his doctorate."

In an aside, she offered, "I spotted the error in a trice, since I communicate with other learning institutions on the Continent quite often, and so I am familiar with all their addresses."

"Of course, you are," said Doyle, with all sincerity.

"It was an error, of course, and I found his correct address by cross-referencing his own graduate work. I know that it is important that the police records be accurate, and so I was just going to leave you a note."

"Thank you," said Doyle rather overwhelmed in the face of such dogged efficiency. "I appreciate that you came by."

The woman offered a thin, happy smile. "No trouble; I was out running errands anyway—I will be out of town for a fortnight, starting tomorrow. Mr. Sergius and I discovered that we both want to travel, but never had anyone to go with, and so we've decided to take a holiday to the Black Sea. Mr. Sergius tells me there are some resorts there that are very reasonable—ones that accommodate dogs." Very pleased, the woman leaned forward to confess, "I haven't been on holiday in years."

Doyle said in a grave tone, "I think you're due, then."

As Williams was giving off the unspoken signs men tended to give off when they were becoming impatient, Doyle thanked the woman, and the two detectives continued on their way across the lobby. Thoughtfully, she asked, "What's it called, Thomas, when somethin' happens even though you weren't truly tryin'?"

"Bad luck?" he offered.

"No, something good and useful, even though that wasn't your intent, and you were all unknowin'."

"Inadvertent?"

She smiled. "That's it—I'm an inadvertent matchmaker; although I've got to give some credit to Bertie too, I suppose."

Confused, he looked down at her. "And who is Bertie?"

"Never you mind, Thomas; it's not important—I'm just thinkin' aloud."

"Well, I'm off to Detention. Do you think there's anything of interest in Navarro's address? It sounded like an entry mistake on the University's end."

Unfolding the Administrator's neatly typewritten note, Doyle perused the contents. "Why are foreign addresses always so complicated? Some long names with too many hyphens, and then 'Andalucía'."

He nodded. "Give it to over to Munoz, then, to make the correction on the record."

Suddenly struck, Doyle looked up to contemplate the far corner of the room. "D'you know, Thomas, I think this place is the same place where Munoz's relatives live, remember? They were going to take-in Elena's baby, but she wasn't havin' it, and married Habib, instead." She paused, frowning. "I wonder if Munoz's relatives know the Navarros."

"Spain's a big place, Kath," Williams offered diplomatically.

She made a wry mouth. "I know, I know—I sound like those people who always think I should know every blessed soul in Dublin. But it just seems such a coincidence."

"Got to go," he interrupted, checking the time. "Circle back later, and we'll see if Munoz or the surveillance team has come up with anything of interest."

"I'll give your regards to Gabriel," she reminded him.

"Oh—right; thanks. Tell him we need him back in the traces."

Thoughtfully, Doyle walked outside, dawdling a bit before she rang up the driving service—she'd best coordinate with Munoz, since she didn't want to be buttonholed alone with Gabriel any more than the Spanish girl did, and therefore it would probably behoove the both of them to arrive at the facility at the same time.

But before she scrolled for Munoz's number she paused, staring at the mobile for a long moment. Coming to a decision, she sheathed it, and then pulled her personal mobile to phone Acton.

CHAPTER 26

A s always, Acton answered their personal line promptly. "Kathleen." "Ho," she said. "I told Williams that if you had your druthers, you'd live alone, and keep bees."

"In Sussex South Downs, perhaps?"

She frowned slightly. "I'm not sure where that is."

"No matter. Would you live there, too?"

"Not if you're livin' *alone*, Michael—please pay attention."

"Then definitely it would not be my druthers."

This was true, and she smiled into the phone. "I don't know how you manage it—soundin' so posh, even when you use a word like 'druthers'."

"I'm a crackin' wonderment," he replied, in his best imitation of her.

She laughed, but then decided that she mustn't get distracted by sweet-talk from her husband, since then she'd be at it all day. "I wanted to check in with you because there's something here in the Navarro case that we're missin', but I'm not sure what it is, and so I'm wonderin' if a brainstormin' session might be in order."

"Lunch?" he suggested. "I can push back a meeting."

She made a face. "I can't—Munoz has roped me into visitin' Gabriel at lunch."

"Has she? That is a shame. Shall I give you a lift?"

Frowning, she squinted up at the trees. "Best not, because then you'd have to give Munoz a lift, too, and I'm not sure she should be listenin' in to what I have to say."

As could be expected, this remark caught his full and undivided attention. "Can you speak of it now, or do you want to come to my office?"

She sighed. "I'll speak of it now, mainly because I don't have much, Michael—it's just one of those feelin's that's nigglin' at me. I keep thinkin' that Elena Munoz's abduction is tied up in all of it, even though that doesn't make much sense—in her case, Navarro would be the hero, not the villain."

There was a pause whilst he thought this over, and she was silent whilst he did so. One of the endearing things about her husband—one of the many, of course—was that he gave a full measure of respect to anything she suggested, no matter how off-base it might seem at first glance.

He offered, "Because they are both Spanish, perhaps?"

"Oh—oh, yes; that's the part I need to tell you. Remember the HR Administrator at the University?"

"I do."

"Well, she came into Headquarters to correct Navarro's address—they had the wrong one in their records—and I wonder if it that wasn't a mistake, but an attempt to hide somethin'. His true address is in Andalucía."

"Yes," he replied, and she was given to understand that he already knew this. "And it only stands to reason; Seville is the region where the Carlists tend to congregate."

Doyle wracked her brain. "The Carlists bein' the hard-core noble people who aren't allowed to be nobles anymore?"

"The very same."

Trust Acton to already be aware of the address-switch, and so she moved on to play her next card. "Well, here's the wrinkle; that's also where Munoz's relatives are from—she mentioned it once, because they were goin' to take-in Elena's baby, but Elena married Habib, instead."

There was a small pause, whilst she knew he was thinking, yet again. She offered, "I know the connection sounds a bit sketchy, Michael, but I truly think there's somethin' there."

In a level tone, he asked, "Do you think Munoz is implicated, somehow?"

"As part of the vengeance-gang?" For a long moment, she thought this over with her best neutral-detective hat on. "No, I don't. But for some reason I keep thinkin' that it's all connected to Elena's kidnapping, and that doesn't make any sense a'tall."

"Let me have a look, then."

"I'm sorry I don't have anythin' more concrete, Michael, but it's been nippin' at me."

"I'll get to it as soon as I can."

She ventured, "Any chance you have a spare hour, so as to relieve Reynolds at home? Edward should be goin' down for his nap soon, so you could get a bit of work done there, if you wanted."

"I will be happy to," he agreed.

"I wouldn't want Reynolds to throw down his oven mitts and quit," she explained. "We'd never survive on our own."

"A good point, although I think he'd have to search long and hard for another household with a Romanov within."

"He's a terrible snob, and shame on him," she agreed. "Lucky for you, that your marriage to me has saved you from such a fate."

"You'll be the Countess of Aldwych in another week's time," he reminded her.

She made a face into the phone. "Now, there's as strange a turn of events as you'll ever hope to see. We've gone down the rabbit-hole indeed, and no mistakin'."

He teased, "Perhaps we'll have your portrait painted, and hang it in the gallery."

"There you go; I can hold a globe, and wear robes."

"You are quite fetching, in a robe," he agreed.

"It wouldn't matter; the other portraits would refuse to hang near mine—your ancestors would be all up in arms, and small blame to them."

"My ancestors may be damned," he replied.

She laughed. "Don't say it too loud, we don't want to jinx anyone."

"I imagine that ship has already sailed."

Reminded, she said, "You know, Michael—I don't remember seein' a portrait of the heiress—the one who married your grandfather, and saved Trestles. I'm surprised she's not displayed in pride o' place, somewhere." Now that she thought about it, it did seem strange—the woman was rather vain, after all, and just the type who'd want the fanciest of portraits, all decked out in the fanciest of jewels.

"I don't think she ever had one done," he admitted. "If you'd like, I could ask Hudson to show you a photograph."

Doyle paused in surprise, and then said, "Not worth the trouble; it was just a thought, Michael."

"I will see you soon."

"Cheers."

Thoughtfully, she rang off. Now, that was strange; there were no photographs of the heiress, and Acton knew it. Mayhap her no-account son—Acton's father—had destroyed them all, or something. After all, her son didn't have his portrait hanging on the wall either, and with good reason.

It all goes back to what I keep saying, she thought; there must be as many bad bloodlines as good ones—it only stands to reason, after all—and so everyone needs to just get over it.

With a mental sigh, she brought her attention back to the matter at hand, and rang up Munoz.

CHAPTER 27

Doyle sat next to Munoz and tried to hide her dismay; Officer Gabriel was indeed looking a bit down-pin, and didn't seem his usual self at all.

The two girls were visiting with him in the rehab clinic's garden, seated near a warbling fountain and smiling brightly as they cast about for subjects to speak of that did not involve love triangles or drug addiction. It was no easy task, as Gabriel seemed disinclined to speak, himself.

"Have you managed a demure dress for the Baptism?" Doyle asked Munoz, thinking that this would be a safe topic. "I can always lend you one of mine."

"It wouldn't fit," Munoz pointed out with a hint of superiority—Munoz had a very fine figure, whereas Doyle was on the less-buxom side. "I've got to go find something boring and neutral. I'll go have a look tonight."

"What is this, the Army?" Gabriel teased, showing hints of his old self. "You should defy them all and wear red. Short, and cut down to there."

Munoz made a face. "You don't know my grandmother; she'd bar the door and have me excommunicated."

"She's fearsome," Doyle agreed. "I met her, once."

Munoz drew a resigned breath. "I shouldn't complain; Elena's dreading it more than I am. On the bright side, my grandmother will give them a nice christening gift—she's got tons of money."

"She wanted to give some of it to me," Doyle remembered. "When you were in the hospital, remember?"

"When was this?" asked Gabriel, trying to show an interest.

"It was after the bridge-jumpin' incident. Munoz stayed overnight in the hospital and the family came out in full force—it was a bit dauntin', I have to say."

"Don't remind me," said Munoz.

"It was mighty impressive," Doyle continued. "They were there in a pig's whisper, all stoic, and determined to show their support—oh," she said, suddenly struck, "*that's* who Mrs. Navarro reminds me of—your grandmother. I suppose it only makes sense, since they're both old-school Spanish, and from the same area. D'you suppose they're related?"

"Everyone's related to everyone, there," said Munoz, a bit glumly. "It's like they're all biding their time and waiting for the sixteenth-century to come back."

"Parts of Persia are like that," Gabriel offered. "Only they're waiting for the thirteenth-century to come back."

"Well, none of them can trump me," Doyle declared. "I get to wear a stupid tiara to a stupid Investiture ceremony, and if that's not positively *medieval*, I don't know what is."

Gabriel perked up, and asked, "How does that work? Is it all pomp and ceremony, like the Order of the Garter? Or is it skull-and-bones secrecy, with animal sacrifices and blood-oaths?"

"I've no idea, and I try to think about it as little as possible."

Munoz chided, "You shouldn't complain; I don't know anyone who wouldn't love to have a tiara."

Gabriel reached for the other girl's hand. "I will buy you one, then."

Since this romantic gesture would be entirely unwelcome to Munoz, Doyle hurriedly intervened. "You're welcome to mine—I don't like it much. When I wear it, I think I can feel thousands of generations of Doyles, rollin' over in their graves."

"You worry about all that stuff way too much, Doyle," Munoz advised. "Just be happy that Acton was willing to marry you."

Doyle decided she was willing to allow the implied insult to slide, since they were being all polite-and-kind, here in the clinic's garden, and anyways, if she told Munoz the true tale with no bark on it, the other girl would probably fall off her chair.

"Acton's the lucky one," Gabriel offered chivalrously. "He's a happy man."

"Thank you, Gabriel." She smiled her appreciation, wishing it were true, but knowing that such was not the case; Acton was not the sort of person that one could ever describe as "happy"—bitten by too many demons, he was.

I wish I knew what was best to do, she thought for the hundredth time; and it didn't help that there was unlikely to be any advice in a marriage manual that would be remotely helpful. Hard on this thought, her private mobile pinged.

"No mobile phones," Munoz reminded her with a hint of censure.

Doyle checked the screen. "It's Acton, and since he's home with the baby I should see what it is," she apologized. "I'll just go out to the lobby for a mo, and then I'll be right back."

But as it turned out, Doyle didn't need to phone Acton, because as she headed toward the facility's lobby she could hear her son's happy babbling—liked to hear himself, he did—and had to smile, despite herself. Something important must have come up, and Acton must need to hand-off the boyo, which was fine by Doyle because she was that ready for an excuse to leave.

But it appeared that her husband had other motives, as she greeted him and Edward, who immediately reached out his arms for her. "We thought we'd surprise you with a visit," Acton explained. "But they do not allow children back in the patient area."

"Ah well; you meant well."

She firmly held the squirming Edward—who wanted nothing more than to crawl about on the questionable floor—and decided that there was not the smallest chance that Acton didn't know the rehab facility would not allow children within, and so she was left with the conclusion that Acton's true purpose was to give her an excuse to extricate herself—which was kind of him, and mighty tempting, besides.

With a twinge of guilt, she confessed, "I'd love to clear out, Michael, but I don't know as I can leave just yet; I don't think Munoz necessarily wants to be left alone with Gabriel, but she can't snub him outright since he's supposedly her boyfriend."

He glanced up toward the door that led into the facility. "Shall I go in, and tell her I've a pressing issue she must research?"

"Good one, but best not," Doyle decided as she handed him the baby back. "She doesn't want Gabriel to know she's a temporary Processor, and thereby livin' snug-as-a-stoat in Geary's back pocket. "I'll go make my excuses, and she'll just have to face the music."

And so, Doyle went back into the garden to announce, "Acton's brought Edward to visit you, Gabriel, but it turns out that it's not allowed, so instead I will leave you, my friend.

Take care; Williams sends his regards, and says he needs you back in the traces."

Gabriel offered a wan smile. "Tell him I'm champing at the bit."

"You do look a bit tired," Munoz offered. "Shall I go, too?"

"Yes—sorry," the young man replied. "I'm a little short on energy. I should take a look around, and pilfer some amphetamines—they must have a stash here, somewhere." With a fond smile, he reached for Munoz's hand. "Will I see you tomorrow?"

"I hope so," Munoz hedged, and it was not true.

CHAPTER 28

Doyle watched as her husband strapped the baby into the car seat, and asked, "Shall we venture out to a restaurant. Michael? We can always do a Code One, if Edward goes to pieces." Unfortunately, the baby was at a troublesome age for going out in public—too old to stay quiet, and too young to obey instruction.

Acton slid into the driver's seat, and started up the car. "Perhaps we should go home, instead."

"Reynolds isn't there," she reminded him.

He gave her a look with which she was well-familiar. "Exactly."

She laughed aloud, and leaned in to wait until he'd the chance to quickly kiss her. "I see how it is—leapin' into bed the moment an opportunity presents itself. I'll not balk; we can stick Edward in his crib, and he'll be none the wiser. I haven't had lunch, though, and so I hope there's a ham-and-butter sandwich in the offin'."

He smiled as he navigated into traffic. "You are cheaply bought."

Wickedly, she teased, "Only try to imagine what I'd be willin' to do for a blood puddin'."

"I confess that it is hard to imagine anything that would be worth it."

She laughed again, and wondered if all this sex-talk was a distraction—heaven knew that she was easily distracted—and the fact that Acton had brought Edward to fetch her away from Gabriel produced a feeling of uneasiness within her bosom. Clearly, he didn't want her to be there, but surely he must see that she needed to show support to poor Gabriel. Acton was not one to feel obligated, though—so perhaps he couldn't relate.

To show that she hadn't been distracted, she offered, "I feel badly about him—about Gabriel, Michael. You'd think with Munoz's attention wanderin', he'd have plenty of incentive to get himself back up on his pins, but instead you can tell that he's not doin' too well."

Acton expression turned a bit grave. "Yes; I visited him a few days ago."

With a twinge of guilt that she'd gone and spoilt the impending-sex mood, she half-teased, "So I heard, and that's very sweet of you, Michael."

"I can only hope the situation resolves itself," he replied.

This remark made her antenna quiver for some reason, and Doyle idly watched out the window, trying to decide why it would. Acton had taken drastic measures to put Gabriel in the hospital as a means to keep him away from the consequences of the Met's drug-running scandal, and Doyle could only surmise that her husband's guarded remarks meant that the jury was still out on whether the young officer would pass through that particular tangle-patch unscathed.

Acton's attitude is a bit like Munoz's attitude, she realized; *neither one of them is truly unhappy that poor Gabriel is sidelined for the nonce*—although they'd different reasons for it. Acton's reason had to do with the rolling-up of the smuggling rig; the only other possibility was that Acton was purposely trying to throw Munoz and Geary together, and that was a bit hard to believe—he couldn't care less who wound up with who—he only wanted to wind up with the fair Doyle.

Her scalp prickled, and before she could consider why this would be, her mobile pinged and she saw that it was Williams.

"Cheers," she answered. "I'm dossin' about on my lunch break, so whatever it is will have to wait." She paused, and then added with all due respect, "sir."

"I thought you were going to visit Gabriel, on your lunch break."

"Cut short, it was. And anyways, Acton's bent on drivin' me home for lunch and he outranks you—or at least for the time bein'. We're goin' to have a quick bowl of cereal." Out of the corner of her eye, she saw Acton smile.

"All right then; if you would, come report to Detention as soon as you're back; I need a third for an interview."

A "third" was needful when a detective wanted a chaperone for an interview or an interrogation; it protected the interviewing officer from being set-up for harassment or entrapment. "Right then; I should be there in an hour or so."

"Ping me when you're on your way."

She rang off, and explained to Acton, "Williams needs a third, so as to protect his virtue."

"Did he name the case?" Her never-negligent husband tended to keep careful track of his overly-negligent wife.

"Not to worry, Michael—he wouldn't dare put me in the same room with someone you'd object to, and anyways, there are no Santeros left in the city, I think." This, in reference to a very uncomfortable hour she'd once spent in Detention, whilst in the company of a witch-doctor.

"A faint hope, I imagine."

"To each his own," she replied philosophically. "I suppose if our Mr. Navarro could find a decent Santero who'd grant him absolution, he'd switch right over; he'd compare practices to see who offered the best results."

"That's a bit cynical, for you."

"He worships at his own altar, my friend—never doubt it." She paused, thinking about it. "Which is another reason to believe that he can't be the one who's in charge of this vigilante-gang; he's incapable of seeing past himself."

"Well-said," her husband agreed. "A weakness, indeed."

CHAPTER 29

A fter a round of hurried-yet-steamy sex—one tended to skip immediately to the good parts, when one was pressed for time—Doyle managed to set herself to rights before Reynolds returned, although she'd the sense the butler was discreetly amused, behind his wooden expression.

Can't sneak much past Reynolds, she thought. Ah, well; it was the price one paid for having servants always underfoot, and let it not be said that she didn't appreciate Reynolds; he'd helped her out of many a tight corner, and on many an occasion.

Upon her arrival in Detention, she was met by DI Williams, who was all on-end, for some reason, and attempting to hide this fact from the fair Doyle, who knew him too well to be fooled for an instant. "What's happened?" she asked with some alarm. It took some mighty doing, to get the stoic DI Williams all on-end.

"Something's come up, and I wanted to ask a favor." He took a quick look at the personnel who were walking down the hallway, and then steered her into the gallery, where they could speak in private. The gallery was a tiered room adjacent to the main interview room, where detectives could watch and listen to an interrogation through a one-way window, unseen by the suspect.

As he carefully shut the door behind them, Doyle made an attempt to soothe him. "No need to ask for favors, Thomas;

I'm your assist, remember? It's akin to bein' a slave on a slave-ship."

But he didn't respond to her teasing, and instead studied the floor for a moment, trying to decide what it was he wanted to say.

Into the silence, she offered, "If I was Acton, I'd say, 'you alarm me'."

He lifted his head, and explained, "Something unusual has come up, and I was wondering if you'd listen-in on an interview with me. It's not my case, but I'm sitting in because it might be connected to one of my pending financial cases."

"Poor you," she sympathized. "Yet another connected case—at this rate, every open felony in greater London is goin' to end up on your docket."

He nodded. "Yes; well—I'd appreciate your opinion."

"Be happy to. What's the case?"

"Grand theft, but the DI who's assigned thinks it may be connected to my tax-evasion rig. The suspect is accused of stealing high-value jewelry."

"Oh—they think the jewelry is connected to a money-launderin' scheme?" Although financial crimes were not Doyle's area of expertise, they taught you at the Crime Academy that the purchase and exchange of expensive art and jewelry was often a means to disguise where questionable funds had originated. The expensive items were easily transferrable, and it was a time-honored technique to avoid any and all marked-currency traps that could be set-up by law enforcement.

Doyle asked the obvious question, since jewelry-thefts were an everyday occurrence in their fair city, and a time-honored pastime for the villains. "Why would they think it's connected to your money-launderin' case?"

"Because the suspect's solicitor is Sir Vakili."

Doyle raised her brows. "Oh." Sir Vakili was a high-powered defense solicitor who tended to represent only the most well-heeled of villains, since his services were very expensive. In turn, prosecutors tended to step very carefully whenever he deigned to appear on a matter, since any missteps on their part were shrewdly and ruthlessly turned to the suspect's advantage, and to the Crown's general humiliation.

Williams added, "I think that's the main reason they believe this theft may be connected to the money-laundering rig. He's also represented the other suspects who've been questioned."

"Is Acton involved in this one?" Doyle posited the question with a bit of trepidation, because Acton was like a hound to the point, whenever large buckets of illicit money were sloshing around with no one to claim them.

"No—DCI Raddison is the SIO."

"Got it," said Doyle. "So, you are a 'third' and you need me to be another 'third'?" She was still not clear on why Williams was all on-end—stepping like a cat in a briar patch, he was.

Tilting his head, he made a gesture toward the one-way window. "Have a look."

Willingly, she stepped down the stairs of the gallery so as to get a view of the detainee through the glass, and then stopped dead in her tracks, blinking in astonishment. "Holy *Mother*, Thomas. Isn't that Martina Betancourt?"

He stepped down to stand beside her, his hands on his hips. "Yes—at least, I'm fairly certain. She gave a different name, though."

With no small excitement, she turned to him. "Holy saints—here's a piece of luck. We should tell Acton, and straightaway."

But her companion only frowned, slightly. "I'm not sure that Acton doesn't know, and I'm not sure whether I'm supposed to."

But his reluctance seemed a bit strange, and she frowned right back at him. "If you're worried that it's Acton's doin', why wouldn't he tell you she's here? The Navarro homicide is your case, after all, and you put out the APW on her."

"I don't know," her companion replied slowly, and it was true. "But either way, it doesn't make much sense."

This was a good point, and—with some confusion—Doyle tried to piece it together, but found that it fell beyond her powers. "Another far-fetched connection? A witness in the Council-murders also happens to be workin' for a high-level money-launderin' rig, on the side?"

"The Council itself was laundering the sex-trafficking money," he reminded her. "So I suppose it's not that much of a stretch—that some of the players are still at it."

Slowly, she shook her head. "Still makes no sense; if that was the case, then she'd be workin' for both sides at once—the Council-members and the vigilante-gang who's murderin' the Council-members." Not to mention that the bulk of the sex-trafficking fortune had already been recovered—in a manner of speaking—with law enforcement none the wiser, but this was a little item that she probably shouldn't share with DI Williams.

"This may be a set-up," he said, concerned. "Someone's setting her up to take the fall."

Doyle frowned. "Then why would she give a false name?"

He shrugged. "She may be scared. Or maybe Martina Betancourt was a false name, for some reason."

Doyle turned her attention back to the girl, sitting idly at the interview table. "If we're worried she's in danger, that's even more reason we should hand it over to Acton with no further ado."

But Williams reminded her, "Acton's holding back on bringing in Navarro, remember. He might be moving pieces into place."

This was another good point, and gave Doyle pause. Martina's unexpected presence in Detention could very well be Acton's doing, although why he wouldn't inform Doyle or Williams of this little happenstance was not very clear.

"Aye, that," she slowly agreed. "If this has Acton's fine hand behind it, he won't appreciate our crashin' in and muckin' about." Thinking this over, she offered, "There's little enough harm in lettin' Acton know you noticed she was here, though? If it's a delicate matter, he'll just ask you to button your lip, and carry on."

Stubbornly, Williams insisted, "I'd like to ask her a few questions, first—just to size up the situation."

The penny finally dropped, and Doyle stared at him in abject surprise. "You want me to listen in, and tell you if she's lyin', don't you?"

He flushed slightly, and didn't respond, which was answer enough.

Thoroughly annoyed, she retorted, "No, I won't, Thomas—and you mustn't ask it of me; I'm not a dancin' bear, to perform for your entertainment."

"Kath—"

"Shame on you, Thomas Williams."

"Hear me out, Kath—it can't be a coincidence that she's here, with Sir Vakili representing her." She caught a flare of emotion from him, and he continued, "I wouldn't be surprised if she's being framed-up to take the fall—maybe Navarro's working a diversion, so that he can disappear with the bulk of the money. It seemed to me that she was genuinely bewildered by the charges, and that's why I wanted you to have a listen."

There was a nuance to his voice that caused her to regard him with full exasperation. "*Of course*, she's actin' bewildered, Thomas—recall that we think she's one of those honey-jars, or whatever Acton called her, and here you are, fallin' for her act like a green-stick *lamb*. She probably senses that you're a nice, sympathetic boyo, and is therefore castin' her lures at you so as to save her from her wicked fate. It's ready to wash my hands of you, I am."

He was a bit quick to take offense, was Thomas Williams, and he replied in a stilted manner, "No—it's not like that at all. I'm worried that she's in more danger than she realizes."

Ruthlessly, she observed, "You wouldn't be half so worried if she weren't such a pretty girl."

This hit a nerve, and he retorted, "That is *nonsense*."

Making an impatient sound, Doyle turned her attention back to the suspect. "It isn't nonsense, it's true, and you're askin' me to do somethin' you know you shouldn't because she's usin' her wiles on you, and you are fallin' for it like a grouper on a sink-line."

Very much nettled by this accusation, Williams replied, "I would like to find out if this is Navarro's doing—this theft accusation. If it is, she's in danger—remember that we think he's killing off his team, one by one. On the other hand, if its Acton's doing, then she's not in danger, and I'll leave it alone.

I just need to know which way; if she winds up dead, I don't want it to be because I guessed wrong."

But Doyle could only observe in exasperation, "You're always fallin' for the wrong girl, Thomas Williams. I'm that ready to knock you in the noggin."

Stung, he retorted, "That's *ridiculous*, and I hope it's not because you're being territorial."

Incensed in turn, she fired back, "You're the one who's ridiculous, because you are not my territory to begin with, You couldn't rescue your poor cousin, so now you have to rescue every damsel-in-distress that you happen to run across—faith, it's one of those white-knight complexes that they warn you about in the Crime Academy."

Angrily, he retorted, "That's not it at *all*, and you are *way* out-of-line."

"No, *you're* the one who's way out-of-line, and I've seen this play too many times. Go—marry Lizzy Mathis before another *moment* passes by."

But William's response to this particular taunt remained unspoken, because their low-voiced shouting match was suddenly put to a halt as Acton came through the door, and then shut it carefully behind him.

CHAPTER 30

H is expression impassive, Acton's gaze moved between them, as he stood at the door for a moment. "Is everything all right?"

Faith, Doyle thought crossly, now it's me, who's the one with the divided loyalties. In a stilted voice, she offered, "We're just fightin' about the Kingsmen's other midfielder. I think he may be even better than Renzo."

"Rizzo," Williams corrected, his gaze fixed on the floor.

"I see," said Acton in a mild tone.

Doyle immediately decided that her loyalties weren't so very divided, after all. "Martina Betancourt is holed-up in Detention, as cool as the flip side of the pillow. Williams and I weren't sure how to proceed, since Williams wondered if mayhap it was your doin'." This seemed a plausible explanation for their quarrel, and it was within calling-distance of the truth, after all.

His brows raised, Acton strode down the steps so as to regard the detainee through the glass, and Doyle could sense his genuine surprise. "No, it is not my doing. And it is a very interesting development; I presume she has given a different name."

Williams advised, "She's in for jewelry theft, but hasn't yet been formally charged. I was called for a sit-in, on a possible cross-reference due to the jewelry angle. She gave her name as Susanna Hilkiah."

"Ah," said Acton.

"Knows her Old Testament, she does," Doyle agreed.

At Williams' puzzled expression, she explained, "Susanna was a Bible character who was wrongfully accused of a crime."

"Oh. I see." A bit heavily, Williams turned to regard the witness. "That puts a different light on it, I guess, if she's having fun with her false names, again."

"She's no victim," Doyle agreed. "Should we go grill her, and shake her up?" Acton tended to come in hot, so to speak, and take matters head-on, often hoping to throw the guilty party off-balance.

But Acton's answer surprised her, as he crossed his arms and reviewed the young woman thoughtfully. "I think not—or at least, not as yet. I need more information, and it may be to our advantage, if we allow her to believe we are none the wiser."

"Sir Vikili's her solicitor," Williams advised.

Acton nodded thoughtfully. "All the more reason, then."

As Williams had not said it, Doyle explained, "We were worried that mayhap she was next on Navarro's list, and that's why she's been brought in on a phony charge."

Acton turned to ask Williams, "How many hours held?"

"It's been two days, sir; they've renewed her twice—which is unusual, for this type of crime, and for one of Sir Vikili's clients."

This did seem unusual—a twenty-four-hour hold was normally the limit, unless there was a serious crime involved. And it was doubly unlikely that her illustrious solicitor would allow her to languish in Detention, alongside the general riff-raff.

Doyle warned, "Are we worried, a'tall? We've had more than our share of deaths in custody, and the PR people will jump in the river, if there's another."

But Acton tilted his head. "Not this time. Instead, I imagine it is just the opposite situation."

There was a small silence, and Doyle ventured, "So—you think she's stashed herself here on purpose, safe as houses? If that's the case, then my hat's off to her—no one would think that the subject of an All Ports Warnin' is goin' to be sittin' it out in Detention."

Acton nodded thoughtfully. "Yes. I would not be surprised if she's been placed here specifically for that purpose—to protect her."

Doyle ventured, "So—mayhap she *is* important to Navarro, if he's willin' to go to such lengths. Mayhap she's truly his girlfriend—or a relative, just like we thought."

But Acton only offered, "Recall that we don't believe Navarro is the person who planned out this particular enterprise."

Williams suggested, "Maybe Castellano's the one who's behind it all, and he's trying to save her from Navarro?"

But Acton disagreed. "It seems unlikely that the muscle would also be the mastermind—too much risk, one would think." Coming to a decision, he turned to them. "Let's hold off, and I will try to discover what is at work, here." He glanced at Williams. "What does surveillance say?"

"No movement," Williams replied. "Navarro rarely even goes outside."

"Has he stopped tendin' his garden?" Doyle asked. "That's a 'tell', I think; if that's the case, then he's gearin' up to do the next murder, and then depart these shores with all speed."

Acton nodded, and glanced toward Martina again. "I would agree. Advise the team that we expect movement soon."

Doyle followed his gaze, and said thoughtfully, "Mayhap Castellano's gone doggo in the bowels of Detention, too; waitin' it out."

"It wouldn't hurt to double-check," Williams agreed.

"I'll get Munoz on it," Doyle suggested, happy to have the ordering of Munoz, for once.

"Shall I back out of the interview?" Williams asked Acton, indicating Martina.

But Acton shook his head. "No; I think not. Sit in, and let's continue on as before—you are investigating any connection with the money-laundering rig. No need to raise any alarms."

Williams glanced at the clock. "I'll go, then; we're reconvening soon."

Doyle immediately gave Acton a look that hopefully communicated to him her desire to mend fences with Williams. She could see that the message was received, but that her husband wasn't at all happy about this—after all, mending fences was a foreign concept to him—and as he made for the door he said to her, "Text me as soon as you are ready to return home, Kathleen; I've no more meetings today."

Now who's being territorial? she thought with exasperation. Men; honestly.

CHAPTER 31

Immediately after Acton closed the door behind him, Doyle offered, "I'm that sorry I'm such a shrew, Thomas."

He shrugged in embarrassed chagrin. "My fault, Kath; I'm sorry too."

Hoping to regain their usual footing, she teased, "Martina's probably a very nice girl, for a cat-burglar."

"I just didn't like the set-up," he insisted stubbornly. "You're not the only one who has feelings about things."

"No argument, there," she said easily. "Go listen to what she has to say, then, and see if you can decide what made you so uneasy in the first place."

He lifted his head to glance at the detainee. "No—I think Acton is right. She's been placed here to keep her out of the arena, for some reason."

Doyle decided she'd best point out the obvious, in the event her smitten companion was too smitten to see it; hopefully, he'd not snap her head off again. "If that's the case, she's probably in on it."

He nodded in acknowledgement. "Yes. And I suppose her representation only confirms it."

As though on cue, Sir Vikili re-entered the room, his brief held in the crook of an arm as he conferred quietly with the Crown Prosecutor.

Williams let out a breath. "I should go," he said, and met her eyes. "Are we all right?"

"We are, and we always will be," she assured him. "Be off, before I start in on you again; it doesn't take much to get me to pullin' caps—it's in the blood."

"See you later."

He left, and Doyle was left standing in the silent gallery for a moment, wishing she'd held on to her temper, but also wishing that stupid Williams hadn't stepped over the line—it was beyond annoying that she'd had to slap him down, and you'd think he'd know better.

Of course, there was the pretty-girl angle, and men tended to lose their grounding-tethers when it came to the pretty-girl angle; she'd seen it often enough, in this line of work. Although she wasn't one to talk, since she was Acton's grounding-tether like no other.

Her scalp prickled, and she paused. What? She was the center of her husband's universe, being as the poor man was a bit nicked—this was no news-flash. But more to the point, she'd been given an opportunity to lord it over Munoz, and was not going to let the grass grow under her feet before seizing on it. As she made for the door, she texted the other girl, "You here? Have assignment."

"Here," came back the unenthusiastic response.

I shouldn't enjoy this as much as I do, Doyle thought, and tried without much success to remember that humility was one of the Seven Virtues. I'm not so very terrible, she assured herself as she made for the lift. After all, I've two ghosts plaguing me that are much, much worse in the no-humility department.

Munoz was duly typing at her cubicle, running some sort of spreadsheet, and did not even bother to look up as Doyle leaned on the partition.

With the air of someone who was brimful of secrets, Doyle revealed, "We've an interestin' wrinkle, on the Navarro case."

"You're not supposed to discuss it with me, Doyle."

A bit deflated, Doyle pondered this. "Oh. You're not official, yet?"

"No." The other girl kept typing.

"Mayhap I can give you a hint."

"Suit yourself." The other girl's fingers hit the keys a little harder.

"Faith, you're in a foul mood," Doyle observed.

The other girl made a face, as she swung her hair over her shoulder. "Of course I am; the relatives are in town for the Baptism."

Doyle shrewdly decided that much of Munoz's unhappiness stemmed from the fact she couldn't sneak off to be with a certain Irish Inspector, and so observed in an innocent tone, "Poor you. Are they puttin' pressure on you to get married? Elena's way ahead of you, after all."

But rather than take the bait, the other girl scowled at the screen. "If it was up to them, they'd just choose a husband for me. Some older man, with lots of money."

"Like Acton," Doyle noted, in a mock-remorseful tone. "A shame, it is, that your grandmother missed that window of opportunity by a whisker."

Munoz slid her gaze toward Doyle. "I doubt it; Acton's not Spanish enough."

Doyle frowned. "But weren't the English nobs all Spanish, too, way-back-when? Weren't the Normans Spanish?"

Munoz sighed in exasperation. "French, Doyle. The Normans were French."

"Then why didn't they just call themselves plain 'French' instead of 'Norman'?"

"That's a great question," Munoz replied, in the tone of someone wishing that a pestering child would go away.

"It's that confusin'," Doyle insisted. "Although it hardly matters—they're all the same, underneath."

Her companion glanced up at her. "Just don't let *them* hear you say that."

Suddenly struck, Doyle leaned in, and ventured in a low tone, "How do they get along with Habib?"

Munoz paused to consider this. "Not how you'd think. They respect him, in a weird way."

With an air of wisdom, Doyle nodded. "Just as I said— they're all the same, underneath. It's that 'debt of honor' thing that Acton natters on and on about."

The other girl nodded. "Yes—I suppose that's it. They respect him because he saved Elena—despite everything, and then he took on Sofia—despite everything. It *is* a debt of honor."

"Old school," Doyle declared, and then made a face because she did not necessarily approve. "Like Trestles, where everything's just so, and everyone's so house-proud, every wakin' moment. Faith—I'm like to break out in hives just thinkin' about it."

The Spanish girl shrugged in resignation as she returned to her project. "I don't see my relatives very often, so I can handle them in short bursts."

"Small doses make sweet tempers," Doyle agreed. "D'you have to take everyone around to see the sights?" Hard to imagine Munoz acting the tour-guide, with her top-lofty relatives in tow.

"No—thankfully. My grandmother hates going anywhere, and she especially hates London; she'd hardly even arrived before her jewelry was stolen."

Doyle raised her brows. "Oh? I wish someone would steal my stupid tiara."

"You and your tiara, Doyle. Who cares?"

Startled, Doyle realized that someone did indeed care about the stupid tiara—someone cared very much. But who?

She frowned, trying to catch at the elusive thought, but Munoz interrupted, "So, what's the assignment? I haven't got time to talk."

Agreeably, Doyle cut to the nub. "We were wonderin' if an All Ports Warnin' suspect has gone doggo by hidin' out here in Detention, under an assumed name."

This disclosure caused even the impassive Munoz to pause and stare, her brows raised. "Really?"

"I told you we'd a wrinkle," Doyle said with an air of superiority. "We'll need a facial search done on the quiet— we've already stumbled across one of Navarro's APW people sittin' in Detention under an assumed name, and so we want to check to see if the other one's here, too."

Munoz began typing. "All right—what's the ID on the APW?"

"Castellano."

Munoz dutifully keyed in the request, and a copy of the APW warning appeared on her screen. She then paused for a moment, and leaned in, scrutinizing the photograph that was displayed on the bulletin.

"Let's do a rule-out of everyone currently held in Detention, usin' their bookin' photo," Doyle prompted. "That should tell us if there's a hit."

"Wait—wait; I think I know who this is," Munoz said slowly.

Doyle blinked. "You *do*?"

"I think—he looks a lot like one of my grandmother's servants, back in Spain. When I was younger, I had a massive crush on him." She closed her eyes, thinking. "*Señor* Trevallion."

Doyle stared at the girl in surprise. "I don't know, Munoz—could it be that he just looks like him? This fellow Castellano is the Council-member who's fled—unlikely it's the same man."

"That's true," Munoz agreed thoughtfully. "The resemblance is uncanny, though."

"A lot of Spanish men look alike," Doyle suggested.

Munoz quirked her mouth. "Again, don't let *them* hear you say that."

She began to overlay the facial recognition program, whilst Doyle tried to dismiss the fantastic idea that yet another Spanish manservant had surfaced in this investigation—it was ludicrous, to think there was a connection—although—although, lest we forget, Castellano had already been caught-out moonlighting as a flippin' doorman. It was an unbelievably far-fetched coincidence, but on the other hand, Doyle had learned at the feet of the master to be skeptical about coincidences.

Aloud, she ventured, "It *can't* be the same man, Munoz—can it? And besides, Elena was internin' at the Council—surely, she would have noticed if one of the high-and-mighty Council-members was actually your grandmother's servant."

"That's true," Munoz agreed, as she watched the facial recognition program skim through the detainees. "Although Castellano came on about the same time she was abducted—just a few days before, if I remember the timeline correctly. But I'm sure you're right; it's someone who looks a lot like him—I haven't seen him in years, after all."

Frowning, Doyle raised her gaze to contemplate the far wall, unable to let it go, as her instinct continued to prod her. "Didn't she have a connection, though? I think you told me that Elena got the internship through a family connection."

Munoz blew out a breath. "I hate to even mention it, now. It was Severon; he was a family friend, which is kind of embarrassing. We'd no idea he was a Section Five, of course, and the less said, the better."

Slowly, Doyle observed, "Yes. Severon was the first Council-member who was murdered, for his sins."

"A creepy pedophile," Munoz proclaimed. "Good riddance."

Doyle had a sudden urge to hold her head in her hands, because there was something here that she needed to figure out—it felt as though a slate of random facts was orbiting around something that tied them all together—but what? A lot of the players appeared to be Spanish. Was Martina Spanish? Were any of the other Council-members? Severon was—and he was the first Council member killed by a vigilante, but they already knew who'd killed him, and that murderer was now dead—no question about that. So; why did Doyle have the strong sense that the other Council spite-murders were somehow connected to that first one?

Because they were *all* murdered by vigilantes, she decided. That must be it; Navarro's night class had taken up the mantle—perhaps inspired by the nasty revelations that had emerged with Severon's death—and then they had carried on, serving out a rough justice because the powers-that-be were seen to be dragging their feet. Although—although, Acton didn't think Navarro had the wherewithal to mastermind such a crackin' good plan—

"No matches with Castellano," Munoz pronounced.

Doyle nodded, and decided this was not a surprise. After all, if the protocol for manservants held true, the only place Mr. Castellano was lying doggo was in a morgue, somewhere, as a regrettable-but-necessary murder.

CHAPTER 32

Doyle was being driven home by her husband, and she was pretending to gaze out the window with supreme indifference even though she'd a good guess as to what was coming, and she was sick to death of always having a good guess as to what was coming.

"I am concerned," he began in an even tone, "that Williams was attempting to take advantage of your friendship."

She quirked her mouth, as she continued to gaze out the window. "Can I change the subject, like you always do when you don't want to answer me?"

He tilted his head. "There was no need for Williams to call you in as a 'third' on an interrogation, when there are Detention officers at hand for that very purpose."

With a sigh, she decided there was no point in trying to protect Williams—Acton had already put two and two together, after all. "He was wonderin' if the witness was lyin'. But I told him I wouldn't do it, and I scolded him, besides, Michael—truly, I did."

"Has he ever asked such a thing before?"

Again, the question was asked in a deceptively even tone, but Doyle was quick to assure him, "No—he was that fashed-out about Martina Betancourt, for some reason. I think it's a bit like the Morgan Percy situation, where he sees a good-girl-gone-bad and thinks he's just the one to try to save her from herself." She glanced over at him. "It's lucky, you are, that you've no such worries."

"I may have to disagree," he replied mildly. "I do save you from yourself, on occasion."

"*Touché*," she admitted with a smile. "Good one."

The ensuing silence seemed a bit ominous—she hadn't managed to tease him out of his somber mood—and so she ventured, "Are you goin' to give poor Williams a bear-garden jawin'?"

"No. I don't think it is necessary. I hope you are not upset."

She lifted her palms. "Not at all; I have the occasional shoutin' match with Williams so as to let off a bit o' steam, Michael—it's good for the soul. You and Reynolds would never even *think* to raise a hand to me."

"I hope Williams doesn't."

This seemed a strange thing to even suggest, and she turned on him in full exasperation. "No, of *course* not. For heaven's sake, Michael, it's just a turn of phrase, and you're bein' over-prickly, yourself. Everyone just needs to get over it—another thing the Irish are excellent at; you English people are *such* a pack of mopin' brooders."

"None more than me," he admitted, and reached to take her hand. "I am sorry, Kathleen."

The statement hung in the air for a moment, and she was a bit surprised at the turn of the conversation—it seemed that he was venturing into the forbidden territory of his mental state, which he never did, and with good reason; talk about going down a crackin' rabbit hole, the last thing either of them needed was for Acton to have an honest bout of self-reflection and wind up back in bed, staring at the ceiling again.

To set things to rights, she cautioned, "Don't you *dare* change a blessed thing, Michael—I wouldn't have the first idea what to do with a cheerful Acton." Pausing, she pretended to consider this. "You must promise me—on your sacred honor—that you'll never be like the man at the corner news-stand, constantly smilin' and showin' an interest in everyone. I wouldn't be able to run to divorce court fast enough."

He smiled, as she'd intended. "I can make no promises."

"Best watch yourself," she said darkly. "No larkin' about, or I'll not be answerable."

He squeezed her hand in contrition. "I am indeed sorry. With hindsight, I realize that I should not have intervened in your quarrel."

"No—it was just as well; we needed to consult with you about how to proceed with the fair Martina—short of havin' me point a dramatic finger, and accuse her of lyin'—and Williams needed a rankin' officer to settle him down."

Acton nodded. "I do think it best that we not let on that we've twigged her, and instead try to ascertain who is behind the scenes, moving the pieces."

With a knit brow, Doyle ventured, "Could it be Sir Vikili, himself? He's very clever—and he's well-placed to hear all the gossip on the high-profile cases. Could he be the one who's behind this vengeance-gang?"

He cocked his head. "Why do you think this?"

This, of course, was the pertinent question, and so she blew out a breath, trying to decide. "Nothin' major—it's not one of my feelin's, or anythin'. He just has the air of—of someone with suppressed knowledge. Although I suppose that describes every solicitor, ever."

Slowly, Acton said, "I will admit I had a similar feeling, and so I attempted to trace the source of the payments from his clients in the money-laundering rig—whether the funds came from a single source, or from multiple sources."

She eyed him sidelong. "Muckin' about in a solicitor's bank account doesn't sound very legal, Michael."

"No," he agreed.

She decided she'd skip over that little aspect. "And?"

"Interestingly enough, I could trace the payments back through several blind accounts to the Kingsmen football club, where the trail disappeared."

Doyle blinked in surprise. "Truly? The *football* club?"

"Yes; as it turns out, Sir Vikili is one of the owners of the team."

Doyle shook her head in wonder. "Is he? Never would have guessed it—he doesn't seem to be the type to be hangin' out a coach window and shoutin' insults at the other side."

"Not as surprising as it seems; each team has many such backers, and to be involved in such an enterprise would put him in contact with potential clients."

Seeing the logic in this, Doyle thought it over. "So; Sir Vikili's representin' the blacklegs in the money-launderin' rig out of his own pocket? Next, you'll be tellin' me he's got a heart o' gold, or somethin'." This said with some cynicism because, in general, high-powered defense solicitors were not known for being an altruistic breed.

Suddenly struck, she added, "And it's doubly unlikely that he's behind all this, because—lest we forget—Navarro's vengeance-gang is a pack of vigilantes. You'd think the *last* thing a defense solicitor's goin' to do is get into the vigilante business—talk about makin' a dent in the client list, that would do it."

"All good points," Acton agreed. "We need more information."

"The story of our lives," she acknowledged with a sigh. "Which brings me to the next subject, and bear with me, since it sounds as though I'm barkin' mad and should be shriven, besides."

He smiled slightly, as he turned into the parking garage at their building. "Let's hear it."

"I went to see Munoz—to have her run the facial recognition assignment for Castellano—and when she pulled up his APW, she thought she recognized him; she thought he was one of her grandmother's servants, back in Spain."

"Ah," said Acton.

With some surprise, she turned to him. "'Ah' what?"

He set the gearshift, and turned off the car. "The pieces begin to fall into place."

There was a small silence, and Doyle decided she'd every right to feel a bit cross, since the men-folk in her life had all decided not to be forthcoming, and apparently all on the same day. "Well, that's all very well and good, Michael, but throw me a crust, if you will. I can see that there's a manservants—menservants?—angle, and I can see that there's a Spanish angle, but I haven't a *clue* how it all fits together. I feel as though I'm seein' all the spokes, but I'm not seein' the hub of the wheel."

Acton rested his hands on lower part of the steering wheel for a moment. "I am afraid to say any more just yet; it may be a delicate matter."

This, however, was a verse she'd heard sung many a time before, and she did not appreciate hearing it yet again. "Holy *saints* and angels, husband—it's *always* a delicate matter, and if you don't give me chapter-and-verse this very instant, I will take up with the corner news-stand fellow without a *single* shred of regret."

Acton bent his head, and offered slowly, "I believe the hub of this particular wheel is the fact that the Council was using its position in the community to illegally launder the proceeds from the sex-trafficking rig."

She eyed him sidelong. "Yes. We already knew that, of course. Although that didn't work out very well for them—they wound up losin' it all."

"True," Acton agreed, mild as milk.

Gazing at him, Doyle knit her brow, trying to puzzle it out in the face of her sphynx-like husband doing his usual sphynx-like deflections. "So—the Spanish players were involved in the money-launderin' rig that Williams is investigatin'? D'you think the two cases are truly tied together—the night-class murders, and the money-launderin'?"

"Tangentially," he agreed.

Doyle decided not to ask what 'tangentially' meant, and instead stick to the bones of the conversation. "So—where does that leave us? Who's next to be murdered?"

"A very good question," said Acton, which was a non-answer if she'd ever heard one.

"You will tell me," she warned in an ominous tone. "I'm countin' to three."

But he met her eyes with all sincerity. "I honestly don't know, Kathleen. I imagine Castellano will not survive, but I do not believe he is dead, as yet. If they are waiting to commit one more murder, he is probably needed to perform it."

Doyle turned to consider the concrete wall before them. "I don't know, Michael; I wouldn't be surprised if Castellano is already dead. I should have had Munoz do a facial recognition for the 'John Does' in all the morgues."

"It is done automatically, whenever there is an APW," he reminded her. After a pause, he then asked, "Did you happen to show Sergeant Munoz the APW for Martina Betancourt?"

Doyle blinked, and turned to stare at him. "You think Munoz might know who *she* is, too?"

He nodded. "I would not be surprised, but I imagine we've missed that opportunity, since I would rather not revisit the issue and raise any alarm. It is unfortunate that Sergeant Munoz has been on suspension, and thus did not see the APWs; we may have been able to make this connection much sooner."

"You're sayin' there's a connection between the vengeance-gang and *Munoz*?" Doyle asked, thoroughly alarmed.

"I'd rather not say more," he admitted.

But Doyle could not be content with such an answer—not fresh on the memory of other recent, harrowing events—and so she asked in some distress, "Holy *Mother*, Michael—is Munoz in danger?"

"No," he said, and reached to squeeze her hand in reassurance. "I believe it is quite the opposite, in fact."

CHAPTER 33

D oyle was trying to coax Edward into eating a spoonful of peas but he was having none of it, as the green-spattered table-top gave testament. Takes after his mother, he does, she thought as she put down the spoon in defeat. I'm with you, my son; vegetables are an abomination.

Reynolds was preparing the evening meal in the kitchen, and she called out to him, "No more peas, Reynolds; the boyo's saying no, and no it ever shall be."

"Very good madam."

She turned back to her son. "You've got to eat your vegetables, Edward. I know they're a sorry excuse, but otherwise your da will leave me for some smart woman who eats arugula, and such."

Reynolds could not appreciate the tenor of this jest, and pointed out, "Master Edward does enjoy sweet potatoes, madam."

"I don't know as that counts," Doyle said doubtfully. "I think the 'sweet' gives away the game."

The servant considered. "Perhaps we could attempt a spinach soufflé."

Reminded, Doyle lifted her brows. "Or creamed spinach? If it's prepared properly, you can hardly tell its somethin' so nasty—plenty of clotted cream, and brimful of butter."

"Perhaps a soufflé would be more healthy, madam," the servant repeated rather firmly.

Crossly, Doyle warned, "Don't start quarrelin' with me Reynolds. The menfolk are all pullin' at my tail today, and I've had my fill."

"Certainly not, madam."

He made a diplomatic retreat into the kitchen, and with a sigh, she repented of her sour mood and glanced up in the direction of her husband, who was seated at his desk in the bedroom, engrossed in whatever it was he was researching— no doubt something having to do with the care and feeding of manservants—menservants?—in Spain.

Watching him, she entertained an uncharitable twinge of annoyance; he'd clearly had a breakthrough on the case—that much was evident—but he wasn't certain that the wife of his bosom should be kept in the loop, which—come to think of it—was the exact same feeling she'd had from the first, when he'd been bowing-and-old-school with Navarro; he wasn't certain whether he should share his suspicions about what he thought was going forward.

Leaning back in her chair, she shifted her gaze out the windows whilst Reynolds served Edward some apple slices— acceptable fare, and therefore immediately consumed with great relish.

Acton's breakthrough had to do with Munoz recognizing Castellano—that much was clear. So; it seemed that perhaps the vengeance-gang was a group of Spanish servants who answered to Navarro, who in turn answered to someone behind the scenes—the mastermind, who was orchestrating the means and manner of operation. But this seemed to beg the initial question they'd had from the very first body-in-the-garden; why would this ultra-Spanish contingent take such an interest in righting English wrongs?

Severon—the first pedophile killed—was Spanish, but since him, the other Council victims *hadn't* been, so it wasn't some sort of Spanish blood-feud being played out on English soil. There seemed nothing to tie the Council-murders together, save the unarguable fact that its members were out-and-out blacklegs, and the authorities had been reluctant to wade into these particular waters.

Acton knew, though—she'd bet her teeth that Acton knew what tied it all together, and he seemed to think it had to do with the illegal money that had been washing around the Council in massive quantities.

Doyle frowned slightly as she continued to gaze out the windows, listening absent-mindedly as Edward happily crunched away. But—strangely enough—that didn't seem right, to her; this case wasn't the usual situation, where money was the motivator; it was more *personal* than that. These were nasty spite-murders, after all, and spite-murders were always personal.

"May I pour you more coffee, madam?"

She smiled warmly, to show that she harbored no hard feelings over the soufflé scuffle. "If you would, Reynolds. I've got to get my thinkin'-cap on, and in my current state I can't outthink Edward."

"Master Edward is quite bright, madam."

She ran a fond hand over the baby's head. "Small comfort, my friend—he's another wily one, and between Edward and Acton I don't stand a chance."

Hearing his name, Edward paused to smile at her, and she leaned in to kiss him soundly. "You'll be on Edward-watch again tomorrow whilst we're at the Baptism, Reynolds; I'm that sorry Mary's away when we've so many events lined up."

The servant refilled her cup, careful to keep the hot pot out of Edward's reach. "Not at all; I quite enjoy our time together, madam."

"And there's my problem," she replied, only half-joking. "I can't duck out of any of these events by usin' Edward as an excuse, because everyone knows I've you here at home, mannin' the ramparts."

The butler raised his thin brows. "I thought you were looking forward to Miss Sofia's Baptism, madam."

"I am, I am," Doyle hastily assured him. "Sorry to be such a crosspatch, Reynolds; it's only that I hate havin' so many things to do in a row. First there was Mary's weddin'—which was a double hardship, since we went to all the trouble but there was no cake to be had—and now we've Sofia's Baptism, and then—hard after that—the stupid Investiture."

"You've forgot the fête, madam," Reynolds reminded her. "The Trestles fête will be held on the eve of the Investiture."

Her foul mood returned with a vengeance. "Oh—that's right; the wretched fête at wretched Trestles, lest we forget. You must *promise* me there will be wassailin', and the roastin' of an ox—I hope they don't cut any corners, when it comes to fêtes."

"I quite look forward to it, madam," the servant remarked with a touch of censure. "An historic occasion."

But she could only shake her head. "I can't agree, Reynolds—I think its all *way* over-done, and a bit silly, truth to tell. To think that people should be celebrated based on nothing more than their bloodlines—faith, it's akin to ancestor worship, and that's completely wrong."

Reynolds paused, holding the coffee pot, and offered, "Perhaps not ancestor-worship, madam, as much as the hope that a bloodline will produce descendants who are as worthy as their antecedents."

Doyle took a guess at what "antecedents" meant, and pointed out, "But isn't it just as likely there are as many bad bloodlines as there are good ones? Although I suppose there's a very blurred line betwixt what's a 'good' bloodline and what's not; after all, back in the day the titles were given to the people who were willin' to kill whoever the king told them to, whether by an army or otherwise. They were rewarded for bein' ruthless."

She paused, much struck, as she considered this insight. "That's what this fête is all about, when you get right down to brass tacks; it's a celebration of murder-in-the-blood."

Perhaps remembering her admonition about quarreling, Reynolds hid his extreme displeasure at such a characterization, and instead offered in a conciliatory tone, "I hope we have become more civilized since then, madam."

Quirking her mouth, she glanced up at him. "I don't know, Reynolds; there may not be kings givin' the orders anymore, but nevertheless you've the sense that the aristocrats don't think they're answerable to the same rules as us peasant-folk. They do whatever they think's best, and if people get killed in the process, it's just regrettable-but-necessary."

With some disapproval, the servant offered, "That is rather a dark view, madam."

She decided not to mention that the head of the household held exactly such a view, and instead offered an olive branch. "Don't mind me, Reynolds; with all this Investiture fussin', I'm feelin' like a duck out of water."

"I believe the expression is a *fish* out of water, madam. Ducks can do quite well out of water."

With a mighty effort, she stifled a sharp retort. "Oh—oh, right. And please don't start speakin' of ducks, or you might bring down Emile on our heads, like Old Nick."

"A very exuberant child," Reynold observed diplomatically, as carried the coffee pot back to the kitchen.

Doyle rose to her feet, and unbuckled Edward from his booster seat. "Let's hold out the fond hope that Emile's father stays out of prison for the nonce, else the wretched boyo will be right back here, livin' cheek-by-jowl with the rest of us, and we've no spare room as it is."

She hoisted Edward to her hip, and took him over to the window so as to distract him whilst Reynolds scrubbed him off with a damp towel.

"Speaking of which, madam, Mr. Savoie has kindly sent passes so that I may take the children to the Kingsmen matches, this upcoming season."

This was of interest; the notorious Phillippe Savoie—a French underworld figure—was laying low in France, as he'd been the subject of a small dust-up at Wexton Prison. Doyle knew that he'd enrolled his son at St. Margaret's for the coming term, and Reynold's remark seemed to verify that they would soon be seeing Savoie and his small son on these fair shores.

Doyle could not look upon this development with a benign eye, but she couldn't complain, either, since Savoie had saved her life, once, and she owed him. I'm as bad as Acton, with his debts-of-honor, she thought; I should instead bar the door to Savoie and then dust off my hands as a job well done.

Reynolds' voice interrupted her thoughts. "I must say that I quite look forward to seeing Rizzo play."

Doyle pulled Edward's grasping hands away from the window-cord, and decided she should no longer be surprised about who was a football fan, and who was not. Instead, she asked, "I wonder if Savoie could be persuaded to slide a ticket or two Father John's way. He said he'd like to see Rizzo play, too."

Reynolds paused at the sink. "It should not be a problem, madam; I believe Mr. Savoie is one of the principals backing the team."

"Of course, he is," said Doyle. "Knock me over with a feather."

CHAPTER 34

After Doyle put Edward down in his crib, she decided to prepare for bed herself, with her husband assuring her that he'd join her as soon as he'd finished up with whatever-it-was he was doing at the desk.

She lay in bed, idly watching him, and decided that whatever-it-was, he was keenly interested, but not being pro-active, or issuing orders. He's monitoring something, she decided; mayhap all the Spanish manservants get together for a pint, somewhere, to plot-out their next take-down.

Unable to keep her eyes open, she drifted into sleep but was almost immediately confronted by an agitated Claudia Peterson, who scowled at her like Sister Luke used to scowl when the fair Doyle couldn't remember her times-tables.

Doyle wasn't having it, and directed with full scorn, "Away wi' ye—tryin' to drive a wedge, what with all your nonsense. Be off."

The ghost scowled harder. "You don't outrank me. You can't tell me what to do."

"You don't outrank me, either, and I've half a mind to report you to whoever gets the reports, now."

Exasperated, the ghost retorted, "Don't you care? He's going to *kill* the baby."

Again, the words rang true, and—pausing before she fired off the next round—Doyle contemplated the ghost who stood before her with some bewilderment. "*Why* do you believe this? After all, he's had plenty of opportunity to kill the baby—if that's his aim—but he hasn't done it."

As though speaking to a simpleton, the ghost explained, "He has to wait until the baby's been baptized."

Doyle blinked in confusion. "But Edward's already been baptized—he had to wear a *ridiculous* lace gown."

Now it was the ghost's turn to regard her in confusion. "What? Who cares about Edward?"

"*I* do," Doyle retorted, immediately outraged. "And so does Acton, despite your nasty accusations."

"What do you mean? Edward's neither here nor there."

"He is *so*," Doyle protested, and wished she could stamp her foot.

"No, he's not." the ghost said. "The baby's the one who's important."

There was a small silence. "Oh," Doyle breathed, staring in astonishment. "Holy *Mother*, but I've got hold of the wrong end of the stick."

"You're not much of a detective," Sergeant Peterson observed bitingly. "Get on it, Sergeant."

Doyle's eyes flew open. "*Mícheál*," she called out, "*Bhí mé mícheart—*"

But the lights had been dimmed and Acton wasn't at his desk, and so she struggled to pull her wits together, fumbling to pull back the covers. "*Mícheál*," she repeated, and swung her legs over the side of the bed.

"Hold, Kathleen; I'm coming." He appeared at the entry to the bathroom, wet, and in the process of wrapping a towel around his hips as his alarmed gaze focused on hers. "It's all right, Kathleen," he soothed, and crouched before her to hold her hands in his. "English, please."

"Holy *Mother*, it's—it's Navarro; it's not you," she stammered in acute distress, her eyes wide. "I had it all wrong—I'm that dense—it's Navarro, who's goin' to kill Sofia, not you who's goin' to kill Edward. Faith, I can hardly be blamed—she just spoke of 'the baby' and who would have guessed such a thing?"

Acton gazed up into her face, and she could sense his deep surprise. "Navarro is going to kill Elena's baby? Are you certain?"

She bowed her head and nodded, her hair falling in a curtain around her face. "Yes—she came back—Claudia Peterson, remember? And she's that annoyed that I'm such a knocker." Doyle paused, and took a deep breath to calm herself down. "I suppose I *am* a knocker, though—thinkin' there's only one baby in the world."

"What did she say?" he asked gently.

As was always the case, Doyle battled the urge to clam-up; she was never supposed to speak of her dreams to anyone, and it was always a struggle to describe them, even to Acton. Instead, she offered, "Not much. She didn't understand why I wasn't acting on orders, and then I told her she was far afield, and then she said that he was waiting until after the baby's been baptized, and then I realized we were speakin' at cross-purposes."

Acton dropped his gaze to contemplate her hands in his, and into the silence Doyle observed in wonder, "We can hardly be blamed for not seein' this one comin', Michael; this one's not a vigilante-murder by any stretch."

"No," he agreed slowly. "But it does make sense. They are all descended from the Carlist remnants in Spain—including Munoz, and her sister."

Doyle blinked, and stared in astonishment at the top of his bent head. "Never say Munoz is a *nob*?"

"No, but there is a familial connection, and bloodlines are very important to these people. Their heritage is everything to them."

"Not to Munoz," Doyle pointed out, thinking of the Spanish beauty's current love interest, as well as those from her recent past.

"No—but it is especially important to the older generation, the ones in the direct line of royal descent."

Carefully, Doyle decided to refrain from making a smart remark about people who thought too highly of their heritage, and instead blew a tendril away from her face. "So; they want to kill Elena's baby because—because of how she was conceived? That seems harsh; it's still Elena's baby, after all, and no one knows that Habib is not truly the father."

He lifted his gaze to meet her eyes. "It is more than that; I believe the baby represents a defeat, for them. They were outmaneuvered, and Sofia is the reminder." He paused, and then added, "That, and I imagine they are concerned that her father's evil will continue on in the baby's blood."

"Why, we were just talkin' about this—me and Reynolds," she exclaimed. "That's why it's all such a pack o' nonsense— this 'bloodlines' mania; there would be just as may bad ones as there are good ones."

Suddenly recalled to the fact that the man who crouched before her was probably not the best audience for the bad-bloodlines theory, she hastily changed the subject. "So—if you put yourself in their hidebound and old-world mindset, you can sort of understand why they'd want to do away with poor little Sofia, but I still don't understand why they're killin' the

Council-members in the first place. Why do they care about a pack of English blacklegs?"

There was a small pause whilst her husband rubbed a thumb across the back of her hand, and then he offered almost apologetically, "I am not certain how much Munoz knows, and so I am reluctant to say more."

"Because I'm a weak link—not to mention a gabbler of the first order," she acknowledged without rancor. "But I can hold a secret if it's needful, Michael—truly I can."

He bowed his head, thinking, and so she prompted, "Is this vengeance-gang related to Severon's murder? He must be another one of their top-lofty Spanish relatives, because I found out from Munoz that he's the one who got Elena her internship." Knitting her brow, she tried to remember the timeline. "Then Castellano came on, posin' as a Council-member, but he wasn't truly—he was the inside man for the vengeance-gang. Were they takin' a vengeance for Severon's murder—was that their aim?

She paused though, puzzled. "Faith, that theory doesn't make much sense, either; why would they take their vengeance out on all the other Council-members? The others had nothin' to do with Severon's murder."

Apparently, Acton had decided to entrust his working-theory to his better half—weak link or no—and so he explained, "I believe Severon's murder was indeed the triggering event, but it wasn't his murder, as much as it was what his murder revealed."

"The sex-traffickin' rig," Doyle promptly replied. "That's how it first came to light; when Severon was murdered, that's when the reporter's investigation revealed how the Council was thoroughly corrupt."

Acton nodded. "Yes. And I imagine it was quite a shock to many people. The Council was hiding the money it made from its illegal enterprise by using false-front investment firms, and we can presume that many of the investors were not aware that their lucrative returns were, in fact, proceeds from sex-slavery."

"Our Mr. Navarro, for example," Doyle offered. "He'd be horrified, by such dishonorable goin's-on."

"Indeed. I imagine all the wealthy Carlists were allowing Severon to make under-the-table investments on their behalf—using his connections on the Council—without knowing precisely how he was accomplishing such lucrative profits. He was one of theirs, after all, and they trusted him completely."

Doyle made a wry mouth. "Not to mention they were gettin' bucketsful of money, which tends to discourage people from askin' too many questions." This, of course, being a truism of human nature that any veteran detective had witnessed many a time.

Again, Acton nodded. "And we can presume much of the money went to bribing the authorities, which is yet another layer of criminality."

"Aye," Doyle agreed. "Law enforcement and prison guards, for starters—and judges, too. Without the corrupt judges, none of it could have happened, and the shame falls on them the hardest."

"We can speculate that the Carlists were passive investors, and these revelations would have been extremely distressing to a passive investor, who had taken no part in the criminality."

Doyle knit her brow. "So; *that* was the vengeance-angle? These Carlist-people were that angry they'd been exposed as involved in somethin' so—so *unholy*, and as a result they went scorched-earth on everyone who set it up?"

But Acton tilted his head in disagreement. "Not exactly. I believe Castellano was placed on the Council as damage-control; to keep a tight lid on any potential exposure for the Carlists, and to do a bit of threatening against the other Council-members, so as to keep them quiet."

The penny dropped, and Doyle stared at him. "And the next thing you know, the Council-members arranged to have Elena abducted."

Gravely, he nodded. "Yes. I imagine they were desperate for leverage against Castellano, and Elena was the perfect pawn."

"Holy *Mother*, Doyle breathed; "*such* terrible people."

"It all falls into place. You will note that as soon as Elena was rescued, the spite-murders of the Council-members promptly commenced."

"Bloody vengeance, for what had happened to Elena," Doyle agreed. "Even though no one would ever know why."

Acton rose to sit beside her on the bed, and drew her to his side as they gazed out the windows into the night sky. "Yes. The spite-murders were planned to impose maximum suffering on their targets, and were carefully executed so that the motive would be obscured—even the CID believed that these were vigilante murders, carried out by a frustrated public."

He paused, absently running a hand down her shoulder. "Which was probably an extra-helping of vengeance; the murders focused the public's attention squarely on the Met, who were to blame for allowing the whole rig to exist in the first place."

"A diabolical plan of revenge," she agreed. She then asked in an even tone, "Was it you, behind it?" Such a plan—laid out in all its glory—sounded very reminiscent of something Acton would concoct.

"No," he said immediately, and it was the truth. "It was not my plan, and indeed, I was somewhat stymied as to motive, until just now."

"Happy to have been of help," she teased, and lifted her face to kiss his neck. "So now, the only loose-end is Elena's poor baby, who is a reminder of the price they paid."

Acton tilted his head. "Yes; if the premise behind your dream is correct, they feel they must eliminate Sofia. They would think it was regrettable, but necessary."

Strangely enough, he didn't seem over-worried about this alarming conclusion, and so she prodded, "Shouldn't we send a field-unit over to Navarro's house, straightaway? There's nothin' like a late-night raid to make one see the error of one's ways."

But Acton shook his head. "I think not; a temporary solution, only, and these people—obviously—are prodigious planners."

She regarded him in surprise. "Then how do we stop them?"

"We stymie them. I will phone Habib in the morning."

But this remark did not exactly calm her fears, and she eyed him a bit anxiously. "You'll phone Habib? Remember, there's to be no more bloodbaths durin' a Sacrament, Michael—I shouldn't have to keep tellin' you."

"No bloodbaths," he soothed, and kissed her temple. "My word of honor."

"Not reassurin', my friend," she pointed out a bit darkly. "Everyone's stupid honor is how we got into this mess, to begin with."

CHAPTER 35

D oyle had almost forgot about her other ghost, and was therefore a bit surprised when the heiress appeared later that night, casually drawing on her elegant cigarette holder and regarding Doyle with a half-smile.

"Oh," said Doyle. "Hallo."

"You're a busy little thing," the woman said, and laughed lightly.

Doyle offered, "It was me and Acton, together. Together, we figured it out."

But the heiress only smiled indulgently as she shook her head. "*Such* a wasted effort; I told you—it's all complete *nonsense*."

Doyle pointed out, "Acton doesn't deal in nonsense."

The heiress eyed Doyle in amusement. "And yet, you've got him wrapped 'round your finger."

"I love my husband," Doyle protested, not appreciating the tenor of this remark.

The woman tapped a long red nail on her cigarette holder. "He wouldn't have interfered, but for you."

Frowning, Doyle disagreed. "I think you're wrong—I *hope* you're wrong. He'll not mourn the Council-members, I think, but an innocent child's a whole 'nother kettle o' fish."

In response, her companion only lifted a skeptical brow. "No; he's cold as ice—you don't know the half."

"Perhaps," Doyle suggested, "you're a wee bit jaded."

The woman's pretty face was suddenly transformed into an ugly mask of fury, as she retorted, "And do you blame me? I was treated *horribly*, even though I'm the best thing that ever happened to this family." Angrily, she drew on her cigarette. "Me and my money."

"No arguin' with that," Doyle soothed, and wondered at this sudden show of temper; her mother would say the heiress had a short fuse, easily lit.

Almost immediately, the ghost seemed to regret her outburst, and gave Doyle a rueful smile. "Sorry; I was never as important to them as the money was, and it still rankles."

"It must be satisfyin' though, to know that you saved Trestles." A bit doubtfully, she added, "It's all so important to them—this heritage business."

The woman chuckled, and regarded Doyle fondly. "You're such a funny little thing; *what* does he see in you?"

"Loves me, he does."

With a sympathetic smile, the heiress slowly shook her head. "No; he doesn't know how to love anyone. Trust me on this."

"But he does love me," Doyle insisted. "We may not be your ordinary mister-and-missus, but he does love me." She paused, and admitted honestly, "Sometimes a bit too much."

"No arguin' with that." The woman parroted what Doyle had said, and then smiled, as though at a private joke. "You don't know the half of it."

Doyle decided that she'd like to bring this particular conversation to a close, and offered, "So you see, the other ghost—the police officer—she was right all along; she just didn't explain it very well."

The ghost threw back her head and laughed. "No—she is full of *nonsense,* my dear. *No one's* going to kill any baby—it's *completely* ridiculous." She waved her cigarette lighter at Doyle. "Only think how *foolish* you'll seem, if you even accuse them of such a thing."

"I don't mind lookin' foolish," Doyle replied. "It would be well-worth it."

The ghost blew out a frustrated breath, and then gazed into the distance for a moment. "I never had much use for babies," she admitted.

"You had one, though," Doyle pointed out.

"A *huge* disappointment. Everyone was, really."

"Oh," said Doyle, who wasn't certain how to respond to such a remark.

"Suit yourself," the ghost said, and shrugged her shoulders. "But if I were you, I wouldn't make such a *cake* out of myself; *no one's* trying to kill any baby."

"It's not me who's got the plan—it's Acton," Doyle explained. "And—say what you will—Acton's very unlikely to make a cake out of himself."

"I hope not—a lot of things could go wrong," the ghost warned. "Just a word to the wise."

"I did tell him no bloodbaths," Doyle remembered with a worried frown, "but I don't know if he was listenin'."

"Silly," the heiress laughed. "There's *nothing* like a good bloodbath."

Doyle looked up in surprise. "Faith; that's a strange thing to say." But she discovered she was speaking to the wind, as it blew, soundless, around the rocky outcropping.

CHAPTER 36

"Nice dress, Munoz," Doyle said. They were seated at the front pew in St. Michael's, waiting for Sofia's Baptism to commence, and the dress was indeed a nice one; modestly cut, and with a demure neckline rarely seen on DS Munoz.

"I'll probably have to elope in it," the other girl groused. "Can you imagine trying to throw a wedding, with this group?"

"No," Doyle said honestly, not at all surprised that the other girl had used Doyle as an excuse to come over and escape the daunting Spanish contingent for a moment. "Terrifyin', is what they are."

Her gaze slid over to Munoz's relatives, who sat, regal and unmoving, in the pews on the opposite side of the aisle. Munoz' parents were ably hiding their general disapproval of daughter Elena's new situation in life, and Munoz's grandmother looked much as Doyle remembered her, formal and straight-backed, except that her hand now rested on an elegant Malacca cane. The elderly woman's shrewd old eyes rested on the altar, and Doyle would not have been the least surprised to discover that she was busy issuing instructions to the Almighty, who'd best listen up if He knew what was best for Him.

Now that she'd seen the older woman again, Doyle could easily see the resemblance to Mrs. Navarro—there was no doubt they were related—but thankfully, the Navarros were not present today, as this would have been aristocratic

216

overload for the fair Doyle, not to mention for poor Father John, who'd been a bit overwhelmed as he apologized for the scaffolding that still bedecked the nave.

Several other Munoz family members were also in attendance, including cousins from Spain, who were slated to stand as the baby's godparents.

A daunting crew, thought Doyle, bringing her gaze back to the front; and no doubt the Navarros didn't attend because they didn't want to take the chance that law enforcement personnel—who were front and center—might start connecting some troublesome dots.

Munoz's voice recalled Doyle to their conversation. "You eloped with Acton, after all," the girl reasoned aloud. "It wasn't a big deal."

"Not a'tall," Doyle agreed, and hoped she wouldn't be struck by lightning on the spot.

"*So* much easier than having to deal with all the drama."

Tentatively, Doyle ventured, "Are we speakin' of Gabriel?"

"Don't be an idiot, Doyle."

"Right," said Doyle.

After a moment, her companion sighed. "But do say a prayer for Gabriel, while we're here. He's not recovering very well, and I think his family's starting to get very concerned."

Doyle made a sympathetic sound. "Withdrawal's a beast, they say. It doesn't always take, the first time."

The beauty's brow knit in a small frown. "He seems to be getting more and more lethargic, which is very unlike him— it's almost as though he's not interested in going home. He's not interested in much of anything."

"Even sex? Mayhap that will help snap him out of the dismals." Having found this tactic useful in her own marriage, Doyle knew of which she spoke.

With a full measure of incredulity, Munoz hissed, "I'm not going to have sex with Gabriel in a rehab facility, Doyle."

"Good point," Doyle said hastily, as several pairs of dark eyes skewed their way in alarmed admonishment. This was exactly what she deserved for speaking aloud any spare thought that happened to cross her mind, and she'd best button her lip with the boyfriend-advice-giving. Former boyfriend, it seemed.

Hard on this thought, Munoz whispered in an aside, "Geary wanted to come today, but I told him no."

Doyle couldn't resist. "Speakin' of not havin' sex." Geary was withholding his favors, no doubt hoping to spur the fair Munoz into the aforementioned elopement.

Hotly, the girl retorted under her breath, "It's not *funny*, Doyle."

Fearful of being on the receiving end of yet another admonishing stare, Doyle hastily assured her companion, "I know, I know—and I shouldn't tease you, Izzy. It will work itself out, it's just troublin' right now, with everythin' on hold. Wait till Gabriel's back on his feet, and then go from there."

The two girls fell silent as Father John approached the altar, accompanied by the new parents—Elena, holding baby Sofia in a pretty white christening gown, and Habib, looking much as one would look if one were a Hindu participating in a Roman Catholic ritual that did not include even a passing reference to the reincarnation of souls.

He truly doesn't care, Doyle decided; he's that happy, with his new family. Let's hope Acton can keep it that way.

After Father John invited everyone to rise for the opening prayer, the new parents and the baby were maneuvered to stand behind the baptismal font. The priest then glanced up at the congregants. "Will the godparents please join us?"

Nothin' for it. As calmly as she was able, Doyle stood and moved to stand beside Elena, smiling as Elena carefully handed over the sleeping baby.

Immediately, there was a stir amongst the Spanish contingent, and Munoz's cousins were seen to hesitate as they made their own way to the font.

"Elena," said her mother in confusion. "Your cousins—"

Acton then addressed them, and—rather to Doyle's surprise—he appeared to be speaking directly to Munoz's grandmother. "My wife has asked to stand as godmother, *Señora*. I hope that is acceptable; she is very fond of the child, and I am very fond of my wife." There was a slight emphasis on his last words, as though they contained a barely-discernable threat.

The elderly Spanish woman stood very still, her hand clenching the head of her cane as the two locked eyes.

Oh-*ho*, thought Doyle, trying to maintain her countenance; *this* is who was pulling the strings? But there was no mistaking the waves of frustrated chagrin—liberally mixed with surprise—that emanated from the grandmother's small frame.

There was a small, tense silence. Another thousand-years-bloodline stare-down, thought Doyle, as she waited for whatever was to come. You've got to give it to the English, they're good at this sort of thing.

"Give over, *Abuela*," Munoz broke the silence, embarrassed. "It's Doyle—we owe her a million times over."

The old woman's unreadable gaze rested on Munoz for a moment, and then returned to Acton's. "*Bien*," she said, and bowed her head slightly.

"*Muchas gracias*," said Acton humbly, with his own bow in the grandmother's direction.

The two masterminds, Doyle thought, watching them; game respects game.

As the cousins moved into position to stand beside her, the baby in her arms stirred slightly, and Doyle lowered her gaze to see tiny dark eyes, looking into hers

Holy Mother of God, she thought in astonishment, and found that she was suddenly blinking back tears. Holy Mother—a living saint; pure and spotless, even though she was conceived of human misery and despair.

The baby closed her eyes again, and—struggling to control her emotions—Doyle raised her head to listen to the words of the ancient ceremony, imbued with fresh meaning due to the small, shining light she held in her arms. There'd been a pitched battle to keep Sofia alive, and—for this round, at least—the forces of evil had been beaten back. *"Their leaves shall not fade,"* Doyle repeated along with Father John, *"nor their fruit fail."*

CHAPTER 37

After the ceremony, Nellie—who ran the administrative side of the Church—invited everyone to have refreshments in that portion of the hall that was not under construction, but her invitation was regretfully declined. Munoz's mother explained that they'd planned to have a small reception at their home, and—as her mother was quite elderly—they'd best take her there straightaway, so that she that could rest.

More like she'll outlive us all, thought Doyle a bit sourly, as she dutifully accepted warm handshakes all around, and posed for photographs. If the grandmother is anything like Acton, she gets invigord—invigin—she's gets crackin' energized by all of her scheming.

Much struck, she watched Acton from under her lashes for a moment, as he said all that was appropriate to the other attendees. He'd some scheme going forward—after all, when did he not?—but he didn't seem quite so—quite as *keen* as he usually was. This particular scheme, whatever it was, wasn't *invigorating* him—there was the right word—and she suddenly had the strong sense that it would behoove the man's wedded wife to shake her stumps and discover why this was. Acton hadn't quite recovered from his recent bout of mind-troubles, and whatever-it-was that he was up to, it was not helping matters.

Her gaze rested on Munoz's grandmother, who was carefully hiding her extreme frustration as the younger generation respectfully escorted her from the church nave. It can't be easy, being a mastermind; you must take your setbacks very hard—you can't control *everything*, after all, no matter how careful your plan.

Her scalp prickled, and she paused, trying to decide why it would. Acton had been troubled, lately, but surely he'd no recent mastermind-losses to speak of—or losses that she knew about, leastways. In fact, one might say that everything seemed to be coming up roses for the illustrious Chief Inspector, what with another shiny title to hang on his bedpost, and the evildoers at the Met all rolled up—not to mention the evildoers at the Council, too. And not to mention further that the selfsame Chief Inspector was miles the richer, as a result of all the aforesaid rolling-up.

Her thoughts were interrupted when her husband bent his head to hers. "Ready to leave?"

"I am," she readily agreed. "Sorry—I was woolgatherin'."

"Shall we take a walk? The weather is quite fine."

She considered this. "Is there any cake in the offin'? I'm mighty sharp-set, after all the various crossin's-of-swords, and I'll not be denied my cake for the second time in a fortnight."

He smiled as he steered her toward the door. "You *are* cheaply bought."

"Nothin' to be ashamed of," she said easily. "We Doyles aren't at all steely-eyed, death-before-dishonor people, like some others I might mention."

"Let's go, then, and find you that cake."

As soon as they emerged onto the portico outside, Doyle asked, "How did you know it was the grandmother who was behind all this? I was that surprised."

Acton took her arm as they descended the stone steps. "I knew it wasn't Navarro, but I presumed it had to be someone of that generation."

Doyle nodded thoughtfully. "I can see that; the youngsters wouldn't have her steel." She paused and then added with a touch of derision, "Or her arrogance."

But he tilted his head in polite disagreement. "Not arrogance as much as ruthlessness, perhaps."

But Lord Acton's wife wasn't having it, and shook her head. "That's drawin' too fine a line, Michael. She's ruthless only as a direct result of her arrogance—thinkin' she's superior to everyone else, and that she knows best who should live or die."

"A very good point," he said in an indulgent manner.

Promptly deciding that she didn't want to get into another discussion about whether having a blooded aristocracy was a boon or a burden—and after all, Acton had saved the day, yet again—she changed the subject. "That was some good detectin', Michael. Well done."

He offered with all modesty, "It wasn't much of a leap, after I discovered it was the grandmother's jewelry that had been reported stolen by Martina Betancourt."

"Ah," she said, in her best imitation of him.

"No doubt that charge will be dropped forthwith."

She agreed, "No doubt. Although I was half-expectin' the whole vengeance-gang to show up at the Baptism, and wouldn't that have been a dilemma, for us law-enforcement types?"

But Acton pointed out, "Unlikely, that anyone who was involved would want to draw attention to the connections— they weren't aware that we already knew of the Carlist angle, and of Elena's role. Discretion was advised, and it was not as though they were planning to kill the baby at her Baptism."

Troubled by this grim reminder, she glanced up at him. "It's horrifyin' to even think about it, Michael; I wonder what their plan was."

"Whatever it was, it involved Navarro, since he could not yet return home."

Doyle thought about this as they walked along the narrow pavement. "I suppose; although if Gran had Martina locked away for safekeeping, mayhap she didn't trust Navarro not to double-cross her. He's brimful of arrogance, himself."

"Yes, I imagine she was being careful not to allow him any leverage," Acton agreed, in the tone of one who'd have done the same thing. "In fact, I would not be surprised if Navarro himself does not survive to tell this tale."

Doyle decided she wouldn't be surprised, either. "Aye that; Gran is a hard one."

"Yes."

Worried, Doyle glanced up at him. "D'you truly think she'll abide by the cease-fire? She'll not come after Sofia, as soon as our backs are turned?"

He seemed surprised she'd even asked the question, and covered her hand on his arm. "No—I am certain she will not."

"I suppose it's this 'honor' business," Doyle observed, making a wry mouth. "You speak the same language, the two of you."

He conceded, "Perhaps."

Doyle smiled with the memory. "She was that surprised when she realized that you'd twigged her out."

"I imagine it does not happen very often."

Pot, thought Doyle, meet kettle.

They walked along in silence for a few minutes, until Doyle finally said, "Out with it, husband. What is it you're workin' up the nerve to tell me?"

He raised his head to consider the tree tops. "I am afraid you will be required to wear a cape, at the Investiture."

She stared at him in unmitigated dismay. "A *cape*?"

"Yes."

He was withholding information, and so, with dawning horror, she exclaimed, "Saints and holy angels, Michael; tell me it isn't red."

"I am afraid I cannot do that."

Closing her eyes in acute distress, she replied, "I'll be needin' that slice o' cake, and *immediately*."

"I'll have one, too," he offered in a meek tone.

CHAPTER 38

The Dowager Lady Acton rested her wrists on the table's edge for a moment, and addressed Doyle. "Have you a cape for the ceremony, my dear?"

"I do," said Doyle, and pinned on a smile. "It's wondrous fine."

She could feel her husband's gaze rest upon her for a moment, and so she added, "Nothin' like a cape, to add a bit of dash to an Investiture."

As the fête was taking place that evening, they were partaking of an informal luncheon at Trestles—informal meaning there was only one servant to attend them, and that Doyle was actually allowed to sit next to her husband. Unfortunately, informal still didn't mean that Edward could join them, and so poor Reynolds had been conscripted to attend to the baby despite his eagerness to prove his mettle in helping Hudson prepare for the festivities.

The older woman's gaze rested thoughtfully on Doyle's hair. "Perhaps you could wear a snood, my dear; you've so very much hair."

I'm half-inclined to strangle you with it, thought Doyle, and then cautioned herself not to think such thoughts, lest she accidently speak them aloud. "That's the truth, ma'am. Not to mention it's as red as the Pope's shoe."

The dowager returned to her meal. "Such a quaint little saying, my dear."

Stop it, Doyle commanded herself before she was tempted to make another smart remark. You're in a foul mood, and there's no winning, by taking her on. Not to mention poor Acton doesn't want to have to throw his mother out on the day of the stupid fête.

Doyle's foul mood had commenced the moment she'd crossed the threshold of Acton's ancestral estate, and it continued unabated, which was unusual for her—usually she could find the humor in the situation and did so, since she didn't want her husband to feel torn; Acton loved Trestles, and—since she loved Acton—she always put on a good face, whenever they visited.

The ghosts did not help, of course—a wide variety of ghosts inhabited Trestles, and they tended to congregate in the rafters whenever she was on site, jabbering amongst themselves and watching her movements with acute interest.

And there was a further ghost-annoyance, this time, in that she was going to have to explain to the medieval knight that she was no further along on the marry-off-Lizzy-Mathis plan than when he'd first commanded her to find the girl a husband. It might be beyond her powers to explain the modern woman to such a person, and she wasn't looking forward to making the attempt.

With a conscious effort, she settled herself down, and said in a more conciliatory tone, "There's to be music tonight, I understand."

"A string ensemble," Acton offered. "I have asked them to include some Irish folk songs in their repertoire."

She smiled at him, touched by the gesture. "That's grand, Michael. "Will there be dancin'?"

"If you'd like."

Thoroughly alarmed, the Dowager's elegant hand paused in lifting her fork. "It will not turn into a romp, I hope."

"Fah, I do luv a foine fiddle," Doyle replied in the thickest accent she could muster.

"Of course, you do," said the Dowager in a pleasant tone. "Might I have a word, Acton?"

"In a moment, Mother."

With a mighty effort, Doyle remembered she was supposed to be her husband's helpmeet, and therefore she sought to steer the conversation toward calmer waters. "Will you play, Michael?" Acton played a fine piano, and had installed one here at Trestles, recently.

"I hadn't considered it," he replied diplomatically.

"We do not play for company, my dear," the Dowager explained, as though to a child. "It would be vulgar."

"Can't have that," Doyle agreed. "It's bad enough Edward's goin' to be paraded around, when he's truly not fit for company." The Dowager had been aghast at the idea that an infant would attend the festivities, and so, as a compromise, they'd agreed that the heir would be presented for a brief interval before he retired for the night.

The Dowager said generously, "Nonsense, my dear; I quite look forward to Edward's appearance tonight; such a lively, vigorous child—why, he quite enjoyed crawling through the Tutor flowerbeds." She paused, and added carefully, "Reynolds will see him bathed, first?"

"Reynolds will see to it, ma'am, never fear," Doyle assured her. "Edward'll be as clean as the robes of the just."

With a precise movement, the Dowager lifted her tea cup, and remarked, "You are so very droll, my dear."

The meal concluded as the servant cleared the china plates, and then Acton's mother glided toward the drawing room, clearly expecting her son to attend her, and—just as clearly—Acton evidenced no intention of leaving his wife's side.

In the hope of preventing an outright tug-of-war, Doyle whispered, "Go, husband; I'm crosser than a crooked pin, and unfit for company. I'll go straight up to have a lie-down whilst Edward's nappin', so that we'll both be presentable for company—fingers crossed."

He bent to kiss her forehead. "If I have the chance, I may join you."

"You shouldn't give your mother the impression we have sex, Michael; she'll think it very vulgar indeed."

He smiled, as she'd intended, and then turned to follow his mother into the drawing room.

With a small sigh, Doyle walked out into the grand foyer, and saw that Hudson was supervising the placement of a huge flower arrangement, centered on the entry way's parquetry table.

She paused in admiration for a moment, breathing in the scent of roses and lilies. "It's lovely, Hudson—smells like heaven."

Pleased, the Steward turned to her with a correct little bow. "Thank you, madam. We plan to assemble a formal receiving line here, so that you may greet your guests upon arrival."

"Oh. Well, that is crackin' excellent." She decided she sounded a bit snarky, and so hurriedly added, "And very appropriate, too, what with all the old family portraits, hangin' here on the walls."

"Indeed, madam. Perhaps we will soon make arrangements for your own portrait."

Holy Mother, she thought; he's been speaking with Acton, and the two of them are conspiring behind my poor back. "Perhaps," she agreed doubtfully. "We'll see."

"Just a suggestion, madam," her companion temporized, no doubt reading her aright.

Thoughtfully, Doyle continued, "Speakin' of which, I don't remember seein' a portrait of the heiress—Acton's grandmother, the one who saved Trestles. You'd think she'd be front and center, in pride o' place."

There was the barest hesitation before the Steward bowed his head slightly. "I cannot say, madam; she was from my father's time."

Doesn't want to discuss it, thought Doyle. Fair enough; I can draw my own conclusions, having met the woman. "I'm off for a lie-down, then, Hudson."

"If you will let me know when you wake, madam, I shall have a coffee-tray sent up to your room."

She smiled her thanks. "If you would; I'm like a starvin' castaway, without it." Since coffee was considered a new-world contrivance, the Dowager forbade it at meals, and Doyle didn't have the heart to remind the older woman that she no longer issued the orders, here.

The Steward offered, "Lord Acton mentioned that you were fond of a particular Spanish brew, and asked that we serve it when next you were in residence."

Doyle had to laugh. "He's coddlin' me, that man. I have to be careful I don't admire the Eiffel Tower, or somethin'."

Her companion unbent enough to offer a dry smile. "Indeed, madam."

"Is Lizzy about? Without our nanny, we've no one to hand-off Edward to, and I imagine Reynolds is itchin' to help you out."

The Steward explained, "Mathis is indisposed, unfortunately, but I will arrange for a maidservant to oversee Master Edward's nap."

"Oh—poor Lizzy; I hope it's nothin' serious."

"The flu, I believe. She will be disappointed to miss the fête."

Lucky thing, Doyle thought uncharitably, as she bade Hudson goodbye and began to mount the stairwell. Although Lizzy was another one who thought all this was worth more than the sum of its parts—she'd murder-in-the-blood, too, as past events had well-proven.

Her scalp prickled, and as she ascended the massive stairwell, Doyle gazed upon the various ancestral portraits that lined it. Yes, no question that Lizzy Mathis had murder-in-the-blood, and—since she was distantly related to the knight—this was not a surprise a'tall, because the knight himself was a pattern-card for murder-in-the-blood.

Not that she couldn't see the case for it, in all fairness; it was not necessarily such a terrible thing—to have the wherewithal to kill people, if circumstances were indeed dire, and evil had to be defeated. After all, the Church itself allowed for an exception, depending on whether innocents had to be protected.

Stubbornly, she frowned slightly, as she passed by the generations of Actons who gazed down upon her, and listened to the flutter of anxious ghosts overhead. Surely, though, this kind of thinking was where it all could easily go awry; who gets to choose which is the greater good? Who gets to choose which life is more worthy? The only one who had a bird's-eye view was God, which was why it was best to leave such matters up to Him.

Reaching the top of the stairs, she turned down the hallway and wondered at her own gloomy uneasiness—even the ghosts in the rafters seemed a bit subdued. Nothing like a medieval fête in a medieval house to make a person start at shadows, especially if that person was trying to convince herself that nothing was amiss.

There's trouble afoot, she conceded; even the ghosts are expecting trouble. So is Acton, for that matter—small wonder that I'm snapping at the Dowager; I feel as though I'm sitting on a flippin' powder-keg.

Once in her room, Doyle was greeted by Lizzy's replacement, who then turned down her bed upon being informed that the mistress was hoping for a nap. Doyle noted that her evening gown—complete with the wretched tiara— had already been laid out, and she eyed it askance.

The girl bobbed a respectful curtsy, and then moved toward the door. "Please call me if you need anything, madam."

With a sigh, Doyle stretched her arms over her head. "If I were King David, I'd ask for wisdom."

The young woman hesitated. "I believe King David asked for an understanding heart, madam."

"Oh. Oh, I stand corrected, then." Thoughtfully, Doyle stared out the windows at nothing in particular, as the maid quietly closed the door.

CHAPTER 39

It was with no surprise at all that Doyle discovered she was to be visited by a ghost the moment she drifted off to sleep. Yet again, she stood on a rocky outcropping and observed the dim figure of Claudia Peterson, standing before her.

"Mother a' mercy, but I need a decent nap," Doyle groused. "Leave me be."

"You'd be bad for morale, if you were a bobby-on-the-beat," said the ghost, "what with all your complaining."

Doyle retorted, "You're one to speak—you're the one who should be repentin' like a prophet in ashes, after all the trouble you've caused. Begone—I'll have no more of your sauce."

But Sergeant Peterson stood her ground. "No need to be so unpleasant, Sergeant. I only wanted to give you a 'well done'."

"Oh," said Doyle, feeling a bit ashamed. "Sorry—I'm in a foul mood."

"You shouldn't be; you saved the baby."

"We both did," Doyle pointed out. "Good on us."

"It's a start."

Puzzled, Doyle ventured, "Who else needs to be saved? I'm crackin' busy just now, what with all the rituals, and such."

"Exactly," the ghost nodded. "You're distracted, and *'if it were done when 'tis done, then 'twere well it were done quickly'*."

There was a small pause. "Not a clue," Doyle admitted.

233

"Pay attention to the facts on the ground," the ghost urged. "You need to work on your situational awareness."

But Doyle responded crossly, "You can't give me orders—you don't outrank me."

"No," the woman agreed, and then—with the air of someone not used to apologizing—she offered, "And I should have explained things better. I should have been clearer about which baby. My fault."

Doyle made a wry mouth. "It all worked out, even if it took some doin'. Gave me a bit of a scare, of course."

The ghost was silent for a moment, and then confessed, "I used to be annoyed that you got all the good press."

"No one was more annoyed than me, *believe* me."

But her companion slowly shook her head. "You deserved it, though, and I didn't. You're the one who's a good copper."

"We both are," Doyle insisted. "Mission accomplished; AIO." She then raised her hand in a respectful gesture, as though she were saluting a superior officer. "Well done, *ma'am.*"

For the first time, an answering smile rested on the other woman's lips as she made the same gesture in return. "Well done to *you*, ma'am."

And then Doyle was alone again, standing on her rocky outcropping, and noting that the wind that whirled around her had suddenly gone cold. Mentally, she girded her loins.

"Hallo," the heiress said, and smiled.

"You should go back to where you came from," Doyle said steadily. "I'll not listen to the likes of you."

"*Such* a shame," the young woman lamented. "You're not at all what you seem; I suppose appearances *can* be deceiving."

"I could say the same about you. They won't hang your portrait, and—considerin' some of the out-and-out blacklegs who are hanging there—that's truly sayin' somethin'.."

"No need to cast insults," the young woman said mildly, and idly fingered her cigarette lighter. "To each his own."

Doyle decided it wouldn't hurt to ask. "What did you do, to be stricken from the books?"

"Nothing of consequence," the heiress insisted. Thinking about it, she pouted, her pretty mouth drawn down. "It was *ridiculous*, how they came down so hard; I saved them all, and *this* was the thanks I got."

In a steady tone, Doyle noted, "The kennels were empty, for as long as Acton can remember. In fact, there were no animals here at all, which seems a bit strange, for an estate like this one."

Her brow still knit, the young woman gazed off into the distance for a moment. "No—they had to clear everything out, and they wouldn't let me have even one little dog. Or a cat, or—or *anything*, really. *So* unfair."

"Well, you'd best be off," Doyle said in her best police-officer-voice. "I'm wise to you."

The woman regarded her with amusement. "You can send me off, but what about your husband? You can't send him off."

"Take your trouble-stirrin' elsewhere," Doyle replied. "I may not have wisdom, but I've an understandin' heart—in spades—and I understand that man like you never could."

"*No one* understands me," the heiress complained, and then, with a dramatic sigh, she disappeared.

With a start, Doyle opened her eyes and stared at the canopy that stretched over the bed for a moment, trying to pull her scattered wits together. As she pressed her hands against her temples, she tried to decide why she still felt so anxious; after all, it seemed clear that she'd put an end to the wretched ghost-visits, and thank God fastin'. But she'd the sense—she'd the rather daunting sense that she hadn't truly solved anything; that she hadn't yet seen the main act, in this circus.

And—hard on this thought—Doyle became aware that she wasn't alone in the room. Propping herself up on an elbow, she stared at the Trestles knight, standing in the corner by the windows and watching her with an expression even more grim than his usual, which was very grim indeed.

After staring at him in silence for a long moment, she drew her brows together in patent disbelief. "Faith, it's roundly mistaken, you are. How could you even *think* such a thing?"

But the knight only fixed her with his implacable gaze, the livid scar that ran across his face standing out in stark contrast to his pale skin.

Completely taken aback, Doyle ventured, "I understand that *you* may have had to be a bit ruthless, now and again, what with all the conquests and such—but that's not how it is, nowadays. Nowadays, we're much more civilized."

Doyle was given to understand that the knight considered her an idiot of the highest order.

"I'll see what I can find out," she temporized. "But I do think you're barkin' up the wrong tree."

Doyle was informed in no uncertain terms that she was not to question her betters, but instead she was to do as she was told.

"But—"

Her voice trailed off, because she found that she was addressing an empty room.

Wide-eyed, she pulled herself upright in bed, and clasped her bent knees. Mother a' mercy; *could* it possibly be true?

Yes, said her trusty instinct; *you know it is.*

All right, then; she thought a bit grimly, and buried her face in her knees for a moment. All right; it's up to me to do something about this, even though I'm heartily *sick* of always having to face the fire; I'm not cut out to be this brave—it's not in my nature.

Much struck, she suddenly lifted her head to gaze toward the windows, where the knight had stood moments ago. That was the very point—that was the point, *exactly*. She may be a weak link, but the knight—and Acton—were the opposite of weak links, because that's what they felt they had to be. After all, *someone* had to be hard as nails, so as to protect all the weak links. And there was the nub of the problem; you might argue that they'd no right to make decisions on behalf of the weak links, but they didn't much care what you thought—they were protecting their own, because that's what they did, and by any means necessary.

With a renewed sense of urgency, she slid off the bed.

CHAPTER 40

The first order of business was to get dressed, and—since her evening gown was lying close at hand—Doyle distractedly pulled it over her head, the soft black velvet settling in luxurious folds around her body. Lifting her mobile from the bedside table, she paused for a moment, considering, and then texted Reynolds. An ally was needful, and hopefully Reynolds would stand buff.

With commendable promptness, Reynolds appeared in the hallway just as she closed the master-suite door behind her, and the servant did not betray by the flicker of an eyelash his extreme surprise upon viewing the Countess-to-be lurking barefoot in the hall, dressed in a long velvet gown with her hair in disarray around her shoulders.

"Ho, Reynolds," she said, wiggling so as to finish zipping the zipper. "Can you help me with the hook?"

"Certainly, madam." With efficient fingers, the servant performed this task, and then asked rather pointedly, "Shall I call for your maid, madam?"

"No. Follow me, please." As she strode down the hallway, she asked over her shoulder, "Where's our lord and master?"

Reynolds hurried along behind her. "I believe Lord Acton has escorted the Dowager to the Dower House, so that she may prepare for the evening's festivities."

Doyle threw him a look. "That, and he's threatenin' her within an inch of her life."

His expression wooden, the butler offered, "I cannot say, madam."

Doyle faced forward again as they came to the end of the hallway. "Well I could use a bit of help; I have to go find a tiara that's hidden in a well."

Behind her, the servant was silent for a few strides. "I beg your pardon, madam?"

Doyle threw him an over-bright smile, as she began descending the servant's back staircase. "Come along, Reynolds; there's a well in the original keep where the archives are kept—Acton mentioned it, once. The keep was where they'd lock themselves up durin' a siege, and there's an old well, somewhere 'neath the floorboards, so as to keep them in water."

Unable to completely mask his alarm, Reynolds ventured, "It may be best to seek permission from Mr. Hudson, perhaps."

Doyle nodded at the footman who'd quickly stepped out of her way as she descended the narrow back stairs. "Hudson's busy as a bee, Reynolds; never say you've no interest in a treasure-hunt? Faith, I love a good treasure-hunt."

The various servants who were busy in the kitchens halted in surprised silence as the lady of the house walked though in her bare feet, holding the tail of her dress in one hand as she smiled a greeting.

"Perhaps—" Reynolds ventured, hurrying in her wake.

But Doyle cut him off as she rounded the corner, and headed down the back hallway toward the keep. "What's a 'snood', Reynolds?"

With the air of someone who is aware this particular subject might be fraught with landmines, the servant carefully explained, "It is a *résille*, madam."

"Not helpful," she declared. "Try again."

"A snood is rather like a small sack, to contain one's hair. Some consider a snood very smart," he added, in a vain attempt to pour oil on troubled waters.

"I thought it was somethin' like that," Doyle retorted grimly. "I should use a henna rinse, and then braid it all about with beads, like the Jamaicans do."

Reynolds could think of no reply, which was just as well since they'd reached the heavy doors that let into the original keep. "Here we are, Reynolds. Now, let's find that well."

Dutifully, Reynolds pulled open the ancient wooden door, but as he did, he made one last attempt to curb his wayward mistress. "We may wish to enlist Mr. Hudson, madam; he could be very helpful, in fact."

But this was the wrong thing to say to the current Lady Acton—soon to be the Countess of Aldwych—whose mood was a bit questionable, at present. "Who rules the roost, in this crackin' pile of stones, Reynolds?"

The servant bowed his head in contrition. "Lord Acton, madam."

"He's going to back me up, Reynolds. Never doubt it."

"Of course, madam. I do beg your pardon."

She made a wry mouth, as they entered the circular stone room. "I've never had to pull rank on someone before. How'd I do?"

"As though to the manor born, madam."

"That's not necessarily a compliment, my friend. Let's go."

The entered the ancient keep—transformed in the present day to an archives room—and Doyle stood for a moment, trying to decide how best to proceed, and wasn't it just like the wretched knight to play least-in-sight when instructions were needful.

"Well, you take that side of the rug, and I'll take this side, and between us, we'll roll it up. I imagine Acton is going to hot-foot it over here as soon as he catches wind, and I'd like to get as far along as we can."

"Certainly, madam."

Fortunately, their efforts were rewarded almost immediately, because the stone floor beneath the rug was revealed to have a wooden trap-door, with an ancient iron pull-ring centered upon it.

"The well," pronounced Doyle with immense satisfaction. "D'you suppose it still holds water?"

Reynolds leaned over to consider the trap door with interest. "I'd not be surprised, madam. The area is rife with rivers."

"Let's pull it open, then, and see what's-what," Doyle urged.

But Reynolds was seen to hesitate yet again, and lifted his face to hers to plead his case. "If there is indeed a treasure to be found—not that I doubt you for a moment, madam—I believe it would be far more appropriate if Lord Acton were the one to secure it."

She made an impatient sound. "Don't go all feudal on me, Reynolds; time's a'wastin'."

"Please reconsider, madam. It is his heritage, after all."

But Doyle found that she was in no mood to discuss the illustrious Lord Acton's illustrious heritage. "For the love o' Mike, Reynolds these people are no better than anyone else, and—as a matter of fact—some are much, much worse."

Warming to this theme, she expressed aloud a thought that had crossed her mind, and more than once. "I've half-a-mind to convince Acton to reject the new title. There were some very dodgy people involved in gettin' it in the first place, and we shouldn't be a part of it."

This heresy, of course, did not sit well with Reynolds, who was shocked to the core, and had trouble finding his voice for a moment. "Oh—oh, please reconsider, madam."

"Everyone's *awful*," she pronounced. "Your hair would stand on end."

Considering this, the servant offered, "That may well be, madam, but the title represents something noble—aside and apart from the people who might temporarily hold it. After all, England has suffered through bad kings, but those kings cannot alter England's goodness."

She eyed him for a moment. "Mayhap Ireland would have been a better example to use, my friend."

After the barest hesitation, Reynolds responded, "But I don't believe Ireland has had any bad kings, madam."

Doyle couldn't help but laugh. "Faith, Reynolds; you're a smooth one."

"The principle is the same," he insisted.

Doyle cradled her head with both hands, and took a deep breath. "I know I sound like I've run mad, Reynolds, but it's truly a wonder I haven't well-before now."

"It is understandable that you are a bit overwrought, madam."

Understatement of the century, thought Doyle. "All right, Reynolds, you win; I suppose I don't want to be the one to throw-over the stupid title, all on account of a few bad apples."

"Very noble, madam," her companion replied, much relieved.

"More than some," she observed darkly. "Now, let's open 'er up."

But they were interrupted when the chamber door opened, and Acton stepped within, looking very handsome in his formal frock.

"Faith, Michael," Doyle said admiringly, as he carefully closed the door behind him. "You look as fine as five-pence."

"Thank you, Kathleen." With an impassive gaze, he took in the strange tableau laid out before him.

"There's a treasure, hidden in the well," she explained. "We were hopin' to surprise you."

"You have succeeded," he replied. "Might I offer my assistance?"

CHAPTER 41

Reynolds offered, "Perhaps I should call for a footman, sir; I imagine it will be dusty work."

"No need; I will take off my coat," said Acton, who suited deed to word as he casually shrugged out of his coat, and laid it rather negligently over a chair.

"If this project involves any length of time, we may need to postpone," the servant ventured. "We must allow Lady Acton sufficient time to prepare herself for the receiving line."

"First things first," Doyle insisted, in a tone that earned her a measuring glance from her husband. He thinks I've finally gone off the deep-end, she thought; and the irony's thick on the ground, because I don't think it's me, that's gone off the deep-end.

Acton stepped over and grasped the ring. "On my count, then."

The two men heaved, and the heavy wooden trap door lifted and fell back onto the stones with a resounding thud, exposing a dark recess beneath. The three of them peered into it, and Doyle could feel fresh air on her face.

Acton said, "Still operative, it would seem."

"That's because it's 'rife with rivers'," Doyle explained. "Whatever that means."

Acton crouched down to gaze thoughtfully into the opening, and Reynolds took the opportunity to caution Doyle, "There may be nothing of value left, madam. Over the centuries, the water will have had a deteriorating effect."

"Gold doesn't deteriorate," Acton reminded him. "And I would imagine there is a dug-out recess in the wall, somewhere close to the surface. Any hiding place would have to be easily accessible in the event of a sudden attack, and I doubt they would have risked contamination by submerging any items in the water."

"As you say, sir," Reynolds agreed.

Reaching in, Acton ran an exploring hand along the interior, feeling his way until he paused. "Ah," he said. "Here is something. Lend a hand, Reynolds; I don't want to risk dropping it."

With careful hands, the two men removed a leather satchel from the nook in the well's wall, where it had presumably lain undiscovered for centuries—the leather itself flaking apart with age. After laying it on the stone floor, the three observed it for a moment.

"Told you so," said Doyle.

"Let's see what's inside." Acton teased the knotted draw-cord, and then he carefully shook out the contents.

The shaft of sunlight that slanted in through one of the narrow windows glimmered on the small heap of metallic objects, as Acton reached to pick up a gold coin, and held it up between his fingers. "Nobles. Richard the Second, perhaps."

With great reverence, Reynolds added, "I believe I see a jeweled chatelaine, and a tiara, sir."

Acton lifted the tiara, which was of burnished gold and fairly plain, decorated only with several small, cabochon rubies embedded along the crown. It was far less ornate than Doyle's modern one, and seemed a bit crude by comparison.

"Fifteenth-century, perhaps?" Reynolds guessed.

"That would be in keeping with the coins," Acton agreed.

Fourteen-twelve, thought Doyle. Not that anyone's counting.

Acton lifted his head. "Thank you, Reynolds; I will be up shortly."

Recognizing a dismissal when he heard it, Reynolds rose and discreetly shut the door behind him, his impassive expression masking his extreme gratification at having been present to experience this brush with history.

In the ensuing silence, Acton continued to crouch for a moment, his gaze on the ancient artifacts, and Doyle could sense his consternation. "How did you know about this, Kathleen?"

"The ghost-knight told me," she said promptly. "He's that angry about my wearin' the heiress' tiara, and thinks you're a sorry excuse for even suggestin' it." She paused, and then added, "It's lucky you'll never have a stare-down with him, because I can't say as you'd carry off the palm."

But her unusually unruffled husband was ruffled, for some reason, and slowly rose to his feet, his brows drawn together. "I am certain Hudson didn't know of this. Did Reynolds?"

She stared at him in surprise. "No, Michael; for heaven's sake, I had to practically rope Reynolds into helpin' me—although he's not much of a henchman, because he spent the whole time frettin' like a schoolgirl about what Hudson was goin' to say."

In an uncharacteristic gesture, her husband rubbed his forehead with a hand. "You *must* have heard it mentioned. Perhaps you came across a reference in the archives?"

The idea that she'd researched the archives was so ludicrous that the penny dropped, and she stared at him in dawning astonishment. "You don't *believe* me, do you? You don't believe me about the knight."

Slowly, he replied, "I don't know what I believe," and it was true.

She could feel the color rise in her cheeks as she tried to hang on to her temper with both hands—the last needful thing was for the lord and his lady to engage in a donnybrook just as company was coming over.

Unfortunately, she was largely unsuccessful in this effort, and her voice rose in angry disbelief. "So—you think I've been barkin' mad, this whole time."

Immediately contrite, he stepped over and ran his hands down her arms in a conciliatory gesture, taking her hands in his. "No—no; forgive me, of course not. But I think we can assume that your subconscious mind gathers information without your being aware—"

"Oh—oh, I've half a mind to wash me hands o' ye," she raged in a fury, yanking her hands away. "Go; hurry down to the street-corner and find some other Countess—one who doesn't need to wear a flippin' *snood*." Crossing her arms, she whirled to turn her back to him.

"No," he soothed, and stepped so that his voice was very close to her ear. "I am so sorry, Kathleen; I spoke without thinking."

"But you truly don't believe me. After *everythin'*, Michael."

"It is—it is a little hard to process."

He gently placed his hands on her shoulders, and she allowed him to, trying—with a mighty effort—to calm herself down. There was no mistaking that she was overreacting, and she was overreacting because she didn't want to face the music, and have it out with him. But needs must; she may not be very brave, and she may not be very wise, but she'd an understanding heart, and—truth to tell—that was worth more than everything else put together.

"We've got to have a discussion," she said steadily. "There's nothin' for it." Acton famously did not like discussions, and small blame to him, his being a mastermind, and all.

"Can I opt out?" he teased, trying to regain their usual footing.

But she would not be teased, and turned to face him, lifting her gaze to his. "I know I make you stew, sometimes, because of—because of how I am. But I don't want to have to guard what I say, Michael—I honestly don't know as I'd know how. And—" here, she had to pause to press her lips together for a moment. "And you're the only person that I can talk to— you're the only person I've *ever* been able to talk to."

"Then let's have a discussion," he agreed gently, and kissed the top of her disheveled head.

"Sir?" It was Hudson, standing outside the door, who'd no doubt been delivered the extraordinary news that the fête honorees were digging around in an abandoned well when they should have been posing for formal photographs in the foyer.

"In a minute," Acton called out.

With some exasperation, Doyle said, "This is where it would be helpful to be an ordinary mister-and-missus, so that I could rail at you like an archwife without worryin' about the Steward of the Estate trackin' us down."

"It is quite private, in here," Acton offered. The walls are quite thick."

She blew a tendril from her face. "No—everyone has us cornered, and I've a better idea. Let's slip out separately, and

I'll meet you down at the pond in twenty minutes, with no one the wiser."

He raised his brows in surprise. "Now?"

"Yes, now. Faith, *no one* around here can do anythin' on impulse— it's all been bred out of you." She paused. "And I'm afraid what I have to say can't wait."

"By all means, then," he agreed, searching her eyes.

Stepping away from him, she smoothed her rumpled skirt with damp palms. "I've got to fetch a few things, and you should probably fetch a bottle o' scotch, since you'll be needin' it."

He lifted a brow. "You alarm me."

"You deserve every moment, my friend," she replied a bit grimly. "Now, go."

CHAPTER 42

Soft-footed, Doyle slipped out the tradesmen's door at the back of the manor house and hurried out the graveled driveway toward the back acres, hoping she hadn't been spotted and wishing she'd worn shoes, since the gravel hurt her feet.

Reynolds had greeted her return to the room with ill-concealed relief, and had immediately gone to fetch her maid, which allowed Doyle to quickly gather together the items she sought and speed down the gallery, so as to avoid the servant's quarters. Hopefully, everyone was so busy preparing for the fête that they wouldn't notice a runaway Baroness, and even if they did, she could tell them to leave her be and they'd do exactly as she said, which would be rather nice, for a change.

Fortunately there was a gibbous moon out, since Doyle had only a hazy idea of where she was going and small blame to her, since the whole place seemed to consist of acres and acres of nothing-much. There was a gazebo next to the pond, however, and it would serve as a marker—she probably should have mentioned the gazebo, but hopefully Acton realized that was where she'd meant. He'd find her, one way or another—he always did.

It's a two-sided blessing, she thought, as she began walking along the grass instead of the graveled path so as to save her poor feet; he loves me to pieces, that husband of mine. Let's hope I can turn this around before that's exactly where this ends up.

Gauging her direction, she struck out across the lawn until she topped a small hill and then paused for a moment, catching her breath as took in the scene before her. It was rather magical, between the stars in the sky, the still body of water that reflected those stars, and the sensation of carefully-staged beauty, standing as it had—exactly thus—for hundreds of years. Doyle was one who liked her countryside untamed, but there was something to be said for such a purposefully tranquil setting; it quite took one's breath away, here in the quiet stillness of the eternal night.

Breaking from her reverie, she made her way toward the water's edge, found a likely spot to sit on the bank, and awaited her husband.

After a few minutes, she spotted him circling round the pond—he must have taken a roundabout route, too—and smiled in reassurance as he settled in beside her. He was on-end, of course, because the poor man's wife had run mad.

"Where's the scotch?" she asked.

"Later," he replied easily, but she could sense his concern, as she scrutinized her face. Gently, he asked, "Are you all right?"

"We just need to have a heart-to-heart, Michael." Now that the moment was upon her, however, Doyle found that she wasn't certain where to begin. I've got to be as subtle as a serpent, she realized; else he'll shut himself up in his fortress, and mayhap I'll never be given another glimpse within.

This would be quite the challenge, since subtlety was not Doyle's strong suit, and as she struggled with it, her husband—as always—sought to help her out. "Reynolds mentioned that you'd thoughts of rejecting the title."

Trust Acton to have interrogated Reynolds so as to have some idea of what his crazed wife was so upset about. "No—I was just blowin' off a bit o' steam, Michael. Reynolds said the title is more important than the people who hold it, and I didn't have the heart to tell him that I think it's just the opposite—it's the people who are eternal, not the titles, or the estates—or even the kingdoms. It's the *people* who are eternal."

She lifted her face to his, and said with all sincerity, "There's the you-and-me-ness, Michael. The you-and-me-ness is written in the stars, and it will never go away; my hand on my heart."

"Yes," he agreed, and lifted her hand to kiss its back.

Returning her gaze to the moonlit scene that stretched out before them, she continued, "It's truly lovely, Michael, and I can see why everyone fought so hard to keep it, what with the battles, and the kowtowin' to whichever king was in charge, or marryin' a truly awful woman, so as to pay all the war-taxes."

At this last reference, he tilted his head slightly. "Has Hudson been telling tales?"

"No—but your grandmother's portrait's not up, which speaks volumes."

His gaze resting on the water, he offered, "I never really knew her; they kept her away from everyone. The rumor is that she was put away after having been caught trying to drown her baby—my father—in this very pond."

Not the only thing she's drowned in the pond, thought Doyle, but decided that was a bit too much information, and not really on point, besides. She put her hand on her husband's arm and squeezed slightly. "She's not you, you know. I know you, back-and-edge, husband, and you're not a cruel man. You just—you just think you're actin' with just cause, when you go about killin' people."

He was silent, and she could sense his wary withdrawal—he wasn't ready to speak of it, as yet, and so it was time to try a different tack.

"I do see ghosts," she offered. "I don't tell you who they are, because I don't think I'm supposed to—except for the knight," she amended, "because he's more for you than for me."

"I see," he said slowly, and it was not exactly true.

She glanced at him. "Do you believe me?"

"Somewhat," he hedged.

With a sigh, she rested her head on his arm. "Now, there's a weasel-word if I ever heard one, Michael."

He offered, "I do know that you are extraordinarily perceptive. It may be that your subconscious presents these—these perceptions as dream-figures, to help transfer them over to your conscious mind."

"The knight would knock you down, if he heard such tripe," Doyle informed him.

"He does sound a bit formidable."

"He told me where the hidden treasure was," Doyle reminded him.

Her husband lifted his gaze to consider the water, and chose his words carefully. "It may be, Kathleen, that you heard something, somewhere, and didn't understand the significance of what you'd heard."

She made a wry mouth. "And then my brilliant mind turned it into a handy ghost-dream. Does that much sound like me, husband?"

"You are very clever," he defended.

"I'm as thick as a plank," she countered ruthlessly. "On the other hand, I tend to unearth and upend all your careful plans, even though I'm no match for you in any way, shape or form."

"You are very perceptive," he agreed stubbornly. "There is no question about it. As I said, it is extraordinary."

"The Santero recognized a fellow-traveler, remember?" This, in reference to the witch-doctor who'd been held in Detention.

He made no immediate reply, and after a small pause, she added, "The Santero, who's now dead."

He was silent, but she could sense a flare of alarm, quickly suppressed. All right, she thought—now we're getting to the nub of it; my husband may be many things, but he's no fool.

"When you're tryin' so hard to hide somethin' from me—and frettin' yourself to pieces in the process—mayhap you should just consider why you'd want to. I may be short on wisdom, but I'm long on an understandin' heart."

He frowned, slightly. "Are we speaking of the Santero?"

"Not any more; now we're wondering why Martina Betancourt is disguised as my chambermaid."

He lifted his face, and contemplated the opposite bank for a moment.

"I'm one for noticin' things," she noted modestly. "And the poor girl can't resist a Bible reference."

He admitted, "Munoz's grandmother asked that she be secured here, for the time being. I thought it would be in our best interests to be generous."

Doyle made a wry mouth. "Because Gran wants to keep her safe, until Gran does away with Navarro."

"I deemed it prudent not to ask."

"Well—as a matter of fact, that brings me straight to the next point-of-order, Michael, which is this; you mustn't kill Williams."

CHAPTER 43

There was a profound silence, whilst she could hear the crickets chirp along the shoreline. "I'll have your promise, Michael—we're not takin' some stupid holiday out-of-town so that you can have Williams murdered in the meantime."

Whilst it was true that Doyle was no genius, it didn't take a genius to see where this was going, once she realized what was afoot. "And I think it's no coincidence that Gabriel and Lizzy are feelin' down-pin, too. So whatever you're doin' that's makin' them all unwell, you're to stop it, and we'll say no more."

In a quiet voice, he asked, "What makes you believe this?"

She raised her brows and sighed. "It's plain as a pikestaff. You're killin' off everyone who knows or who's guessed about my—my secret. And—whilst I understand that you believe you are actin' with the purest of motives—I've caught you out, and so there's the end to it."

He remained silent.

All right, she thought, cautiously optimistic; he's conflicted, and he's frustrated, but I also think—I also think he's rather relieved.

In a level tone, she continued, "The knight is that worried about Lizzy Mathis—that's why he wanted me to marry her off, as soon as may be. And if she's on your necessary-but-regrettable list, it must mean that Lizzy and Trenton were the ones behind Commander Kozlowski's disappearance, since the Commander was enemy-number-one with respect to catchin' me out. Not to mention the two of them took that little side-trip up to Ireland at the same time that the good Commander disappeared. You're killin' your team, just like Navarro killed his, so that there will be no potential loose-ends. But that's all over, and we'll have no more of it, if you please."

He continued silent, and much hung in the balance, as he tried to decide what to say.

Instinctively, she knew that she should keep talking, so as give him time to decide what to do, and fortunately this was something she did well. "The Santero knew—knew my secret—and he was killed, because of it. And I imagine it was you who killed that poor tech on the task-force."

Slowly, he said, "No one can know about—about what you can do, Kathleen. Surely, you must see this?"

With a gentle motion, she rubbed his arm with her hand. "Allow me to be the judge of that, please. Although I suppose I haven't the best record, since the whole reason I told Williams about it in the first place was to save him from Morgan Percy, and it didn't even matter, in the end. Let this be a lesson to me."

"I'm afraid it is not a laughing matter, Kathleen."

With some intensity, she faced him. "But it *is*, Michael—it is indeed a laughin' matter. No one would believe it; we've only to laugh it off."

Heavily, he replied, "The Commander believed it."

But Doyle scoffed. "Not as yet, she didn't. Recall that she put together the stupid task-force for the express purpose of testin' it out. And she got that idea only because Gabriel made some mention, but Gabriel was takin' drugs at the time, and so was not a reliable witness in the first place." She repeated, "We've only to laugh, and call the whole idea ridiculous."

But he shook his head slightly, and dropped his gaze to contemplate her hand on his arm. "I'm afraid it is much worse than that. The Commander was making plans for you."

He was quite grave, and so she assured him, "I'd just play dumb, Michael. It's not that much of a stretch, after all."

Carefully choosing his words, he revealed, "You would be beyond value, to those who are ruthless, and who want to protect their own interests by any means necessary. Yours would be the last face prisoners saw, before they died in an agony of torture. There would be no escape for you; no quarter given. The people who would conduct such interrogations are without any form of remorse because they have to be; they believe they've no choice."

She stared at him in dawning horror, as he turned to meet her eyes. "If you refused, they'd bring pressure to bear by threatening Edward, or me. A person with your—your talent would be priceless to them, and any means to ensure your cooperation would be wholly justified."

"*Holy* saints and angels," she breathed.

"I'd no choice," he concluded, and looked out over the water again.

They sat together in the stillness for a moment, until she offered a bit stubbornly, "I should be the one to decide, Michael."

"No." He reached for her hand, and brought it to his mouth. "With all due respect, you are rather naive, Kathleen. You don't have the perspective, perhaps, that I do."

"I've no ancient heritage of murderin' people, left and right," she agreed a bit tartly. "And I think that's not a bad thing, all in all. Besides, I very much doubt you'd allow MI 5— or whoever the blacklegs are—to go along their merry way, if such a happenstance were to occur. I know you like the back o' my hand, my friend; you'd rain down so much hellfire on their poor heads that they'd long for those happier days after the openin' of the Seven Seals."

He did not deny it, but said only, "Better to act preemptively, so that such a reaction is never needed."

"I'm well-able to handle anythin' that comes my way," she insisted. "I always have."

"Allow me to make that determination, Kathleen."

But she shook her head. "No—not at such a cost. Someone once told me that you're cold as ice, but I know better. You may pretend you are, but you aren't." She rubbed his arm in sympathy. "Small wonder you've been wracked to pieces, lately, thinkin' about layin' waste to everyone who might be a weak link."

With exquisite frustration, he replied, "I was hoping you wouldn't notice."

"I'm one for noticin'," she reminded him. Gently, she leaned to look up into his face. "I always manage to catch you out, Michael, and I'm the only one who can convince you to stop with all the Commandments-breaking. I don't think that's a coincidence—unless your other theory is correct, and I'm just barkin' mad."

"No," he said quickly, and lifted her hand to kiss it again. "Forgive me."

With a small smile, she settled back again, and contemplated the tranquil water that stretched before them. "Well, then; if you're interested in my subconscious-ghost-transferrin'—or whatever it was that you called it—I can tell you that the old tiara belonged to the knight's wife."

She pulled the ancient object from the velvet bag she'd brought along with her, and held it up so that the moonlight reflected off the dull metal. "He respected her, even though it wasn't a love match, by any means. She agreed to marry him as part of the deal when he conquered the original landowner—she was the daughter of the house, and if she married their blood-enemy, it would help to keep the peace."

Thoughtfully, she fingered the burnished gold. "So, she was another heiress who saved the day—and one who sacrificed more than your grandmother ever did. She was so very brave, but was unsung—like so many women were, back then. I'll be proud to wear her tiara, tomorrow."

"By all means," said Acton quietly.

"Here." She fumbled around in the velvet bag, and then handed him the heiress' more ornate tiara. "Into the pond it goes."

Without hesitation, Acton cocked his arm and threw it into the water, where it landed with a small plunking sound.

She then handed him the rosary that she'd received from Mrs. Navarro. Again, he cocked his arm and threw it as far as he could into the still water.

Silently, they sat and watched the ripples expand across the quiet surface. "I shouldn't be superstitious, but I am."

"You've every right, I think."

"So—no regrettable-but-necessary murders for Williams, or Gabriel, or any stray forensic-tech who listened to me gabble. Agreed?"

"Agreed."

"And Lizzy and Trenton, too."

He did not respond immediately, and so she urged, "Honestly, Michael; they'd never squeak to anyone about the Commander's death, and even if they did, you'd look all askance and say 'tut-tut', and no one would believe them, on account of your bein' *so* much superior to mere mortal men."

"It is helpful, to have a title," he noted.

"Don't start," she warned. "Tell me you agree, husband."

"Agreed," he said, and placed his hand over hers. Almost immediately, she could sense his mood lighten, and with some relief, she gave herself yet another "well-done" for talking her volatile husband down from the precipice.

Aware that it was important to scold him no further, she offered, "I'm that sorry I've turned your life upside-down, Michael, thanks to my gabblin' tongue."

"Nonsense," he replied. "I am quite fond of that tongue."

"Again, don't tell your mother," she warned. "And whilst we're tacklin' touchy subjects with a vengeance, I do think it may be time to move someplace with more room. At heart, you're a solitary soul—this I know—and you've no quiet place to retreat to, amidst our ongoin' raree-show."

He ducked his head for a moment, and then informed her with a small smile, "I have taken care of the matter, Kathleen. I have purchased the floor below ours."

She blinked. "Have you indeed?"

"I was going to tell you on our wedding anniversary."

Fondly, she leaned into him. "The finest day, that was. A shame I didn't realize it, at the time."

"I did."

To reward this full-hearted accolade, she lifted his face for his kiss, and then scrambled to her feet. As she pulled her hair out of the way, she asked, "Help me with my hook, will you?"

Willingly, he stood to undo the hook and zipper. "You don't swim," he reminded her, as he helped her wriggle out of her dress.

"You do, though. Come along, husband."

Willingly, he shrugged out of his formal coat and began undoing his cuff links. "Careful," he warned. "I think the shore falls off quickly."

"You'll have to jump in to save me, then—and wouldn't that be irony and justice, shakin' hands?"

She waded in to the water, taking a quick breath because it was cool against her skin. Lifting her face, she admired the myriad stars shining overhead, and sank down all the way up to her shoulders as her husband hastened to join her.

EPILOGUE

The two men stood silently on the pathway, looking out over the dimly-lit vista that stretched before them. Against the dark water of the pond, two heads could be seen, nestled close together with the moonlight reflecting off a pale arm, flung 'round her companion's neck. A stray breeze carried the faint sound of murmuring voices.

"As you see," said Reynolds, in an even tone.

"Quite," Hudson replied with an impassive nod. "Thank you. I will have footmen posted at the terrace doors to keep the guests within. Perhaps you will be kind enough to inform her ladyship that Lord Acton is indisposed."

"Very good, sir," said Reynolds. "Does the Dowager Lady Acton favor a particular aperitif?"

"Sherry," Hudson replied. "The Manzanilla is appropriate, I think."

Reynolds nodded, and, in perfect understanding, the two men quietly turned back toward the manor house.

www.ingramcontent.com/pod-product-compliance
Lightning Source LLC
Chambersburg PA
CBHW020744250626
47155CB00003B/907

* 9 780999 859696 *